# Caraka's DAUGHTER

# Caraka's DAUGHTER

## Sarasa Hardy

PARTRIDGE
A Penguin Random House Company

ISBN:         Hardcover          978-1-4828-4398-9
              Softcover          978-1-4828-4397-2
              eBook              978-1-4828-4396-5

**To order additional copies of this book, contact**
Partridge India
000 800 10062 62
orders.india@partridgepublishing.com

www.partridgepublishing.com/india

For my grandson
My constant inspiration

# Prologue

*Vaman Bhat looked around at the vast sea of people surrounding him. Although he had been prepared for a crowd, his limited experience had not prepared him for this. He had been to religious gatherings before, events celebrating the greatness and the glory of any number of the millions of gods Hindus hold sacred. But this was no ordinary event – this was the Maha Kumbh Mela, that most holy of holy celebrations that occurred once in 144 years. The lesser Purna Kumbh Mela was celebrated every 12 years, and drew more modest – although still impressive – crowds. But this was the major event of the century. Literally hundreds of thousands of people had gathered at the banks of the sacred Ganga; to bathe in the holy river on this day was to cleanse oneself of all sin and guarantee a place in paradise. Vaman Bhat had never thought to see so many people in one spot ever in his life, and he never would again.*

*Legend had it that a long long time ago, when gods still roamed the earth, they lost their strength and needed to get it back. Their idea was that they would churn the Ksheera Sagara or the primordial Ocean of Milk, and extract from it amrit, or the elixir of eternal life. They were not strong enough in themselves to accomplish this difficult task, and so they*

vii

made an uneasy peace with their arch enemies, the demons, and agreed that they would work at it together and share the elixir equally after they extracted it. All went well, and after assiduous churning they were able to extract a kumbha or urn full of amrit. At this point, unfortunately for mankind, both the gods and the demons forgot all about their pact. A war ensued and lasted for twelve days and twelve nights – which was interpreted to be twelve human years – and at some point the celestial bird Garuda flew off with the urn, leaving the gods victorious while the demons retired bitter and hurt to the nether regions whence they had come. Some drops of the immortal nectar had fallen to the ground, and it was there the Kumbh Mela was celebrated; and the memory of that nectar confered immortality in the after-life to all those who attended the mela. Or so they said.

An alluring idea, and one that had appealed to men, women and children, monks and nuns, ash covered holy men, old and young, the sick and the infirm. Vaman Bhat had decided to attend almost a year ago, and had started making his preparations well in time. He had been forced to leave his wife and 10 year old son behind, although they had both wanted to come with him on this pilgrimage. But the boy had not been well when the time came to leave, and it had not been difficult to persuade his wife that undertaking this journey under such circumstances would be dangerous. After arriving here and seeing the crowds, he was glad they had not come. Sita was not used to this, she had always been delicate – even going into the bazaar in Banavasi sometimes gave her a headache. He shuddered to think how she would have reacted to this mayhem! It was not just the numbers, it was the strangeness of some of the sights and sounds at the mela which he would remember *forever more. It was not for nothing that this pilgrimage was considered to be the most extraordinary manifestation of devotion that a Hindu was capable of – for it was not an easy experience. He recalled the sight only this morning of the Naga sadhus – hundreds of them – naked except for the ash smeared on their bodies, rushing into the river with their mighty roar. It was enough to make the blood run cold! But it was not all terrifying – only yesterday he had participated in a fascinating debate on the source of knowledge – erudite scholars from across the country had argued about the origins of knowledge. Saffron clad holy men – and holy women – milled around, engaging in smaller discussion groups, framing clever questions designed to flummox the speakers, heckling them when they attempted an answer. Vaman Bhat had left the hall with his thoughts in a welter.*

*Out in the open, the atmosphere was anything but intellectual. Above the babble of noise rose the sublime sound of devotional music. Here and there large groups of men and women had gathered to sing the praises of Lord Hanuman, or Ganesha, or Vishnu, or Shiva, depending on their particular preference. Small markets had sprung up selling everything from fruits and vegetables to local handicrafts – embroidered bags, god pictures painted with natural dyes, carved sandal wood figurines, stone sculptures. Most popular of all – bangles! All colors under the sun, made of painted wood and ivory and silver and gold, some with stone inlay. Women struggled to get to the front to try on their favorites from the vast array. And above all of this was the heavenly aroma of food wafting from innumerable stalls. The more orthodox of course looked upon the food stalls with distaste. It was unthinkable for them to eat food cooked like that on the roadside with no regard to rites* or rituals. But for the majority, they were a source of endless mouth-watering variety. They were spoiled for choice, for there were vendors from north, south, east and west. Should they choose the fried gram flour fritters today, or go with the rich sweets dripping sugar syrup? Or perhaps the mixed vegetable stew with fried bread? Decisions, decisions!

And in the midst of all this, a lost child.

As he wove his way through the jostling crowd, Vaman Bhat's eyes lighted upon a small figure dwarfed by the vast sea of people that surrounded her. She was clearly lost, but strangely composed, for one so young - she was neither frightened nor in tears. She was a small quiet little girl who didn't know where she was or why she was all alone. Her father had been with her, holding her hand. But he was no longer there. She was looking curiously around her, but despite her composure, to the man who now stopped to observe her, she looked forlorn. A small lost little girl, pretending that it was all going to be alright.

Vaman Bhat went up to her and sat down on his haunches in front of her. "Hello" he said, "Who are you?"

"I am Devi," she said, without hesitation.

"I see, Devi. Are you alone? Where are your mother and father?"

"I don't know," she answered simply. "My baba was with me from the morning, I was holding his hand. But when I looked at him just now, he wasn't my baba at all…he was someone else."

"You were holding some other person's hand?" Vaman Bhat asked. "Did you know who he was? Was he a friend of your baba's?"

*She shook her head vigorously. "No, I don't know who he was. He also didn't know me. He just left my hand and went away."*

*He put out his hand, and she put hers in it trustingly. The innocence of children! He started walking with her, he hardly knew where. Should he take her to the organizers of the mela – always assuming he could figure out who they were – and see if they could find her parents? Should he take her to one of the many charitable institutions in the city and leave her there, hoping that they would try to locate her parents? He couldn't see his way forward. He started out instead to the ashram where he was staying – at least he could get her a meal and some rest; perhaps something would occur to him when he got away from all the crowds and noise. So they walked to his ashram and settled down in his room. Telling her firmly not to go anywhere, he went down to the common kitchen and got a plate of rice and lentils and some yogurt. The little girl was sitting still on the cot, staring at the door, when he returned.*

*"Did you find my baba?" she asked, quietly, almost as if she knew what the answer would be.*

*"I haven't gone looking for him yet," Vaman Bhat explained. "I thought you would be hungry, so I got you some food."*

*The little girl took the food from him and started eating with an appetite – she was a stoic little thing. Over the next few days, they spent their time wandering about the town, going to all the famous places of pilgrimage, going down to the river, going any where that a crowd had gathered, where they would be seen by a lot of people. But no one came up to claim the little girl, and slowly she began to lose interest in searching for her baba. Gradually the crowds were beginning to thin as well, as the mela wound down, and people started back for home. About a week after he found her, Vaman Bhat also began to feel that perhaps he should make preparations for his return journey. But he was seriously concerned about the little girl. Clearly, reuniting her with her family was now an impossibility. Should he take her home with him? That would mean that she would probably never see her parents again. If he left her here, at one of the ashrams, there was a remote chance that they would find her if they mounted a thorough search. But how would she be treated in the meantime? He had heard horror stories of these so-called holy men and their filthy proclivities – how could he leave her there, alone and defenceless? He tormented himself, contemplating his options, when she made the decision for him.*

*"You can be my baba," she said in her matter-of-fact way. "I don't know how I lost my baba, but then I found you. Do you have a home? Can we go to your home?"*

*Vaman Bhat hesitated for only a second. Already in a week he had grown to love this little girl and worry about her welfare. For ten long years Sita and he had tried to have another child, but somehow that had not happened. Perhaps there is a reason for everything, he thought. Evidently this was the child he was meant to have. She had been born to someone else in a distant land, but by some miracle, she had found him. Vaman Bhat felt a great weight lift from his shoulders. Instead of worrying about how to restore her to her father, he now contemplated joyously the journey home, and of presenting Sita with this unexpected gift.*

*They set out for Banavasi without further delay, arriving home late one evening some weeks later, to find Sita and Udaya sitting down to their evening meal. They both rushed excitedly to the gate and then stopped in their tracks upon seeing that Vaman Bhat was not alone. Sita looked at the little girl and then looked around to see if any others were following them, but she saw no one. She looked at her husband; he was looking at her with a mixture of anxiety and at the same time a strange excitement.*

*"Husband? Who is this?" she asked.*

*"This is Devi," he answered, lifting the child up in his arms, as if that was all the explanation required. And in a way it was, because Sita asked no further questions. She invited the child into her home and her heart as readily and easily as her husband. Only once in all that time did the little girl cry — when Sita took her from her husband's arms and held her, the child clung to her and cried heartbreakingly, as if a dam had burst within her. Sita held her close, comforting her; and then, still carrying her, she stepped into the house with her husband and son and shut the door.*

# Chapter 1

As always, the dream is very vivid. On an elevated platform lies a young man. He is badly wounded, the most obvious of his wounds being inflicted by the arrow head protruding from his chest, the shaft jagged and broken, just about six inches still remaining. Standing above him is a middle aged man, wonderfully kindly and benign, looking down at the young man with sorrow nicely blended with a lively curiosity. Observing both the man and the youth are several young men – watching keenly and respectfully. Two of them stand out – they are clad in flowing saffron robes, their heads shaved clean, clearly foreigners. The other three or four young men are dressed in simple white *dhotis*. In a corner, possibly unseen by any of the group, is a young girl, about six years old. She is watching wide-eyed while the man begins to speak.

"I will now explain the diagnosis and treatment of embedded splinters, as expounded by Caraka in his seminal text on the science and art of healing," the man says. "Splinters can cause great harm and suffering to the human body. There are many interesting facts you need to know about splinters! They can be internal or external. They could be made of metal, bamboo, wood, grass, horn or bone. Of these, metal splinters are the most dangerous, because metal is hard and unyielding, and particularly suitable for being fashioned into objects that stab. And of all metal objects, the arrow is especially dangerous, because it is swift and hits hard, it has a tiny head, and it can fulfill its purpose from afar….."

So saying, the man slowly eased the arrow head out of the youth's body, and held it up for inspection by the observing young men. "There are two types of arrows," the man continued. "Barbed and smooth. When they hit the body, if they have a good deal of velocity, they will penetrate deep ….."

The young girl stares fascinated at the young man lying inert on the platform. He looks strong, his body muscular, the limbs long and well formed. He is very still, and pale, his eyes closed, his face clenched in pain. What could have happened to him? He received his wound during some military skirmish perhaps – or maybe from an attack by bandits.

The man is now continuing with his lecture – he is clearly a professor, holding a class for his students. But the setting is intimate, inside what looks like someone's home. Is it the little girl's home? She doesn't know….. "The wound is in the windpipe – look here". Here the man parts the mouth of the wound and points into the open chest cavity. The students move closer to get a better look. The little girl moves forward as well, but quietly, surreptitiously, so that her presence is not discovered. "Look at the swelling of the flesh. And inside there is blood – the blood has rushed out, impelled by the wind in the pipe. When this much blood rushes out, it is important that the pipe is stitched up immediately. If there is a delay, excess loss of blood results in death."

The truth slowly begins to dawn on the little girl. She realizes now that she has been waiting for the older man to somehow miraculously revive the youth. Maybe she has seen him do that many times before? But now she realizes that is not going to happen. The youth on the platform is not about to rise. She can see the blood oozing thickly out of the open wound. The man wipes it with a fresh cloth and then closes up the gap. He then steps regretfully away from the young man. "He was not brought here in time, poor man."

The little girl realizes the truth.

The young man is dead.

It fills her with a terrible sorrow….she whimpers, and the whole group turns to look at her. The man shakes his head with mock anger. "Are you there, my child? This is not a fit place for you! Come away, come away …" She feels overcome, she begins to cry in earnest, but she doesn't know why.

She was being shaken awake. "Devi, Devi, akka" a voice said loudly. Devi woke with a start and sat up, eyes very wide. She felt completely disoriented, and looked around. This was not the courtyard she was in a minute ago! No, no, of course not. This was her home, and she was not a child, if she ever was the child in the dream. And here was Nagi, shaking her awake.

"Are you awake now?" Nagi asked. "Or are you still dreaming?"

Devi rubbed her hand over her face before replying. It was wet with tears. She wiped them away and looked at her hands. "Same dream again eh?" Nagi asked. "Always makes you cry! What was the man doing this time? Delivering a baby? Cutting open an old woman? Why can't you dream about handsome young men, like other women your age?" She started arranging Devi's bed clothes with affectionate exasperation.

"I did dream about a handsome young man today," Devi said. "Only he was dead."

"Oh goodness!" Nagi exclaimed. "What kind of dream is that? No wonder you cry! Now wake up and get going – enough of this morbid stuff."

"But Nagi, you don't understand. It isn't morbid – it's highly educational. I don't know why I get so emotional every time I have these dreams. It isn't what happens in the dream that makes me cry – it's something else, and I don't know what. Yet…it may come to me sometime soon."

"Well, I hope it does," Nagi grumbled. "I don't much appreciate this – waking up crying is just bad luck. Here, come on – the day awaits you, and so do your patients."

"Also, I learned something very important in my dream – it will help me with that young boy who came in yesterday. I just realized what I need to do for him!"

"Good for you," Nagi retorted, unimpressed. "But not before your bath and breakfast, not if I have anything to do with it." Nagi had looked after her for years now, and Devi's affection for her prompted unconditional obedience to her commands. She got up and began to prepare herself for the coming day. It would be a busy one – they all were. Hopefully, it would be a successful one as well.

## ii

This is the kingdom of the great and good king Kakushtavarman. The place: Banavasi, the capital of the Kadamba Empire, ruling over large tracts of the western Deccan since a young brahmin named Mayurasarman established independence from the powerful Southern dynasty of the Pallavas in a fit of pique more than a hundred years previously.

Legend had it that young Mayurasarman set out for Kanchipuram from Banavasi with the intention of studying the Vedas. He belonged to a family of Vedic scholars, much addicted to Vedic study and the performance of sacrifices. However, upon reaching Kanchipuram, he was confronted by an impudent Pallava guard who questioned his right to enter the hallowed gates of the city, and a furious quarrel ensued between the aspiring scholar and the fractious guard. Mayurasarman supposedly returned to Banavasi vowing vengeance for the insult, and gathered together an army which proceeded to overpower the Pallava frontier officials and established a Kadamba stronghold in the dense forests around Sriparvata after levying tributes from various subordinates of the Pallavas. He and his forces then engaged in guerilla war with the Pallavas, harassing them whenever they came within shouting distance; this finally lead the Pallavas to make some measure of peace with him and recognize his sovereignty over all land between the western sea and the Tungabhadra River.

All sorts of stories commonly made the rounds about the origin of the Kadamba dynasty. One of them recounted how the dynasty was established by Trilochana

Kadamba – the Victorious One – who was endowed with three eyes and four arms. He was apparently born out of the sweat of Shiva, which had fallen under a Kadamba tree – commonly found in this part of the world - and hence his name became Kadamba. Another story dispensed with the many-armed Trilochana and had Mayurasarman himself featured as the three eyed offspring of the Lord Shiva and Mother Earth. The Kadamba tree often played a role in these myths, probably because there were so many of them around – some people also believed that Mayurasarman was born to Lord Shiva and the goddess Parvathi under a Kadamba tree in the Sahyadri mountains nearby and hence the name Kadamba. Some even went so far as to ascribe their origins to the Nanda dynasty: they would have it that King Nanda, who had no heir, prayed to Lord Shiva in the Kailash mountains when a heavenly voice advised him that two sons would be born to him, would bear the name of Kadamba *Kula* (family) and they should be instructed in the use of weapons.

Whatever their origins, the Kadambas were now a proud Kannada dynasty. They were quick to make Kannada the official language. Rumors that they had originally made their way to this region from the north – perhaps as far north as the Himalayas – were summarily rejected. Were the Himalayas endowed with their beloved kadamba trees? The locals were pretty sure they weren't (although none of them had actually been north of the Aravallis). And if not, then how could the proud Kadamba race have originated there? They would then have adopted the name of some tree that was locally abundant there, would they not? The logic was simple yet unarguable – and few people bothered to argue it anyway.

Since then, Mayuravarman (as he was later called) and the Kadamba Dynasty prospered, and now, a 100 years later, after a succession of kings, the great king Kakushtavarman rules over the land. Banavasi, as the capital, is one of the most beautiful cities anyone has beheld. The people of Banavasi were well aware that there were other large cities elsewhere in this large land of Bharat. Some had even visited Varanasi, for example – but they were not impressed. And with reason; the steady influx of admiring and appreciative visitors to Banavasi provided ample confirmation of their conviction that this was heaven on earth.

A large part of the beauty of the city was the river Varada that flowed all around it – causing it to be referred to by some people as Jaladurga or the Fort Surrounded by Water. The sparkling river, largely fringed with lush greenery, was also a haven for many species of water birds. Large trees overhanging the mighty river, heavy with white ibis, pelicans, storks and moor hens were a common sight, particularly during the winter months. All in all, Paradise!

### iii

Devi's house was built in the typical style of village homes, but with a difference. The front wing was taken up by a clinic. The rest of the house was built around a square open courtyard that served many useful functions – it was the meeting place where they all gathered of an evening to chat and exchange the news of the day; it was where Nagi dried the medicinal herbs and sorted out the vegetables to be cooked that day and sunned all the spices; it was where they all ran out into the rain and splashed and played in the water; it was where they received their visitors and held their social gatherings. Around the courtyard were all the rooms. There were five of them in the house, including Devi, Nagi and the three young helpers they had rescued from an orphanage in Banavasi. Devi had her own room, with a smaller room adjoining where she kept her clothes and books and other personal belongings. The kitchen was set in the back, and had a large hall next to it where they all took their meals. Several smaller rooms were ranged around the courtyard, and this was where Nagi and the girls would spread their mattresses out at night.

Devi's morning ablutions were generally perfunctory; it was only when the morning session with her patients was done that she had a proper bath, prior to lunch. The situation was idyllic, however – a private path from the house led down to a hollow, at the base of which was a spring surrounded by a pool. The hollow itself was hidden from view, and there was no evidence of the spring either. It was only when one got quite close that the quiet gurgle of running water could be heard. When Devi had first moved to this remote location, she had walked quite a distance every day to the river. One day Nagi had returned more voluble and excited than usual: it appeared that she had been trying to identify a good location for their herbal garden and while doing so, she had literally stumbled upon the hollow, hidden by an overgrowth of shrubbery. It didn't take long to clear a path to the hollow, and in a few days after that, Nagi had organized some local youths to hammer stones into the earth to create a rough and ready staircase down to the pool.

Devi walked quickly to the pool; this was not the time of day for leisure. Later, she would enjoy the cool quiet by the spring, and the play of dappled sunlight on the water, but now she simply splashed some water on her face and body. Briskly drying herself off, she wrapped herself in the simple saree that Nagi had set out. She walked quickly back to her room to apply kohl in her eyes and a bindi on her forehead. She took down the shiny copper plate and looked at herself to make sure that she had done it right. What she saw gave her no pause, she had seen her reflection hundreds of times before. She did not have any great opinion of her looks, but there were many who would call her beautiful. Her eyes were large, dark brown, set under naturally arched brows. Her forehead was not wide, and this was because she had such an abundant head of hair – thick and lustrous, growing down to her knees, which she usually confined in one thick braid when she didn't make a knot at the nape of her neck. Her best feature was her skin – smooth, with the inner glow of good health, and a natural blush on her cheeks. For the rest, she was of medium height, tending to be buxom, but blessed with a slim waist; had elegant feet, although her hands were roughened with her constant preoccupation with gardening; and had an infectious laugh that brought a smile to the face of anyone who heard it. At twenty one, she was lucky to have this kind of independence: most girls her age would long ago have been married off to a man of their parent's choice. She thought gratefully of her foster father, Vaman Bhat – if it hadn't been for him, that would have been her fate too.

If she had only woken up earlier, Devi would have had time to take a turn around her herbal garden. It was her favorite way to start the day. It had taken a year or more for her to build up the rich variety of plants she had there. Whenever she heard of anyone taking a trip or going on pilgrimage, she would hurry to their house. Depending on the direction of their journey, she would present them with a list of plants for them to bring back. Here she had the help of Vaman Bhatt. He was the most knowledgeable man she knew when it came to herbs and plants, and gave her invaluable guidance on where they would be available and how they could be used in various remedies. He had come by his vast store of knowledge from his guru – the famous Shama Shastri, well known for his medical miracles. He could cure the most dangerous and lethal of conditions with his concoctions – even the bite of a snake or a rabid dog responded to his healing touch.

Now, Devi's growing reputation as a healer was beginning to draw more and more people to her clinic. Too many people, she sometimes thought ruefully, especially when she stepped out and saw the crowd of people waiting already, and it was barely an hour after daybreak. Fortified by the spicy cereal and vegetables that Nagi had made her sit and eat, Devi was now ready to start her day. She stepped out of her private area and into the clearing outside. The area was swept clean every morning by Nagi, washed with fresh cow-dung and then decorated with a rangoli design drawn with rice flour. The design ranged from elaborately flowery to severely geometric depending on Nagi's moods. Devi checked today's effort – reasonably flowery, so probably a reasonably good mood.

Devi had worked out a system for dealing with her patients. She would first examine them all rapidly. Those that seemed particularly sick, with bleeding wounds or feverish or in acute pain she would send to the front of the line. Old people and pregnant women were next. The rest would come towards the back of the line. It had not been easy establishing the rules – at first she had been accustomed to encountering a mob scene every morning, with people shouting and jostling for her attention. After a few days of this she realized that she was exhausted mainly from crowd control, not from the effort of attending to her patients. She discussed this with Nagi.

"What on earth am I to do, Nagi? I am so tired with people pushing me around! Did you see that man this morning? He literally pushed that poor child out of the way – that child was burning up with fever, while there was nothing wrong with the man. Just indigestion! He actually bragged about how he had eaten half a goat for dinner last night!"

Nagi said thoughtfully, "It is because you are so young… they think they can get away with pushing you around, especially the men. You tell me what rules you want to set, and I'll see to it. Let me see who tries to challenge Nagi!" Nagi was taller than most men, with broad shoulders and a commanding air. A shock of curly black hair and flashing black eyes completed the picture. Most people were happy to follow where Nagi led – in fact, most people were too scared to oppose her!

The next day as Devi went out she heard Nagi laying down the law to the waiting crowd. And such was the force of her personality that when Devi emerged she found the group waiting for her round-eyed like a bunch of scolded school children – it was all she could do not to smile. For one thing, they were all lined up; and if this was not enough, they were actually silent, no pathetic hollering with arms outstretched, begging for attention. Maintaining as stern a demeanor as she could muster, she put her system into action. And she had never looked back – now everyone realized that if one day, god forbid, they happened to be the sickest, they would get seen first.

Taking a deep breath, Devi got to work. She quickly scanned the group – about 40 people. A solid morning's work.

# Chapter 2

Vaman Bhat was up before dawn, as usual. He had many things to do before daybreak, many preparations to make. The wee hours of the morning were a busy time for a Brahmin; unfortunately for Vaman Bhat, so was the rest of the day, but that was of his own choosing. His first act was to walk down to the river for his ritual bath. Although it was yet dark, he neither faltered nor stumbled. He had walked this path so many times before, he could do it blindfolded. He had the company of several of his friends and relatives who were similarly up before day break with the same mission in mind. Only perfunctory greetings were exchanged. This was not the time for gossip and chatter – no one was in the mood for it. Later in the day, after the morning rituals were done and the morning meal eaten, when the sun was up and the household was in full swing – that was the time for the men to congregate under the banyan tree and exchange the latest news and their views on life.

Vaman Bhat climbed down the stone steps of the river bank, down to the river. The water was cold, but not uncomfortably so. He dipped himself three times in the water, being careful to immerse his head completely each time. Then, still with the wet cloth wrapped around his waist, and carrying a small silver jar of the water from the sacred river Varada, he climbed back up the river bank and walked quickly home.

His house was simple but spacious. The house had been built by his respected grandfather, Purandhara Bhat, and his family had lived there for three generations already. The garden in front was of medium size, and was planted with three coconut trees and as many mango trees. In between there was a jasmine tree and a hibiscus, both of which provided him with flowers for his daily puja. A broad veranda went all across the front of the house, and served as his meeting room for casual visitors and business acquaintances. The house itself consisted of several large rooms around an airy central hall. The high ceilings and the thatched roof served to keep the house cool even in the heat of the mid-day sun.

The puja room was a special chamber, large enough to fit several people inside, and facing east. His wife Sita had set out all the necessary accompaniments for his puja: the lamps in front of the deities of Shiva, Parvati and Ganesha, filled with oil and with fresh wicks ready to be lit; the fresh palm leaves required for the ritual; the fruits and flowers that would be offered to the gods; the bananas in milk, honey and coconut to be consecrated during the puja and then given to the family as a blessing; and the incense sticks. He set down the jar of water that he had brought with him, and settled himself cross legged on the mat, facing east. The sky was taking on a pink-ish hue, the sun was about to rise: it was time for him to begin.

He began with the first invocations of the Sandhyavandanam, the morning prayer: Achyutaya Namah; Ananthaya Namah; Govindaya Namah.

He had been doing this every morning since he was seven years old, when he was initiated into this rite by the temple priest in the presence of all his family and friends. It had been an occasion of great rejoicing, and after that he had been invited by his father to perform this ritual along with him every morning. That early morning togetherness with an otherwise remote and forbidding figure had filled him with an odd mixture of emotions – mainly pride and importance at now being qualified to be admitted into a club of which his father was also a member; but also some trepidation in case he made some mistake and earned his father's displeasure.

Vaman Bhat sternly brought himself back to the moment. His mind was wandering this morning, and that annoyed him. This was usually a meditative time for him, a time when he composed his thoughts for the day and focused his mind for the tasks ahead. Despite his absentmindedness, he had been going through the motions of the Sandhyavandanam. He now started the most crucial part of all: the chanting of the Gayatri Mantra, conferring wisdom, knowledge and enlightenment.

> Om Bhur Bhuvah Svah
> Tatt Savitar Varenyam
> Bhargo Devasya Dhimahi
> Dhiyo Yo Nah Pracodayat

"We meditate on the glory of that Being who has produced this universe; may He enlighten our minds."[1]

According to his family lineage and birth star, Vaman Bhat was supposed to repeat the mantra 32 times. Quite often, he would be so entranced by the sound of the mantra that he would lose count and continue chanting it until he slowly emerged back to consciousness. Today was not one of those days. He continued to be strangely distracted, and completed the ritual as prescribed but without his usual delight in it.

He rose and gave his wife some of the holy water in the palm of her hand, as a blessing; and then some of the banana and milk. By this time his son Udaya was also up, and he gave him some of the banana mixture as well.

Udaya – dawn; they had named him that because he had been born in the early hours of the morning, and his father had seen the first early signs of dawn as the mid-wife came and informed him of the birth of his first child. As it happened, his only child. Vaman Bhat looked at him with pride. He himself was fairly tall, but Udaya was even taller. Both were light skinned, with a high forehead and a sharp nose; but while Vaman Bhat's eyes were a gentle grey, Udaya had inherited his mother's black eyes. He had also not opted to shave his head, as was the usual custom of Brahmins, and one that Vaman Bhat had followed for many years now. Udaya had a full head of hair which he tended to keep growing until his mother admonished him and packed him off to the barber.

---

[1]     Interpretation of Swami Vivekananda

He too had been initiated into the mysteries of the coming of age ceremony, the Upanayanam. For many years, it had been the father's pride and joy to hear his young son recite the Gayatri mantra along with him early in the morning, after having accompanied him to the river for his early morning bath. In this case, there was no question of a remote and distant father – Vaman Bhat was a loving and even indulgent father, who spent many long hours with his son, teaching him the wonders of astronomy, of plants and birds and nature, or sometimes simply the intricacies of a good game of chess. However, some years before, Udaya had attended the lectures of a learned monk who had come to Banavasi as a guest of the king. Learned men and philosophers frequently visited and gave public discourses on various subjects, and it was common for men of letters to attend such discourses and participate in the debates that followed. Udaya returned from this particular lecture plunged in thought, and for the next several days had spent a good deal of time in close communion with the monk. At last, he had announced that he had been convinced by the monk, and he would henceforth practice the tenets of Buddhism. Vaman Bhat had not been surprised by this, nor unduly upset. This new religion had been spreading like wildfire, and was a highly respected one. The king himself was known to have sympathies with the Buddhists and had given them extensive lands and other gifts. It did not ask one to break from basic Hindu tenets. In fact, Buddha was considered to be a reincarnation of the great Vishnu himself – the Creator of the universe.

What it did mean was that Udaya no longer accompanied his father in the performance of his morning ritual. Buddhism rejected ritualism of all sorts. His diet also was even more stringent than the normal Brahmin diet, disallowing not only all meat and alcohol, but also encouraging the eating of uncooked foods as far as possible, even cereals. It was a bit hard on his parents teeth, but on the whole enjoyable, and extremely healthy. Vaman Bhat was proud of his son; he appreciated his independence of thought, and respected him for it. He was also showing much promise in public service. He was essentially serious minded and quiet, and his job in government gave him the opportunity to benefit the poor and needy with the ample resources of the kingdom. This suited both his temperament and his new religious calling.

But what about marriage? his mother often wondered. He was of an age when most men had been householders for many years already, with a brood of children filling the house with their noisy laughter. But whenever she brought this topic up with her husband, he would hush her up. "Give him time" he would advice quietly.

It always surprised him that she didn't see the truth staring them in their face. He had seen it years ago, just a few years after they had brought the little girl home and before they had formally adopted her. Udaya's love for the little girl had slowly transformed from the indulgent love of an older brother into the passionate love of a man for a woman – Vaman Bhat felt that he almost knew the moment when that transformation had occurred, one fateful Diwali day when they were all resplendent in their new clothes and laughing and playing around the courtyard with their fire crackers. She had been wearing a new red saree that her fond father had got for her from one of his trips to the northern kingdoms; her eyes lined with kohl, with strings of jasmine in her hair, she had been as pretty as a picture. He had then caught a look Udaya had directed at her, and his heart had filled with both happiness and fear for his son: clearly, he did not see her as a sister at all any more, but what about her? Although a marriage between them was the dearest wish of his heart, Vaman Bhat feared that it may never come to pass. Would she ever see him as anything but a beloved older brother?

Not yet, that was for sure. She was completely oblivious to any change in his feelings for her – or so he thought. Udaya was careful never to reveal himself – but it cost the boy an effort. When she left after her weekly visits, he would be plunged in his own thoughts for a long while. There was no hint that the teasing and affectionate relationship they had shared since they were children would change any time soon. And until it did, there would be no marriage for his son, Vaman Bhat was sure of that.

Finishing up the puja, Vaman Bhat sat down to his morning meal. It was the main meal of the day, and kept him going through his long hours at the office. He was very strict, and never ate a morsel or drank a drop that was not from his own home. Today his wife had made his favorite lentils with radish and a salad of mung bean sprouts with fresh grated coconut. Mixed with the red rice topped with hot clarified butter – what could be more delicious? He finished up with a tall glass of refreshing buttermilk and then went to his room to get ready for work.

## ii

The Kadambas were well known for their sound administrative system. Some said that they had learned a lot from the Guptas in the north. After all, King Kakushtavarman's daughter was now married to the son of Samudra Gupta and there was plenty of coming and going between the kingdoms. An annexe to the palace complex was the administrative block, and all the key advisors to the king were to be found there. The king called himself the Dharmamaharaja, meaning that he was both the temporal and the spiritual leader of his people. At the moment, an Ashvamedha yagna was underway, and the king was very preoccupied with it. The six month period of the sacred horse's wanderings would come to an end in the next fortnight, and preparations for that event were in full swing. The yagna had been very successful, and had further expanded the kingdom, which had pleased the king mightily. The noblemen who had accompanied the horse and defended it on its journey could count on some rich pickings when this was over.

The kingdom was divided into nine provinces or mandalas, with a governor for each province. King Kakushtavarman had appointed his son Krishna as the governor to the Thriparvatha Region, and other regions were in the charge of sons of various prominent families. Each mandala was further divided into smaller units, which had proved to be efficient for administration as well as for the collection of taxes. The taxes flowed regularly up the chain of command into the coffers of the king at Banavasi.

In Banavasi itself the king had quite an entourage at his command. He had his Chief Secretary and a Chief Justice. He had a personal physician and a private secretary to take care of his personal affairs. There was a Council of Ministers, headed by the Prime Minister, primarily responsible for ensuring that law and order were maintained, and the needs of the subjects were met. Vaman Bhat's job involved working with the Vidyavriddhas – the scholarly elders. They comprised a group of twelve scholars from around the world. Two were from as far as China and one from Persia. The others came from seats of learning from the great kingdoms of the north and south: from the Gupta and Ganga and Pallava regions. Debates and discussions between the elders were a daily affair; and it was the duty of Vaman Bhat and several others like him to record the main points and distill them into short papers that could easily be communicated to the king. This was a very taxing task, since the discussions were often on obscure texts in the Upanishads or on new ideas that were being aired for the first time. A lot of research and consultation were required to ensure that the ideas were being accurately conveyed; and since the king was a scholar himself, he could easily pick out a mistake, making the task that much more exacting. All in all, it was a wonderful way for a genuine scholar to spend his time, and Vaman Bhat thoroughly enjoyed himself on most days. There were some days when the scholars spent their entire time splitting hairs on some particularly niggling little issue, extremely tedious and petty, but luckily those days were few and far between.

He walked into his office room, one he shared with four others like him, and sat down at his desk. He opened the top and took out a pot of ink and his pen, and the manuscript he had been working on the day before. He needed to edit it somewhat, and bring it down to a page: those were their instructions. The king liked it that way, made for easy reading he said – which was nice for him no doubt, but the very devil to produce.

"Had your breakfast?" Vasudev Bhat, who sat to his immediate right, asked the usual introductory question.

Vaman Bhat assured him that he had had a very good breakfast indeed, and was all set for a productive days work.

In return, he asked courteously after Vasu's wife. "How is your wife? Has her stomach trouble eased at all?"

At this, Vasu's face was wreathed in smiles. He nodded enthusiastically. "Oh yes, sir, I must thank you very much for that. That infusion that you prescribed has done her wonders. Now she is able to take her meals comfortably, and already she has put on some weight again. It is no fun seeing your wife getting thinner and thinner every day, especially when she used to have such a healthy figure earlier."

Vaman Bhat was well aware of the healthiness of Vasu's wife's figure. Some less charitable people might even have called her fat, as indeed was poor Vasu. But she was an excellent cook, that had been her excuse. Then suddenly, some strange malady had overtaken her, triggered by a short bout of fever. Following that she had been listless, unable to enjoy her meals, and had lost weight at an alarming rate. Vasu had approached Vaman Bhat in great perturbation; over the years Vaman had developed something of a reputation as a healer, thanks to his study of the medicinal properties of herbs. Vasu had begged him to come home and take a look at his wife, and perhaps prescribe something that would help.

So Vaman Bhat had gone along after work to Vasu's house some weeks back, and had been quite taken aback to see the poor woman – she really did seem to be in distress and had definitely lost a significant amount of weight. He felt her pulse by placing his index, middle and ring fingers along her wrist on the side of the thumb. Reading the pulse required concentration and experience; Vaman Bhat had both. Was the heart beat swift and light, like a slithering snake? Was it strong and forceful, like a leaping frog? Was it slow and smooth, like a gliding swan? Sometimes it could be all of these. Vasu's wife's pulse was forceful and erratic – definitely a leaping frog. Taken in conjunction with the other symptoms, his diagnosis was a malady of the liver. He would need to put together a special mixture for her.

At home, he had not gone to pick the herbs from his garden, because this was not a case that would respond to the standard types of herbs that grew in his backyard. What he needed was Katuki, a herb found only in the high altitudes of the Himalayas. Luckily, he had some packed away, the remnants of a small store of the precious herb given to him by a visiting monk. To this he added a small trace of copper. Too much could be deadly, but in the right quantity copper was a powerful stimulant to various cells of the body, including the liver. Spooning a generous quantity of honey into a pestle, for both the herb and the copper were frightfully bitter, he ground the whole into a smooth paste. Two spoons of this two times a day on an empty stomach, followed by a cup of warm water should be adequate, was his prescription. Which apparently had proved correct, for now Vasu was a happy man, back to having a healthy wife, who was no doubt back to cooking up all the delicacies he had been missing.

"Good," Vaman Bhat said with satisfaction. "Happy to hear it. If she had not responded, I was thinking of referring her to my daughter. She is a much more experienced healer than I am, you know."

"Yes, yes," Vasu agreed enthusiastically. "I have heard many good things about her, sir. I know of many people who have gone to her and got a lot of relief. But a little out of the way place she has chosen, isn't it? Is it safe for a young girl to live there on her own?"

Vasu had touched a tender spot. "Well, she says she is safe. She is not alone, you know. She has Nagi with her, and also now three young people whom she has trained as her helpers – they live with her too. But she has a large area there for her herbs, the air is clean and fresh and the water is pure – she says she needs all that to do her work effectively. Udaya and I go often to see her and make sure she is well. What else can you do these days? Children will have their way!" Vaman Bhat was resigned to the situation.

"Oh yes, yes, no doubt, no doubt, sir. What cannot be cured must be endured, as they say!" Vasu tried to console his friend. "Young people these days are much more capable and independent than we used to be. It's a good thing I suppose." He didn't sound particularly convinced.

A third voice suddenly intervened, high and slightly shrill. Both Vasu and Vaman Bhat turned in surprise, since it belonged to one who didn't often appear in this part of the palace. "Are you speaking of your daughter?" asked Narayanachar, the king's personal physician.

Both Vasu and Vaman Bhat quickly rose and folded their hands in greeting. With Narayanachar was his colleague Siddayya. Vaman Bhat eyed them both warily. He had had occasion to meet this duo before, under circumstances he did not recall with much pleasure. Narayanachar was reputed to be a good man, but rather too aware of the importance of his position. The king held him in very high esteem: after all, the role of the royal physician was an important one. With paranoia running so high in royal circles, one of the main functions of the royal physician was to ensure that the king was not being poisoned. There were so many ingenious ways in which poison could be administered –through inhalations, such as through the snuff he used frequently through the day. Or through his food and drink, although that was too commonplace for most self-respecting villains. Poison had been known to have been delivered even through ordinary toiletries, such as a toothbrush twig, or a comb, or through the oil used to massage the king before his bath. It was the royal physician's job to guard the king's personal effects, and regularly subject them to tests to ensure their continued safety. All this in addition to alleviating the king's aches and pains and colds and fevers. It wasn't an easy job, but Narayanchar had done it well; and so far, by god's grace, the king had enjoyed impeccable good health.

As a result of the king's regard, Narayanachar tended to put on airs. There was no doubt though that he was extremely competent, and was said to be a man of integrity, at least professionally. Siddayya, on the other hand, had no such reputation. He was well known to be a charlatan and feared by many for the influence he wielded over the royal physician. He was also supposed to be a trained healer, and it was said that he and Narayanachar had met at medical school. However, he did not appear to practice medicine any more; many said that he did not have a healing touch, that all his patients had died. But that was in another kingdom and many years ago, and now Siddayya had abandoned medicine in favor of politics. He had the ear of the royal physician, and the royal physician had the ear of the king. He made things happen.

Vaman Bhat, unfortunately, had been singled out by Siddayya many years ago for a campaign of harassment. The trigger for the campaign had been his daughter, and the fact that he was training her in the science and art of healing. "It is not responsible of you, a senior member of government and a respected member of society, to transgress all rules like this," Siddayya had accused him. "Everyone agrees that this is not a fit occupation for women. If it had been, the Vedas and Upanishads would have said so. You are going against nature, the natural order of things."

In vain did Vaman Bhat point out that nowhere in any of the scriptures did it say that a woman may not be a healer. In fact, women's temperaments – more sympathetic and feeling – were better suited to the profession. But none of this cut any ice with Siddayya. He wanted Vaman Bhat to immediately discontinue the training of his daughter. Narayanachar backed him in this, although not with the same single-minded viciousness. However, Vaman Bhat steadfastly refused to comply with their demands. He was not transgressing any law by training his daughter, and nowhere could Siddayya produce any evidence of a specific ban on women being healers. Under the circumstances, Siddayya had no recourse but to retreat with veiled threats;

and even these he could not really make good, since Vaman Bhat was a respected figure and could not be easily dragged down. So Siddayya had backed off, but Vaman Bhat knew that he was waiting for his opportunity to pounce.

Looking at the men now, Vaman Bhat was filled with foreboding. On the face of it, the men looked friendly enough this morning. Both were younger than him, aged maybe around fifty or so. Narayanachar, being the shorter and plumper of the two, tended to look genial. His round face and light brown eyes gave him a gentle look, which perhaps was not entirely unfounded. He tended to smile a lot, which was also disarming. Siddayya was different altogether: tall and thin, with a broken nose and sly eyes, he looked the quintessential schemer. Maybe there was some truth to the saying that one's nature is reflected in the face, because one look at Siddayya was all it took to glean the direction of his thoughts.

"Good morning, sir," said Vaman Bhat politely. "This is indeed an honor! What brings you to our part of the world? Is there some problem with the documents we sent the king yesterday?"

"No, no, Vaman, nothing like that at all," Narayanachar replied. "I don't concern myself with your texts – it's all too philosophical for me! I like to stick to what I know – which you too have an interest in, I know, although unlike me you never were formally trained in medicine. Nor is your daughter, although she has a roaring practice from what I hear."

"All her training is from her father," sniggered Siddayya. "We are well aware of it. Training a woman as a healer, whoever heard of it! It is mere hair splitting to say that it is not forbidden in the scriptures – so many things may not be explicitly forbidden, but does that mean we go ahead and do them?"

Vaman Bhat drew a deep calming breath. "She has a natural talent for healing, sir," he reiterated gently in his daughter's defense. "People have great faith in her, mostly due to her invariable success in treating even the toughest cases. Her strength is in truly understanding the pulse, sir. She takes great care to spend time on it and it pays off. I have never known her to be wrong in her diagnosis. Besides, although she has a good practice, she is not getting rich on it, that isn't her intention. She treats all the poor people for free."

"Yes, I have heard a lot about the faith people have in her! Any quack can inspire faith if they put their minds to it – give people a pain killer or a mood enhancer and they will go away saying you are a brilliant physician. Well, well, every father has the right to be proud of his daughter, I suppose, although….. I understand she is only adopted." Vaman Bhat had to bite his tongue to stop himself from snapping back. Siddayya was a snake, everyone knew that – better beware of him, and not give into the momentary satisfaction of giving him a set down.

But he could not let Siddayya's last remark pass without comment. "She is adopted, sir, but both my wife and I love her as much as any parent loves their own daughter. I don't think she has ever felt a lack of affection and care in our home. And we have encouraged her to explore her interests and talents far in excess of what most parents allow for a female child."

Narayanachar laughed shortly and said "Yes, well, be that as it may, I have a request for you. Actually, it is a request for your daughter. As you know, the Ashvamedha yagna concludes two weeks from now."

Vaman Bhat nodded, wondering what was to come. How could he or his daughter have anything to do with that?

"Well, on the concluding day, the king will perform the usual rituals and sacrifices associated with the final day of such a yagna. The ceremony will be thrown open to the public – this is not usual, but the king has deemed it so this time. It appears the Council of Ministers has convinced him that his subjects want to participate in his triumph. It will mean a Herculean effort in terms of arrangements and logistics. All the stands to be erected and venue to be prepared, all those mouths to be fed – the next couple of weeks will be a nightmare! Anyway, in the midst of all this, the king has suggested that we set up a tent for a healer. In fact, he is set on it. With so many people coming from all over the kingdom, and all the excitement and crowds, it is likely that there will be some injuries and ailments that will need immediate attention, some first aid."

"That is a good idea, sir. The people will appreciate it," Vaman Bhat said.

"Yes, that is what we thought as well. It has never been done before, so we don't yet know how effective it will be, but it is a good indication of the king's concern for the welfare of his subjects." Clearly, the king was going all-out to curry favor with his subjects. Although Kakushtavarman was a popular king, and a powerful one, the provincial governors were a restless lot, including his own son Krishna.

Who knew when they would decide to foment trouble in the kingdom? "So I thought the best thing would be to have your daughter and her team come and man the tent – or should I say woman the tent – for the day. We will give her whatever she needs in terms of facilities and supplies, and we will compensate her well. It is after all a great day, and the king is in an expansive mood."

"The king has heard all about her, you know," Siddayya added resentfully. "He likes to hear the voice of the people from his Ministers. Somehow word has got to him that she is the talk of the town, that everyone swears by her. No doubt being a pretty young woman doesn't hurt – unlike me, most people are stupid enough to be taken in by a pretty face."

Vaman Bhat gritted his teeth. He must not let the man get to him! But as for the rest of the proposition, he hardly knew what to say – it was the last thing he had expected. It was an honor alright, to be picked by the king among all the healers in the kingdom, to be showcased on a historic occasion such as this. But would it be dangerous?

"Don't worry," Narayanachar seemed to have read his mind. "There will be plenty of security. This is essentially a military triumph. The entire might of the king's army will be present. The chances of any kind of trouble will be very slim. Think about it, but not too long. I need to know by the afternoon. If she isn't available, I will need to find someone else. But the king is keen on her, don't ask me why."

"I will let you know, sir. I will go at once to her house and inquire from her." He almost sighed as he said that. Knowing her, he could scarcely predict what her reaction would be. She might be wildly enthusiastic, or she might be violently opposed. She may see it as a god sent opportunity to show Siddayya up for his narrow minded prejudices; or on the other hand she may not want to be seen to be obliging him in any way.

He crossed his fingers firmly.

# Chapter 3

Asking Vasu to make his excuses in case anyone came looking for him, Vaman Bhat set out immediately in the direction of his daughter. It was a healthy walk, and even at a brisk pace it would take more than an hour. He considered going home and yoking up his bullocks, but then balked at the idea of answering Sita's questions. She would want to know the reason for this mid-week trip, and since he could never resist her cross-examination, would worry endlessly about the implications of this royal request. Better tell her at the end of the day, when it was a done deal. One way or another, it would lay to rest at least half the speculation; and it would spare him a whole lot of futile advice and instruction.

Luckily the worst of both the summer and the monsoon were over. It was not for nothing that this region was called *Malenadu* – the land of the rain. But by this time it normally reduced to an occasional shower, a respite from the preceding almost three months of relentless driving rain which left the paths squelchy with mud.

Devi had finished with most of her patients by about noon. It had been a busy day for Laxmi, her oldest helper, mixing endless batches of cough and cold medicine. All morning Devi had suffered some disquiet. Yesterday a young man had been brought in a serious condition. He had climbed a jackfruit tree, and had been cutting down a fruit from one of the high branches when he lost his footing and fell. His guardian angel had evidently been looking out for him because he had fallen on a grassy verge at the base of the tree, which had spared him any seriously broken bones. He did have a painfully twisted ankle and was badly bruised all over; but the most worrisome was that he had a deep gash in his thigh, and Devi suspected that a sharp twig might have penetrated the skin and buried itself deep inside. The area had been swollen up and too painful to touch. She had temporarily bound up the wound after applying a thick paste of pounded root of the Bhuiamala plant boiled in cow's milk and mixed with a little sesame oil. She had hoped the young man would come back today so that she could check on how he was doing, and guage whether her remedy had been effective.

As she was winding up, there was a commotion in the yard outside, and Laxmi burst into the consulting room. "He's here!" she announced breathlessly.

"Who's here?" Devi asked perplexed.

"That man from yesterday, the one you have been asking about," Laxmi replied.

Devi hurried out. Sure enough, the young man had been brought back, but he was clearly not doing well. She had secretly been hoping that he would walk back into the room declaring himself to be completely cured. On the contrary, he had been carried back in a roughly made litter by a couple of his male relatives. Devi asked them to immediately take him inside and put him down in the inner chamber, which they did. She sent Laxmi to fetch Nagi at once. She went closer to examine the patient. He did not look good. His face was ashen with pain, and he was gritting his teeth to stop himself from crying out. When Devi put her hand out to check the wound on his thigh, he did cry out, and she quickly withdrew her hand.

Nagi entered the room hastily and stopped short upon seeing the young man stretched out on the mat. "What is it?" she asked Devi quietly, "What can we do?"

"Get me some poppy seeds crushed in honey," Devi instructed her quickly. The poppy seeds would soon numb the young man's senses and make him drowsy, which would make it easier to examine him. Nagi returned shortly with a smoothly ground mixture of poppy seeds and honey, and spooned it into his mouth. The effect was surprisingly quick, and within about ten minutes, he became less restless and the tension in his muscles began to relax. Within fifteen minutes he was falling asleep. Devi waited anxiously for him to settle down. The wound on his thigh looked ominous, and she knew that it meant surgery. Clearly something was lodged inside the wound, and it would have to come out. She thought of her dream that morning, and if she had not been so tense, it might have made her smile. Not everyone had the good luck to find their dreams of such immediate use!

Without having to be told, Nagi went out and brought back a basin of hot water with turmeric dissolved in it and some clean towels. Then she laid out the knives, needles and pincers that would be used for the operation. Devi carefully removed the bandage from the wound, drawing her breath in sharply when she saw what lay underneath.

It was ugly, uglier than yesterday even. The ointment had not done much good; but then it couldn't, not with a twig still lodged inside. Devi instructed Nagi to hold the man's shoulders down even though he was heavily sedated, for the pain of extraction would be severe. If he were to jerk or twist violently due to the pain, it might lead to all sorts of unpleasant complications.

The first task was to clean the wound thoroughly with medicated turmeric water. The patient moaned with pain and shifted restlessly. Nagi immediately held him down gently, murmuring soothing words to calm him. Then Devi took up the knife which was kept well sharpened, and made a quick incision to open up the wound so she could see inside. She staunched the quick rush of blood with cotton. The opened up wound revealed that indeed there was a sharp long sliver of wood lodged in his thigh. The pain must have been excruciating. Picking up the thinnest pincers, Devi grasped the tip of the sliver protruding slightly from the flesh. She must take a firm grip and pull hard and surely. If the sliver were to break inside the flesh, it would be a disaster. She would then have to cut even deeper, causing much more loss of blood, many more chances of infection, and it would take much longer to heal. Sending up a short prayer asking the blessings of the great surgeon Susruta, she gripped the sliver and pulled with all her strength. The sliver came cleanly out of the wound, and at the same time the young man shrieked in pain and reared up from the mat. Nagi lunged forward and grabbed him by his shoulders and pushed him back down on the mat with all her strength, while Devi desperately mopped up the blood pouring from the open wound.

Gradually the situation came back under control. The young man subsided, moaning, but much calmer than before. The flow of blood reduced substantially, and finally stopped. Both Devi and Nagi were soaked in sweat, from the exertion and from the stress. But the operation was not yet complete. Holding the lips of the wound close together, Devi anointed it generously with a mixture of ghee, honey and turmeric. She then took a wad of margosa leaves and bound the wound around tightly with them, before covering the whole area with clean bandages.

The young man had drifted back to sleep again. Did he look more comfortable than before? Devi devoutly hoped so. There was nothing left for her to do but clean up the mess, and go take a much needed bath.

When she turned around, she saw Vaman Bhat in the doorway. She was startled by his presence. How long had he been there? Had he been watching her doing the operation?

"Father!" she exclaimed. Then, looking more closely at him, she asked anxiously, "What is the matter? Is everything alright with you? Mother? Why have you come in the middle of the week like this? Why have you left your office to come so far?"

Vaman Bhat smiled at this barrage of questions. "There is nothing to worry about, we are all well. I need to discuss something with you, that is all. But it can wait until you have bathed. You have had a busy morning."

Only then did Devi realize what a sight she must present – bathed in sweat and covered in blood, hardly a sight for sore eyes. Even a fond father might find her less than appealing at this moment!

Nagi chimed in, "You must stay and eat with us, sir". Vaman Bhat agreed, although he said he had already had his breakfast earlier. But he would join them for a snack.

As Devi turned to go, he said quietly, "That was well done. I couldn't have done the operation better myself."

She couldn't agree. "You would have done it better, father. You would have done it yesterday, when he first came here. I sent him off thinking he would heal with ointments. I should have known better. That sliver should have come out at once."

Vaman Bhat laid a gentle hand on her shoulder. "Don't be so hard on yourself, child! Now you have learned, through experience. This is how I learned also, through experience. You have no idea of the mistakes I have made in my career. That young patient was lucky to have you as his healer."

She smiled fondly at him. Always so supportive, always so loving! Then she stepped lightly out of the room towards the bathing pool.

## ii

She stripped her soiled clothes off with relief and waded into the pool. The water was cool and inviting. She wondered again why her father was here. It was not usual. She knew he was kept busy at work on most days, and this unscheduled visit made her somehow uneasy. Why had he looked anxious? Or was she imagining it? She always felt a pang when she saw Vaman Bhat looking anxious. She knew that she had caused him hardship. She was always aware of what her foster parents had done for her. Without their shelter and love, she would probably have ended up as one of the beggars on the river ghats of Allahabad, abused and exploited in unspeakable ways. She would be eternally grateful to them if only for that; but they had done so much more. They had nurtured her and supported her in ways that even real parents often did not do for their children, particularly their daughters. Daughters were meant to be married off as soon as possible, to the best match that they could find.

This would have been Devi's lot under normal circumstances. But it was her good fortune that her parents did not subscribe to the accepted formula. Just as they had been liberal and open with their son when he had chosen to follow the path of the Buddha, in the same way they had observed their daughter's interest in healing and encouraged her in it. At a time when a normal parent would have been looking around for a suitable groom for their daughter, Vaman Bhat was teaching his daughter about the healing properties of herbs and giving her medical texts to pore over. Devi was aware of the opposition that he had faced from very high quarters to his training of her, which he had withstood without compromise.

This had often caused Devi disquiet. Should she have been a more dutiful daughter, less determined and troublesome? If she had just opted to tow the line and follow the path taken by all of her childhood companions, life would have been much easier for her parents, she was sure of that. Many of her friends now were well ensconced in the family fold, looking after their aging in-laws and a brood of babies. They were happy enough, some of them very much so. Why couldn't she have been like them? She could have presented Vaman Bhat and Sita with grandchildren to play with and spoil. They would have been delighted.

And she wouldn't have had to look far for a husband. Despite his best efforts, Udaya had not been able to conceal his feelings from her. He had never been good at pretending anyway. He could not tell a simple white lie without turning red in the face. She had known almost from the very first day that he had discovered his feelings that he had changed in some essential way. She made sure not to reveal her knowledge. Devi simply did not love Udaya in that way, and she knew she never would. He was her best friend, and greatest supporter, but her wayward heart could not be brought to return his feelings, try as she might. In fact, that was what had prompted her to move this far away from home. She knew that had caused her parents some grief, but she had no choice. Her proximity was making Udaya's life hellish, and she herself felt increasingly uncomfortable. Making some excuse about wanting to grow a large herbal garden and needing more space – both of which were true – she had scouted around with Nagi's help and found this spot, which was now proving to be ideal. But it had cost her. She was always conscious of the burden of worry she had placed upon her parents' shoulders, particularly on Vaman Bhat.

Which was why she always felt a pang when she saw the small frown of worry between his eyes.

She emerged from the pool, clean but not too refreshed, still pondering all these matters prompted by Vaman Bhat's unusual presence in her house today. Dressing quickly, she went back to the main room where her father was sitting and chatting with the girls. They got up and ran off when they saw her coming in, leaving father and daughter alone to chat.

"The girls seem to have settled in well – and they have learned a lot! They could answer all my questions without any mistakes," Vaman Bhat said to her, smiling.

"Yes, father," Devi replied. "It's taken a bit of time, but they have been good students. But tell me, I'm waiting to hear. What was it you wanted to discuss with me?"

Vaman Bhat stood up and walked to the window, looking out on the herbal garden. "I don't know where to start," he said. "You know that the king is planning a big celebration to mark the successful conclusion to his Ashvamedha Yagna?" Devi nodded. It was the talk of the town, everybody had heard about it and was making plans to be there on that day.

"Well, as you know there will be thousands of people there, all manner of people. Young and old, sick, infirm, they will turn up to watch the fun, whether they are fit to be there or not. You know our people. They love this kind of public display. Plus it is not everyday that this kind of ceremony is held publicly, so I suppose we should not judge them too harshly."

Devi was beginning to wonder where this was going. What did the king's Ashvamedha Yagna have to do with her?

"Anyway, to cut a long story short, the king has decided to set up a first aid tent at the venue. This is an excellent idea of course, because with the heat and the crowds, chances of people feeling faint or hurting themselves are high. Previously there was no help around, unless some kind neighbor offered to help out of the goodness of their hearts. But this time the king has decided to offer this service to his subjects. I suppose he feels it will increase his popularity a bit also, which is always a good thing these days. There are all sorts of rumors around about rebellion and insurrection and what not."

"Really?" Devi was surprised. "I thought the king was at the height of his popularity and power, what with the successful Ashvamedha and everything."

"Well, yes," Vaman Bhat agreed. "That's true, but you know what they say – uneasy lies the head that wears the crown. The governors have also become quite powerful, and now the king has more to lose than ever before. I am sure he as a few sleepless nights. But I digress. Here's the reason I came today."

Devi waited attentively for him to continue, although he sank into a brief reverie, deep in thought. "Yes, the reason I came today," he continued suddenly. "The reason is that the king would like you to manage the tent. Apparently he asked for you specifically."

Devi was dumbfounded. Whatever she had expected her father to say next, it was not this. "What! What are you saying, father?" she exclaimed, incredulous.

"Yes, yes, child, it is true," Vaman Bhat assured her. "Narayanachar and Siddayya were at my office this morning, and they put this proposition to me. They will give you all the assistance you need, and there will be a good reward for you in this. The king is in a generous mood they claim, and they should know."

"Siddayya!" Devi exclaimed again. "That snake! He means some mischief by this, I'm sure."

Vaman Bhat did not dispute it. "He might, I do not disagree. I too mistrust Siddayya with reason. But

Narayanachar was also there, and he is generally a good man. It sounds like your talents are finally being recognized as they should, and this would mean that you have even royal sanction to continue with your work. All the trouble we have had all these years from Siddayya and his supporters will become a thing of the past. Plus you will get a nice sum of money that you can invest in your clinic – there is still so much more that can be done here."

Devi looked at her father in surprise. "So what are you saying, father? Are you suggesting that I take this up? You know that Siddayya well, he cannot be trusted. This must be some trick! He has always been after my blood, you know that. I cannot believe he has come up with this proposal now – this seems like a very prominent position to be in, quite an honor in fact! Why would he be handing it to me, of all people, on a platter? I smell a rat…"

Again Vaman Bhat could not disagree. "I know, daughter, I know. I have thought about this all the way here. If Siddayya can find a way to get you and me into trouble, he will, I am well aware of that. But on the other hand, I have also been thinking, what harm can come of doing this? It seems like a simple enough proposal. One that is for the public good, in fact, something which we all take seriously in our family. It will give you exposure to a larger set of people, potential clients. It may well be the next step in your career. But I don't want to influence you. You have always been able to make your own decisions, I have full confidence that you will be able to make this one as well. The only hitch is that they want to know by the end of the day, which gives you very little time to think about it. It will need to be somewhat of a snap decision, unfortunately."

Devi was silent. Mainly she was confused: on the one hand, this was a good opportunity. She would get to be seen by the entire town as the king's chosen one, and that would definitely increase her client base. More clients meant a bigger income – not that she wanted to be rich. But more money meant that she could do the kind of work that she really wanted to do. Right now, much of it was restricted because of lack of funds. On the other hand, Siddayya was untrustworthy, and his proposal was sure to have some hidden agenda which they would discover much later when it was too late. He had been gunning for her for years now, causing untold anxiety for her parents. What prompted his jealousy and venom, she had never been able to fathom. It was not that she was taking any business away from him, or causing him any other hardship with her practice. It appeared that she just offended his conservative ideas on the role of women, and her very existence posed some sort of challenge to his beliefs.

But if she were to turn down this opportunity, she could kiss goodbye to any hope of being singled out again by the king. He had evidently heard good things about her from some source, although she could not imagine from whom. He was a man who believed in rewarding talent. And evidently he at least was not mired by traditional ideas on what was proper behavior for young women from a good family. Despite being a liberal and just king, he would not take kindly to having his offer rejected by a chit of a girl. No doubt he thought he was bestowing a huge honor upon her. So what should she do?

Vaman Bhat watched while she wrestled with the problem. "Come, let us eat," he said to her presently. "It's always easier to make a decision on a full stomach. You have had a tiring morning already, and here I am burdening you further before you have had a chance to fortify yourself. Nagi!" he called out.

"Yes sir?" Nagi appeared immediately. Vaman Bhat instructed her to serve food to her mistress at once since she was urgently in need of sustenance. Nagi quickly went out and reappeared with banana leaf plates and copper tumblers, which she set on the floor for both father and daughter. As they sat down, she brought in the steaming rice and beans and vegetables, simply but deliciously cooked, and Devi ate with a hearty appetite. She had such an active day every day that she had no reason to watch what she ate. Everything was burned away in the course of her exertions. Vaman Bhat ate sparingly, although the long walk had given him something of an appetite. They spoke desultorily about household matters, and Vaman Bhat gave Devi some advice on the cultivation of her herbal garden. After they had drunk their buttermilk and washed their hands, he reminded Devi that she needed to make a decision fairly soon. She had not forgotten, it had been in the back of her mind right through lunch. She came suddenly to a decision.

"Yes, I will do it," she said.

"Sure?" he asked. "You won't be able to back out once you agree. Not without a very good reason, anyway."

"Yes, yes, I know that," Devi replied. "But it is a good opportunity, and if I do not do it, it will put me in a very bad position. If it was just Siddayya asking, I would not have any problems with refusing. But if it is the king who has said I should do this, how can I refuse? He will never give me such a chance again. Besides, he may even take it out on you – and you have to meet the king almost everyday. It's probably because he thinks so highly of you that he even spared me a thought."

"Don't worry about me," Vaman Bhat reassured her quickly. "You think about yourself first. I will deal with whatever repercussions your decision may have on me. I was not born yesterday you know. I have a few tricks up my sleeve as well! My only concern is that you do what you feel is right, what you are comfortable with."

"Then tell Siddayya I will do it, father," Devi said decisively.

Vaman Bhat gave Devi a quick hug. "It will all work out for the best, you will see. I will help you in anyway I can, and you know you can count on Udaya as well. We will pull this off between us. It will be your triumph, I guarantee."

Then he hurried away, so as not to delay telling Narayanachar and Siddayya of his daughter's decision.

# Chapter 4

Krishna Rao was a worried man. As the Prime Minister, the task of organizing the Horse Sacrifice, the culminating ceremony of the Ashvamedha celebrations, fell to his lot. He had realized that it would be a massive task, and that was even before the Council of Ministers in their wisdom had declared that it should be thrown open to the public. What on earth had induced them to do this he would never figure out. And they had gone straight to the king with this brilliant suggestion, without following the well-established protocol of running the idea by him first. If he had had any inkling of their intentions, he would have stopped them short with some perfectly good objection. He could have invoked some obscure scriptural reference that prohibited public celebrations after battles, for example, or cited some ill omen which contra-indicated it. But no, they had gone straight to the king, giving ample demonstration of the low cunning of which he had always suspected them. By the time he got wind of the idea and hurried to the king's chamber to dissuade him from this mad scheme, he found it was already too late. The king was all charged up with the idea. Having his subjects witness his triumph, having them participate in his celebration – what could be more rewarding to a monarch? He would hear of nothing against the notion, and pooh-poohed all of Krishna Rao's concerns. "You're an old woman, Krishna Rao," he had laughed. "Think of the spectacle, think of its impact on the people! Hundreds of thousands of them will come to see their king being anointed as the greatest king on earth. How many times does that happen in a person's lifetime? Sometimes not even once. I am giving them something to think about and talk about for generations to come. Have a sense of history, man!"

That was all very well, and Krishna Rao did have a clear vision rising before him of the spectacle and the historic occasion. But all it did was give him a cramp in the pit of his stomach. Thousands of people would certainly show up, and they would all need to be catered to, arrangements would have to be made for sleeping halls, mass feeding would have to be provided for, security would have to be arranged for there were sure to be all sorts of unsavory elements in the crowd, the ceremonial ground would have to be prepared and stands erected all around for the crowds to sit and observe the proceedings in comfort.

All this in addition to the preparations for the Horse Sacrifice itself. Hundreds of priests needed to be organized. Huge numbers of animals would have to be made ready for sacrifice. There were very specific requirements in this regard. All the materials would need to be arranged – the fruit, the flowers, the massive amounts of wood for the fire, the incense and all the myriad other items required for a puja on such a grand scale. It was going to be a nightmare!

It was not that Krishna Rao was not equal to the task. He was the most able man in the kingdom. It was not for nothing that he had become the Prime Minister at such a young age. He had been barely forty when he had been elevated to the post. He had paid his dues for many years, working his way up the system, serving several provincial governors in senior capacities, until he was noticed by the king. Then he had been unknowingly under the king's observation for a year or more before he had finally been offered the post. It was said that he came from an extremely poor family of farmers, but had shown so much promise as a young boy that a local Brahmin had taken him under his wing and tutored him in the scriptures. The boy had no interest in becoming a scholar, but the skills his education gave him held him in good stead. As soon as he could, he got a junior position in the provincial government, and there was no looking back after that. Looking at him now, it was hard to imagine that his beginnings had been so humble. With his wide forehead and patrician bearing, his impeccable silk dhoti and shirt, and the gold edged turban on his thick head of hair, he looked every inch the scion of some aristocratic family.

But this was an altogether difficult time. This Horse Sacrifice was a personal triumph for the king, no doubt, but the kingdom had paid a price for it. The most noble young men in the kingdom had been sent off to accompany the horse in its wanderings. They also represented the families closest to the king and his strongest supporters. The process of picking this small band of warriors to accompany the horse had been a divisive one. There was much muttering and rumor mongering amongst those who had not been chosen, and they had not been placated by the king's subsequent overtures of goodwill. With the announcement of each fresh victory of the horse, the resentment amongst this group had grown. After all, they felt, it could have been one of them who could be even now sharing in the victory if only the king had been impartial in his choice. This, of course, was more a product of their jealousy than a fact. The king had only picked his most able warriors for the Ashvamedha Yagna. It made no sense to allow nepotism or favoritism to dictate that choice. The whole point of the exercise was to assert the king's power by successfully conquering and annexing neighboring kingdoms. This could only be done by the best and brightest. The king had been scrupulously objective in his choices, but the disgruntled ones were not willing to accept this.

If this was not enough, the cost had been high. Ashvamedhas were an expensive business. No doubt, they brought in huge dividends, when successful, in terms of greater territory and wealth. But they had to be paid for first, and this had been done by raising taxes, and the people had not been happy. For several years now, the provincial governors had borne the brunt of the effort to fill the royal coffers to pay for the expenses attendant on the Ashvamedha, and the strain was beginning to show. Unless the king rewarded them richly – and soon – there was no answering for the consequences. Krishna Rao was afraid that even now it was too late. Stories of plots and counter-plots abounded, and it was difficult to decide whether there was any truth to them. His spies had reported secret meetings and confabulations between the governors; and most disturbing of all, some of the reports were from

Thriparvatha region, where the king's son Krishna was governor. If the king's own son was plotting and planning an insurrection, things were going to be difficult indeed.

To top it all, he had received news just this morning that Jayadeva, the son of Ramaraya, one of the king's closest confidantes, had gone missing. He had been one of the bravest and ablest of the young warriors following in the wake of the horse. The loss of this warrior was not only inexplicable, but also going to be the very devil to break to the king. There was no knowing what had happened to the man. Had he been kidnapped, or had he been killed in battle, or had he fallen by the wayside and not been noticed? His informant had not been able answer these questions. All that was known was that Jayadeva was missing, and the group would be returning without him. The king would definitely see this as a bad omen. It remained to be seen who he would hold responsible for it.

It was no wonder that Krishna Rao was a worried man, juggling all these vexed matters, while at the same time attending to the routine administration of the kingdom. He had convened a meeting of all his staff and the Council of Ministers later this afternoon, but first he needed to consult the scholars on a matter of procedure with regard to the actual ceremony. He would go and talk to Vaman Bhat. He could be counted on to give him accurate information. Besides, he liked the man, and could perhaps unburden himself a bit to him.

On the way he stopped to inspect progress with the arrangements for the celebrations. The venue was the famous Madukeshwara Temple, built to commemorate the death of the demon Madhu, killed by Lord Vishnu at the request of Lord Shiva. The temple complex itself was a work in progress. At its center were shrines dedicated to both Shiva and Vishnu. A special feature of the temple complex was the massive stone sculpture of the five hooded Naga or sacred serpent, said to have been constructed by the princess Sivaskanda Nagashri almost two hundred years previously. Alongside this impressive structure was a huge vihara or a covered hall, with an intricately carved roof, often used for important occasions, such as the present one. Next to the vihara was a deep pool, with carved stone steps leading down to it, used by the priests for their ritual baths, and for washing the idols on certain prescribed occasions. The temple complex was enclosed by an elaborately patterned stone compound wall, more than ten feet high and several feet thick. Four massive gates served as entrances on each side of this wall, all beautifully decorated, carved with all manner of human and animal motifs. The most impressive of these gates was the one that served as the main entrance: the East gate. It was extra wide and tall, to allow free access to the temple chariot. The temple chariot was taken on a daily perambulation around the outer perimeter of the temple walls so that the gods could survey their land and their subjects. The people of Banavasi never tired of this ritual, and everyday the great passage all around the temple was lined with hundreds of devotees who gathered to watch the procession and catch a glimpse of their gods out for an evening stroll.

So this was the venue for the Ashvamedha celebration. Krishna Rao had discussed the arrangements in detail with the architects and builders after consulting the priests. Stands would be set up all around the temple for people to sit and watch the spectacle. The victorious parade of the golden chariot drawn by the conquering horse and his accompanying soldiers and nobles would go all around the temple twice, after which the ritual cleaning of the horse by the chief queen and her ladies could be conducted in full view of all the spectators.

After that, Krishna Rao planned to move the operations within the complex, and to close the great carved doors of the East gate. It was agreed that, despite Siddayya's protests to the contrary, the general public would not be allowed inside the temple complex. The rituals that were to take place in there had been explained to Krishna Rao, and it came home to him that only those with a strong stomach would be able to withstand the grisly affair.

He did not think people would be too disappointed. They would have had enough excitement watching the procession, and the carnival atmosphere that would take over the town would distract them into other pleasures. The king was providing food for everyone at massive kitchens to be set up some distance from the temple complex. People who had set out from home very early that morning so as not to miss a minute of the fun would be looking forward to the sumptuous meal. After that there would be all sorts of amusements to be found, especially for country-folk who were on a rare visit to the big city.

## ii

Vaman Bhat was in his office, a prey to doubt. He had come back well in time the evening before to meet with Narayanachar and Siddayya, both of whom appeared to have been awaiting his arrival. He sat them down and told them of his daughter's decision. They had seemed satisfied with the response. Narayanachar had gone so far as to congratulate him. "I am glad that she has agreed, Vaman. This will be a good step forward for her, it will be the making of her career. I hope she is conscious of what an honor it is to be singled out like this. The king does not bestow his favors easily. And she has you to thank for it as well. As you know, the king has a high regard for you, and this is in a way the result. I know she is young, but I hope she has the sense to take this task seriously and apply herself sincerely."

Vaman Bhat assured him that this was the case. He was confident of it anyway. He had never known Devi to do anything in half measures. But having delivered the message, he was overcome with dissonance. He knew that there had been little choice in the matter, and that the consultation – both of Narayanachar and Siddayya with him, and between himself and Devi - had been a mere formality. The king might as well have decreed that Devi take up this task. It would have amounted to the same thing. It would have been madness to have refused a royal request. So why had Narayanachar and Siddayya come to him and put it to him in that manner? Had they hoped that Devi would be foolhardy enough to refuse and thereby incur the displeasure of the king? Quite likely. It was the sort of scheming that was typical of Siddayya! So it might have been a disappointment to the duo to find that she had not fallen into their trap. However, they had seemed pleased enough, and promised full cooperation and assistance to make the project a success. They instructed Vaman Bhat to tell his daughter to give a full list of materials and medicines she would need for the day. "No need for her to bring anything from her clinic," Siddayya had said. "Let her give us a list, we will procure everything she needs. We will get the best of everything, no need to worry on that account."

At home, Sita and Udaya had expressed their fears as well, but they too had to acknowledge that there was no other decision that could have been made in the circumstances. "I will go to Devi tomorrow to ask her what she needs," Udaya said. "I have to go there in the evening anyway, so then we can spend some time discussing this. I will help her of course, she will need all the help she can get. Just Nagi and the three girls will not be enough. Perhaps you should be there too, father," Udaya suggested.

Sita too seemed to agree with this suggestion. But unfortunately Vaman Bhat, along with the other scholars, had already been assigned other duties for the big day. He would need to be in the center of things, as an advisor to the priests performing the Yagna, directing them to the appropriate passages in the scriptures and making sure all the rituals were being properly observed. He would not be able to attend to the sick in his daughter's first aid tent. He regretfully declined Udaya's suggestion; but offered to help in any way he could prior to the actual day, in the planning and preparations.

As he sat awash in hopes and fears, he saw Prime Minister Krishna Rao entering the courtyard outside. He hardly had a chance to wonder where he was headed, when Krishna Rao entered the room. His eyes lit up when he saw Vaman Bhat sitting there alone.

"Vaman, I am glad you are here and I am glad you are alone. We can get a chance to talk."

Vaman Bhat welcomed him with folded hands. He had a very high regard for Krishna Rao, a scrupulously honest and decent man, besides being a brilliant administrator. Their paths did not cross very often but when they did meet, it was with mutual warmth and respect. He asked what brought Krishna Rao to his office this morning.

"It is this Horse Sacrifice, Vaman," Krishna Rao explained with a sigh. "Don't quote me on this, but it is seriously becoming more trouble than it is worth as far as I am concerned. It is not just the ritual itself. That is not a problem. After all we are quite accustomed to making elaborate arrangements for rituals. But making it into a public function? I do not know why the Council of Ministers came up with such a hare-brained scheme, but now the king is all for it, and there is no backing out."

Vaman Bhat made a face. "Yes, I fully sympathize with you. I noticed some stands are being erected around the central courtyard of the temple. All these arrangements must be very time consuming for you, and stressful. Managing these teams of workmen to finish against the deadline is a headache, I am sure."

"You never said a truer word, Vaman. And the expense! Already we have poured money into the military campaign, and now more into this celebration. The king keeps talking about all the money that has been pouring into the coffers thanks to our military victories, but if we carry on spending it in this way, there will be precious little left. I have warned him! If he doesn't watch out, he will have a full blown rebellion on his hands. There is only so much the people will take; putting up a big show for them may placate them briefly, but in the long run the money should be used for their benefit. There are so many pending things that could have been done – roads need to be built, not to mention all types of other infrastructure: aquaducts, schools, community halls, homes for the poor."

"But look at it from the king's point of view," Vaman Bhat suggested. "After all, he needs a celebration, after such a successful military campaign. You cannot deny him that. I suppose the best that can be done is to control the damage as far as possible. Aim for simplicity and elegance rather than opulence, wherever possible. In fact, the king can make a political point out of it, saying that he wants his subjects to participate in the celebrations, but at the same time wants to ensure that they are not cheated of the benefits that rightfully belong to them."

"That sounds eminently sensible, Vaman, and that is what I had also intended to do. But that Siddayya interferes at every turn. Every proposal I make to keep things simple is shot down by him, and replaced with something outlandish. Can you imagine he wants all the streets of Banavasi strewn with jasmine flowers so that when people walk on them, the heady fragrance of the flowers will envelope the city? Heady fragrance of flowers! Heady stench of waste is more like it. I have started agreeing with everything he says, because arguing with him is just a frustrating experience for me! The king invariably agrees with all his suggestions. I have decided to play the game on the face of it. But after all, I am the Prime Minister, and I am the one ultimately responsible for the arrangements! On the actual day the king will be too busy with the rituals to make a note of whether or not all the arrangements have been made according to Siddayya's instructions. By the time Siddayya's spies report to him, it will be too late. Hopefully the celebrations will be successful enough that the king will overlook any shortcomings. Besides, I am counting on the fact that he relies entirely on me for the administration of this kingdom. That should save my neck, even if Siddayya tries to discredit me!"

"Siddayya is a dangerous man, sir," Vaman agreed. "But your plan will work, I think."

"I certainly hope so. Otherwise I have a nice retirement plan ready – go back to my farm, watch my crops grow and spend time with my family. Actually, that's a most attractive prospect! About the only sensible suggestion Siddayya made was to suggest that your daughter set up a first aid tent at the celebration. What did she decide? Has she agreed to do it?"

"Yes, sir, she has agreed," Vaman Bhat replied, but he was puzzled. "Did you say Siddayya suggested it? He said that it was the king's suggestion, and that he and Narayanachar had concurred with it."

"Oh that Siddayya is a crafty devil! He puts his suggestions in the king's mouth in such a way that eventually even the king believes it was his own suggestion. But I was there in the chamber that day – it was definitely Siddayya's suggestion. I was surprised, actually, because I know he has had a running feud with you over the training of your daughter. But anyway, if he is managing to overcome some of his prejudices, it is a good thing. A gifted healer should be encouraged, whether male or female."

Vaman Bhat made some reply, he hardly knew what. This was a disturbing piece of information. Why had Siddayya misled him into believing it was a royal command?

What was Siddayya's reason for suggesting Devi? What mischief was he planning? Vaman Bhat was again overcome with worry.

But he had no time to dwell on it because Krishna Rao had moved on and was asking for the details of the actual ceremony and the rituals that would need to be performed at the yagna. He needed to take down the relevant manuscripts, study them and then explain them to the Prime Minister.

"I understand that the dimensions of the fire altar of the yagna have to be very exact? I am told that there are mathematical formulae that govern the calculation of the length of each side and the number and dimensions of the bricks to be used." Krishna Rao seemed well up on the details.

"Yes, sir, that is indeed the case. My friend and colleague Sridhara is in charge of ensuring that all the calculations are made accurately and that everything is in keeping with the appropriate sutras. He is an accomplished mathematician, sir, trained in Pataliputra under some of the greatest teachers of our times."

Vaman Bhat got caught up in the discussion of the minutiae surrounding the yagna. He would have to leave speculation about Siddayya's schemes and intentions until later.

# Chapter 5

The young man was walking stealthily in the undergrowth, circling the camp. Just a few days ago, he had been inside the camp, looking out to make sure there were no marauders out there, waiting to ambush them. Today, he was outside, looking in, trying to assess the mood of various people within the camp. Usually at this time of day he tended to lie low for fear of being spotted; but in the post-lunch hours, it was fairly safe to be abroad, since most people in the camp would be resting. After the hectic days of warfare in the preceding year, there was a sense of anti-climax in the days leading up to the finale. Everyone was of course excited at the prospect of being back home with their families and enjoying the comforts they had been missing. The campaign had been brutal, and it was only the fact that they had been so successful that had kept them from turning back from some of the encounters. But success is sweet, and with each new win, their determination to complete the operation grew stronger. Some of their enemies had been mighty in their own time, and defeating them had been no mean feat. They had lost many brave soldiers, but those were the wages of war. So many had survived and were still there to enjoy the hero's welcome that was being planned for them. That was the blessing and the miracle.

The young man was Jayadeva, son of Ramaraya, the king's handpicked warrior. He was currently a dead man. Reports of his disappearance must even now be making the rounds in the city and among palace circles, he knew. Why then was he lurking about the soldiers' camp, spying on his colleagues? The reason for this was simple: he was on a special mission, given to him specifically by the king himself. He remembered well the day he had been recruited. He had been attending a high-level meeting in the king's ante-room, discussing military strategy. The meeting ended and the the Council of Ministers and others started filing out when the king signaled for him to stay behind. When they were alone, the king had called him close to his side, and sworn him into secrecy by all that he held sacred. Jayadeva was made to realize that this was dead serious, and whatever followed would mean a great deal of hardship, perhaps even death, for him. But it was a great honor to be chosen by the king for such a dangerous mission, and as a warrior, it was the highest recognition of the king's faith in his bravery and competence.

The king's fear was that there was a rebel faction that was plotting against him, and would strike when he was most vulnerable, soon after the Ashvamedha. His greatest fear was that his own son, Krishna, whom he had raised above all the others, giving him the governorship of the richest region in the realm, was also amongst the rebels. This was a source of grief, and at the same time also of anxiety, because the king knew that Krishna was an able man.

Jayadeva's mission was simple. He was to keep his eyes and ears open and to observe his colleagues closely. Who did they talk to? Were they in touch with anyone outside the camp? Did they receive any messages? Were they forming cliques amongst themselves? As the king's trusted man, Jayadeva's duty was to relay his findings to the king at regular intervals. He was given a special set of codes that he should use when sending his messages. Nobody would know of this arrangement save the two of them. Not even Jayadeva's father, the king's close and trusted friend Ramaraya, was to be told.

Jayadeva had carried out the king's command assiduously throughout the campaign. In the thick of battle, there was not time or opportunity for the warriors to indulge in politics, and their entire energies were focused on winning the next battle and moving on. The encounters had been fierce and frequent, and they had been constantly on the move. For a long time Jayadeva had had nothing to report, although he had been vigilant for any unusual behavior. His reports to the king had been monotonous and repetitive, and sometimes he wondered whether he was justifying the confidence the king had placed in him.

But after the heat of the battles had cooled, and they had begun their triumphant return to the capital, he began to notice a difference in the ranks. The old allegiances started to re-surface as the team spirit faded. At first it was expressed in a couple of warriors belonging to one camp picking on one of the others and starting a fight for the most ridiculous reasons. Gradually, these encounters became more aggressive and polarized. And more frequent. Late night clandestine meetings started to take place. If Jayadeva had not been alert he might have missed them, and slept through the night with the rest of the soldiers. As it was, he had been able to listen in to some extremely revealing conversations, which completely vindicated the king's suspicions. Krishna was indeed gathering his forces, but to what end was still not clear. He could well be mustering his men to dominate over another province, to show his father the king that he had the military might to do so. Or he could be planning something more threatening. Jayadeva's job was not to speculate, but merely to relay the information and let the king and his advisors come to their own conclusions.

Jayadeva's role might have ended there, except for one slip up. He was observed one day, while he was observing the camp. It was a most unfortunate circumstance, and it was no fault of his. It was late night, and he had kept one of the warriors under surveillance all day. He suspected that he was going to make some move today, but wasn't sure when or how. While he waited in the dark, he sensed that there was someone else in the shadows. Could it be the contact that his quarry was waiting for? He maintained a deathly silence, barely breathing for fear that he would be heard in the stillness of the night. The person in the shadows was less adept at this game, and was betraying his presence by small sounds, little shifting and crackling noises that would have gone unnoticed, except Jayadeva was listening for them, trying to guage his exact location.

Jayadeva would most certainly have discovered the identity of this mysterious marauder except for a most unexpected twist of fate. For many days now there had been a rumor that there was a wild leopard hunting down cattle in the vicinity. The camp had been taking adequate precautions against the beast, lighting huge flaming torches around the perimeter to keep it at bay. Jayadeva kept well away from the torches, and remained successful in maintaining his incognito in the dark shadows. But tonight he was not so lucky. Out of nowhere, with a fearful roar, the leopard appeared, charging at him at full tilt. He had no choice but to run, and in doing so, he revealed himself to the other person, whoever he was, also lurking in the darkness. By the time the noise aroused the camp, Jayadeva was well out of sight, but he realized as he managed to evade the leopard's hungry pursuit that he could never go back. The man in the darkness would have seen him, and would tell his partner within the camp who he was and what he was doing. There was a chance that he would not actually guess at Jayadeva's true intentions, but he could not afford to take a chance on that.

So he disappeared permanently, leaving those who remained to speculate wildly about his whereabouts. If there was one person within the camp who knew, or at least suspected, the truth, that person was clearly keeping it close to his chest. The others mounted a concerted search for him in the days to come, but drew a blank. If they had only known, Jayadeva was concealed in a cave quite close to the camp, and they came close to discovering him on several occasions! But eventually they gave up the search, and concluded that he had been killed and perhaps eaten by some wild animals.

Since then, his job had become somewhat easier, because he no longer had to play a double role. He now focused on laying low and staying out of sight, and being very careful to maintain the fiction that he was dead. Tonight was going to be the last night that he would observe the camp. He had received orders from the king to leave immediately for Banavasi, and to set up his operations there. Jayadeva's mission was to adopt a suitable disguise and start gathering intelligence on any unusual movements of people and munitions in the capital city prior to the Ashvamedha celebrations.

At all costs, any disruption of the celebration must be prevented, and all trouble makers silenced. Permanently.

## ii

That evening, Udaya dropped in to visit Devi. He often came to check on her, so it was not an unusual occurrence. Normally, they would have sat down to chat in a companionable manner and then had a meal together. But today Udaya was frowning and looking concerned, not at all his usual calm self.

"What is it?" Devi asked, worried immediately for her parents.

"I believe you have agreed to Narayanachar's request to manage the first aid tent at the Ashvamedha celebrations?"

Devi sighed. She had known this would come up. "Yes, but what choice did I have? Narayanachar and Siddayya put the proposition to father in such a way that it was almost impossible to refuse. If the king requests you to do a thing, I don't see how it would be possible to refuse. Can you imagine the repercussions?"

Udaya raised a questioning eyebrow. "What repercussions? I hope you were not thinking of me. I would rather face any repercussion under the sun than have you placed in the way of danger."

"It was not just you Udaya. What about father? You know he has to work practically within the palace – it would have been most awkward for him. Especially since the king must have suggested this in the first place because of his fondness for father."

"You are crazy if you think father cares about that," Udaya interrupted her roughly. "Father is even more concerned about your safety and happiness than I am, you know that."

Devi tried to calm him down. "Udaya, don't get so worked up! I know father would never jeopardize my safety. In fact, when I said I had reservations about taking up this task, he immediately reassured me that his interests would not be hurt no matter what decision I made. But surely it's not unnatural for me to think about it. Besides, I also had other reservations."

"Such as?" Udaya wanted to know.

"Well, you know that Siddayya! He is nothing but trouble, and he has had his knife into me for years now. I do not trust him as far as I could throw him – I would not at all be surprised if he has some dirty game afoot. But both he and Narayanachar were very insistent that the suggestion had been the king's, so that makes me more comfortable. Perhaps the king is trying to teach these conservative Brahmins a lesson. Challenging their dearly held beliefs on what is not appropriate for a woman to do!"

Udaya laughed at that. "Always speculating wildly, that's you! Someone should tame that wild imagination of yours. Although, come to think of it, in this case you may have a point. The king has more recently been more and more open to new ideas, and been listening to all the intellectuals and religious leaders who come to court. He has been very curious about Buddhism lately: especially the fact that Buddhism does not recognize caste differences. So maybe the king is trying to make a point after all – that Brahmins need not always lay down the law and dictate what can and cannot be done by various members of society, as they have been doing for so long."

"Anyway, whatever his motives, you can absolutely count on me. I will help you in any way you need, just give me my marching orders. I believe there is some spadework to be done. They need a list of supplies and whatnot. I can put that together for you and deliver it to Siddayya if you like. And on the day itself, I will get there early to set up the tent. Father would have been there too, but unfortunately he has already been assigned some other duties."

Devi thanked him gratefully. He was always a rock she could lean on. She wished she could return his feelings – it would have been so ideal. He really understood her so well, and would so willingly support her in her work, defend her as her father had done against all those who criticized and opposed her. But it was not to be; and one day he would come to terms with it too and stop hoping for things to change.

# Chapter 6

The dream visits her again that night. It is the same kindly looking man, surrounded by desks arranged in rows in front of him, with a young man seated at each one. Again the little girl is an insignificant observer, hidden away in a corner, as if afraid of discovery and possible expulsion. This time there is no body on the table, but just several piles of herbs arranged in a row. The man is explaining something and the young men are sitting with parchments and pens at the ready, taking notes as the lesson proceeds.

"There are twelve essential medicines in ayurvedic practice. These twelve by themselves can be used in any number of combinations, either with each other or combined with other herbal medicines, to cure almost all diseases that you will encounter. You will see that some of the herbs that we use very commonly are not here among these twelve. You may ask, where is the turmeric? Where is the holy basil, the tulsi? Where are the ginger root and the margosa neem leaves and the camphor and so on? My reply is this: all those are extremely valuable herbs also, but their power is enhanced when combined with any of these twelve master herbs here on my table. Is that clear?"

All the students nod diligently, and make a note on their paper. "I will now explain the specific qualities of each herb. Look closely at the herb as I talk about it."

The little girl listens intently. It is imperative that she remembers every word said here today, although she does not quite remember why. She only knows that she needs that list of master herbs. She needs to give it to somebody for a very important reason. As unobtrusively as she can, she draws a little closer.

"This is Adhatoda or Vasaka. The leaves of this plant are very bitter, and hence its name – the leaf that a goat will not touch! The flowers as you can see are white and contain a lot of nectar. But we are concerned more with the leaf. What is adhatoda good for? It can be combined with ginger or turmeric or tulsi or with small amounts of all of them to create decoctions that can cure all manner of lung disorders: cough, wetness in the lungs, breathing problems, symptoms of common cold."

"Next we have bark from the Arjuna tree, one of our most sacred trees, named after the beloved hero from the Mahabharata with whom you are all familiar. This bark can be ground up and combined with margosa neem leaves and other ingredients to treat problems associated with heart disorders: pain in the heart, a high temper, nervous agitation."

"Now here is an interesting herb, one that you will not be able to do without: Ashwagandha! It grows as a stout shrub and bears yellow flowers and red berry-like fruit. It can be used for many conditions. It is extremely effective as a rejuvenative tonic for the muscles and bone marrow. You can combine it with margosa neem leaves and yashtomadhu to treat fatigue, weakness, chronic illness. You may call it the king of all herbs, it can be combined with so many other herbs to become almost a panacea for all ailments."

"Another crucial one is Brahmi. I am sure you have all heard of it. This plant was named in honor of Brahma the Creator, so you imagine how powerful it is! We use it primarily as a brain tonic, to improve memory, increase intelligence, and sharpen mental focus, while calming nervous energy. Your mothers have probably soaked it in sesame oil and then applied it to your hair. It prevents hair fall and graying. But most importantly, applying it to your scalp calms nervousness, alleviates headaches and promotes good mental functioning."

All this is very interesting and useful, but the little girl is feeling increasingly anxious. Is this what she needs to know? Is this what they are expecting from her? She needs a list of herbs, but is this list right for her purpose? But wait! The master is saying that these are the twelve basic and most essential herbs, so this must be it. If she gave this to them, surely it would be adequate? She is confused and nervous. What if she is mistaken? What if she gives them the wrong list, and a whole lot of people get into trouble because of her? What if a whole lot of people *die* because of her? It isn't fair! Why have they given her such a big responsibility? She is only a little girl, this shouldn't be her job!

She feels weak with helplessness and overcome with the enormity of her task. Tears slowly gather in the corner of her eyes and begin to trickle down her face. She cannot wipe them away and she can no longer concentrate on what the master is saying. She will fail in her mission, and they will all blame her for it. She feels miserable and afraid.

At that moment she heard a familiar bracing voice. "Goodness, the tears again! Another dream? Wake up now, and shake yourself out of it! I keep trying to figure out what triggers these dreams of yours. Do they come when you are very tired? Or have eaten too heavily at dinner? Or if you over-sleep? What is it? We have to come up with a way to stop them"

Devi opened her eyes and wiped away the remnants of the tears. "No, no, Nagi, I don't want to be rid of them. I know I wake up in tears, but I quite enjoy the dreams, honestly! They're very educational, for one thing, and also I feel oddly comforted by them. I can't explain it."

"Funny way you have of showing your enjoyment!" Nagi snorted, completely unimpressed. "Anyway, get up now, and get ready! This is not a day for staying nodding in bed, you know that."

"Oh heavens! Yes, of course," Devi scrambled out of bed. "What time is it? Don't tell me you let me oversleep! Today of all days, I can't believe this happened!"

"Relax!" Nagi was completely exasperated. "Have I ever done a thing like that to you? Why would I let you down on what is possibly the biggest day of your life? Of course you haven't overslept. It is just about 5 o'clock in the morning. If you would deign to look out of the window, you would see that the sun is barely rising. Now stop jumping around and go and wash. I have brought a bucket of water from the pool for you to bathe in – it is too early for you to go there at this time."

"But you went," Devi objected.

"Yes, I did. If I get bitten by a snake, no one will miss me! But if anything happens to you, who will look after all those sick people who come here?"

Devi went up to her and hugged her fiercely. "I would miss you," she said, smiling.

"Alright, enough of that. Now hurry! I have made some ragi porridge for you, it'll keep you going until lunchtime. Luckily your mother will bring lunch for all of us – something to look forward to! I hope she brings that fabulous okra dish she makes with the tamarind and coconut, I could eat a whole bowl of it." Nagi talked while she started putting together the supplies they would need for the day. A change of clothes, some towels, a mattress and sheets, a jar of boiled water.

Devi laughed out loud. "What a time to be thinking of amma's cooking! I suspect we are going to be so run off our feet that we won't have time to eat. But let's see….maybe nobody will show up." It was disorienting not to know what to expect. She shrugged, trying for a lack of concern that she didn't feel. She so badly wanted this to be a success. It would certainly be nice to have helped some people in need. But she had to admit that it would also be nice to make her father proud, it would be nice to win praise from the king, it would be nice to come back with a purse full of money. She went into the backyard to bathe and get ready.

By the time she had dressed and eaten her porridge, the sun was decidedly higher in the sky, and it was time to go. Udaya would already have reached the appointed spot, where Siddayya's assistant had promised that a tent would be erected and the list of herbs and supplies that Devi had requested would be placed. It would be up to them to arrange things precisely as they wanted inside the tent, but they would be given enough furniture and other materials to help them to be comfortable.

It abruptly dawned on her. "So that's what the dream was about!" she exclaimed.

Nagi struggled to the cart with a bagful of extra towels and supplies. "What dream? What are you talking about?" she asked on her way out.

"The dream that made me cry, Nagi! When I woke up this morning, remember? You wondered what it was about. Well, it was about what supplies we should order for today, and I was getting worried about whether we had ordered the right things and whether we would have enough of what we need."

"Well, I'm taking additional supplies from here, just to be on the safe side. That's my practical approach, and much more useful than simply having nightmares about running out of supplies, if you ask me! Lucky for you one of us is down-to-earth!" Nagi pinched her cheek fondly and then hollered for the girls to come out double quick so they could leave immediately.

Raji, Jaya and Laxmi came running out, still bleary eyed from their early morning wake-up call. But they were excited about going into town, and that too on such an important mission. Not only that, if akka would agree, maybe they could quickly slip out and catch a glimpse of the festivities too. They were confident she would – she was always a good sport. To see the Horse Sacrifice! They would be the envy of all their friends.

They set out quickly, piled into the horse cart that Siddayya's assistant had sent out to them last night. Although they set out briskly enough, soon they had to slow down a bit due to the growing crowd of people on the road as they approached Banavasi. People were hurrying to the venue early so as to get good seats. They were all coming prepared, carrying food and water and even rolls of bedding on their heads, to ensure that they had a jolly day out with the family. Weaving their way through the crowd, getting more and more bogged down as they got closer into town and the numbers of people swelled, Devi and Nagi decided it would be quicker to just get down and walk. Instructing the three girls to stay in the cart and watch over the extra supplies, they jumped down and set off briskly towards where the first aid tent was supposed to be. It was much quicker on foot, and in no time they caught sight of the huge stands that had been erected around the temple complex. Coming closer, they saw that the stands were four tiers high, and beyond them the passage around the temple had been cleared of all the shops and street hawkers and significantly widened. Armed guards had been placed at frequent intervals to manage the crowds and direct them towards the seats and away from the temple complex. As Devi and Nagi slowly walked around the outskirts of the stands, they saw their tent set up quite prominently, across the street from the southern entrance to the temple complex. "Well, that's not too bad," Nagi remarked grudgingly. "When he does something, that Siddayya does a good job of it. I didn't think he would go to so much trouble over this."

"If they are going to do it at all, they might as well do it right! But don't give Siddayya the credit. That must go to my father. He has been discussing this with Siddayya and Narayanachar, and he must have pointed out that there is no point putting up a small tent in the middle of nowhere. Nobody would have been able to find it! At least now everyone knows there is medical help at hand if they need it – see, how everyone is staring at it! Good, good! I think we will get a nice crowd. Not that I want people to fall sick, but you know what I mean!"

And there was Udaya, directing a couple of men bearing a large head-load into the tent. Devi and Nagi went up to him and made their presence known. He looked quite calm and collected. "Everything is under control," he reported cheerfully. "All the materials we had asked for are here, and there is a lot of space inside. Lots of clean sheets and towels and floor mats – in fact, they all look new!"

Devi pushed past him and stepped eagerly into the tent to survey the arrangements. Nagi was already inside, briskly directing the men hither and tither. Udaya had already done a fine job of arranging the medicines and mats and other things, but Nagi knew the way Devi liked things done and made a few adjustments.

Soon it was all in order. The girls also arrived, all three of them in a high state of excitement. "So many people!" Raji exclaimed, wide eyed with wonder. "I have never seen so many people in one place ever before! Can so many people even fit inside the temple, akka? Where will they all sit and see what is going on?"

"All these people are not going to enter the temple! I think the plan is for everyone to watch whatever they can from outside. Look, they have built steps all around the outside of the temple for people to sit on. Only the king and royal family and the priests and other important people will be going inside the temple," Nagi explained to them.

It was Jaya who went up and whispered to Nagi. "Will akka let us go and see also? We will go one by one, and only for a short time."

Nagi snorted. "If you go, it will be all together and with me watching over you. All of you are such country bumpkins, never been outside the four walls of our house, and now you want to go and get caught up in the terrific crowd milling around in the temple. No thank you! You will never find your way back here, and I wouldn't be surprised of there are villains out there looking for just such foolish girls as the three of you. They will carry you off and do god knows what with you all!"

"Shhh," Devi frowned. The poor girls were looking genuinely frightened. Nagi meant well, but sometimes she really went too far. "Don't worry girls. You can go after a while. The parade will not begin until late morning. Nagi will go with you."

As the time for the arrival of the victorious horse and its accompanying army drew nearer, the milling crowd became ever more restless. Rumors were flying around wildly. "They have started towards Banavasi already. I believe they spent the night camped in the forest about an hour away, so they should be here very soon!"

Vaman Bhat stopped by on his way into the temple. He was to be part of the group of priests sitting by the king and prompting him through the yagna. It was a complicated business and Vaman Bhat was preoccupied. He carried a thick sheaf of parchment with him, containing all the instructions for the full day of rituals. He gave both his children a hug and wished them luck and then hastened on his way. Their mother was to come in a little while with their lunch. "She is cooking up a storm!" Vaman Bhat assured them with a smile. Then he left.

This time it was Laxmi rushing in. "They are going to pass by our tent! That's what the guard at the temple door says. He said they will eventually enter the temple through the East gate, but they will go all around the temple two times. They have to go past us!"

"Go past us? You have high hopes if you think you will see anything, with so many people crowding around!" Nagi said grumpily.

"Come on, Nagi, don't be such a sourpuss," Devi laughed. "Why are you so crabby this morning? It is only natural that the girls are excited – it is their first trip into town in months, and that too for such a momentous occasion. Let them have their fun. I think you are being too much of a wet blanket! And I do hope we can catch a glimpse of the horse and the king's army as they go past the tent, even if there is a crowd. It will be my only chance to see some of the pageantry, because I am not leaving this tent all day, that's for sure. Whether or not we have any patients, I will stay here, just in case."

"Me too," Udaya said firmly. "I think what Nagi needs is some food. She was so busy feeding everyone else this morning, I'll bet that she forgot to eat anything herself. Here Nagi – this is your lucky day! I have some peanuts in my bag, have some. They might put a smile on your face!"

"Peanuts for a monkey!" Nagi humphed, but took them with a smile anyway. It did seem to help, and when the girls ran in next to tell them that the cavalcade was less than fifteen minutes away, she did not quell them with a caustic remark.

"I heard a rumor that one of the ace warriors has gone missing," Udaya said to Devi in a low voice. "Jayadeva, the son of Ramaraya, you know him, don't you?"

"No, I don't think I have ever seen Jayadeva," Devi replied.

"No, you probably wouldn't have seen Jayadeva. In fact hardly anyone has seen him, because as a young boy he was sent off to his maternal grandparents' village somewhere in the North. Ramaraya married a woman he met and fell in love with when he had gone with the king to Pataliputra many years ago."

"Yes, yes, I have heard that story. Very romantic! Of course, I know Ramaraya – know of him, at least. I know that he and father meet sometimes to discuss scriptures and other matters. Father has always spoken highly of him."

"You are right," Udaya agreed. "Ramaraya is highly respected by everyone. He has always refused a position in court, and prefers to tend to his farm. But he is a learned man, and the king relies on him for advice on many matters of state. It was because of the king's regard for Ramaraya that Jayadeva was summoned from Pataliputra to be a member of the warrior army accompanying the Ashvamedha horse. The king was very careful when choosing this special force. If he picked Jayadeva, it must have been because he had a good reputation as a warrior in the Gupta army."

"How did he go missing? Was he killed in battle? But then they would have found his body." Devi was puzzled by this story.

"Well, that is just it! There is no body, at least none that they found, and I believe they really looked everywhere. It was well known that Jayadeva was a bit of a favorite with the king, and so special care was taken to ensure his well being. Despite that, he seems to have disappeared. Maybe he was kidnapped or killed by wild animals or something."

"Has the king been told? He must be very upset. Not only to have lost an able warrior, but also because it is a bad omen! The king is very susceptible to omens and signs just now, I believe."

"He has been told alright. Father said so."

"Oh, so father is your source!" Devi exclaimed. "What else did he tell you? When?"

"Just last night," Udaya replied. "He is pretty disturbed about it, because as you said, the king is really jumpy right now. He wants everything to be perfect for today, and of course was completely thrown by this piece of bad news. But what is to be done? Scouts have been sent out to search the forests and question the villagers, and until they return, there is not much information to go on. Ramaraya is devastated of course. He will not attend the festivities today, and that is upsetting the king as well. But you can hardly expect a man to rejoice when he has lost a dearly beloved only son!"

"Oh that is sad! What a price everyone has paid for this campaign to be successful! It makes me angry to think about it. Why does a king have to be so power hungry? Look at the way they had to squeeze the taxes out of all of us. Even father was finding it a pinch, so I can only imagine how it would have hurt the poor peasants! And so many young men dead. And what about the villagers whom the army encountered on the way? I am sure they were massacred as well if they offered any resistance, although they will not talk about that. And now we are supposed to celebrate this blood-thirsty enterprise!"

"No point getting worked up about it," Udaya said mildly. "That is the way it is. If our king did not wage war against others, someone would come and attack him. He would be seen as weak and ineffectual, therefore an easy target. If one has to fight a war anyway, better to be on the winning side, don't you think?"

Luckily Devi was spared the need to come up with a response to this completely pragmatic point of view – honestly, where was Udaya's sense of justice? - because there was a huge upsurge of noise outside and the thundering sound of crowds running past their tent. "They are here! They are here! Nagi akka – see, they will go past our tent, like I told you they would! Come on, come on – hurry! You don't want to miss this!"

The girls' excitement was infectious. Devi, Udaya and Nagi followed the girls out into the street, into the press of people ranged in front of their tent. Pushing through the throng, they managed to get to a spot where they had a slightly better view. The first glimpse they caught of the on-coming procession was a huge cloud of dust.

Out of the dust, figures shadowy at first began to emerge. Leading the procession were the musicians. Colorfully dressed in bright waist cloths and head dresses, they came dancing along, announcing the start of the festivities. Their bugles and conch shells created enough noise to raise the dead, and they were outdone only by the drummers, tens of them, beating on drums of all shapes and sizes. The music was not particularly tuneful, but it succeeded in creating a jubilant mood, and went down very well with the crowd. They were greeted by much hooting and whistling, and many people stood up and danced to the beat of the drums.

Then the roar of the crowd became muted as more figures started emerging from the haze.

First, a phalanx of soldiers appeared. They looked like humble foot soldiers, not part of the army of notables handpicked by the king. They were armed with spears and some had shields. They wore leather vests, but other than that had no other protection. They probably bore the brunt of any attack. It was no wonder they looked so happy – they were fortunate to have survived this long, and if their luck held out, they might get a fat reward from the king for services rendered!

The phalanx was a large one, and took several minutes to pass. They were cheered on lustily by the crowd, the more daring of whom were stepping up and patting the soldiers on the back. Then there was another huge roar as the archers appeared. They were carrying their longbows aloft, and each had on their back a quiver of metal-tipped bamboo arrows. These archers formed the backbone of any attack, and their arrows were legendary. The longbow archers could pick off soldiers on horseback with ease, and were greatly feared during warfare. They would sometimes use arrows with iron shafts, put to deadly effect against armored elephants. The most dreaded were the fire arrows, killing men and animals in the most horrific way possible.

The archers were followed by more foot soldiers, wielding shields, javelins and long swords. It was their duty to give their lives in protecting the archers, who were highly trained and invaluable for decimating the enemy.

This impressive show of strength was a necessary prelude for the main event. Eight ceremonially decorated elephants now appeared, and the crowd gasped at their magnificence.

The armor used during battle had been replaced with gold ornaments, on their foreheads, on their massive breasts and even in their ears. They had been painted all over with scenes from their recent battles, and surmounting each of them was a huge gilded throne in which were seated about half a dozen noble warriors. A great shout went up from the gathered crowd. These were the heroes who had brought home the victory! No accolade was adequate to describing them, or their bravery, their valor. They looked benignly down at the crowd and waved and smiled. Devi wondered what they were thinking. Did they think it was all worthwhile? Perhaps they did. They were warriors after all. Fighting wars was what they did, it was their reason for being. Being killed in war was considered the greatest glory, it meant that the warrior went straight to heaven. But coming back home in triumph was obviously preferable to martyrdom; so presumably they were happy, not to mention relieved.

And then there was another collective gasp. Behind the elephants – finally, finally – came the golden chariot everyone had been waiting to see. The horse, yoked to the gilded chariot with three other horses, was driven by the king. Ceremonies had been taking place right through the year that the horse had been roaming at will. Today was the culmination of all those ceremonies, and the king himself had to preside over this final all-important day. The chariot evoked a mix of emotions among those who beheld it. The horse itself was a magnificent beast. The choice of the Ashvamedha horse was carefully made: it had to be a stallion, between twenty four and a hundred years old, and of certain prescribed proportions. Clearly the horse had to be fit and strong enough to endure the rigors of battle time and time again. Seeing the horse that had been the author of so much good fortune for the kingdom filled the spectators with awe and wonder. And then to see the king as well! It was not often that many of those lining the path had the opportunity to see the king at such close quarters. Many fell to their knees as the chariot passed, some even to the ground, pressing their foreheads to the earth, expressing their veneration for one who was god's representative on earth. The chariot moved forward majestically, keeping the pace deliberately slow, so that the subjects could drink in their fill of the splendid sight.

The golden chariot was followed by more soldiers, but the crowd hardly paid attention any more. It was a tough act to follow! Devi watched until the chariot disappeared around the corner, then turned away and walked back to the tent with Udaya. The rest of the crowd could continue enjoying the show, but she was here to do a job, and she intended to get on with it.

# Chapter 7

A controlled chaos prevailed inside the temple complex. The planning had been meticulous, Krishna Rao had seen to that. He hoped this was the first and last time he would have to go through this process. For the first time in a fairly demanding career, he had become accustomed over the last week or so to getting up with a splitting headache. Nothing had matched this for sheer administrative complexity and political shenanigans. The Council of Ministers, egged on by the likes of Siddayya – he was by no means operating alone – had continually challenged his authority and gone behind his back to the king. Luckily the king was a seasoned ruler, and although he was vulnerable to their blandishments, he yet did not allow them to overrule Krishna Rao. It was by dint of this regard alone that Krishna Rao had been able to contain some of the more ambitious of the coterie's plans. It was almost as if they were deliberately trying to empty the treasury, but why would they want to do that? Maybe it was simple nepotism and graft. Perhaps they wanted the contracts for some of the suggested extravagances to go to their friends and relatives.

But this was not the time for such speculation. Striding through the temple complex towards the prayer vihara where the ceremonial sacrifice and attendant rituals were to take place, Krishna Rao's only thoughts were for the upcoming ceremonies. He was dressed perfectly for the occasion. His cream silk dhoti and upper cloth, and red gold edged turban suited his tall figure well, and struck the appropriate formal note that the occasion demanded. Already he could hear the roar of the crowds outside the temple walls. That could only mean that the procession had arrived, and was making its first circumambulation of the temple complex. The arrangements for the washing and anointing of the horse had been made outside the temple's main entrance, and he would go there after checking on the arrangements at the vihara.

As he went, he was reminded of Vaman Bhat's stories about Horse Sacrifices done in the past. It was quite the rage for kings down the ages to crown all their achievements with a sacrifice like this one. The Ramayana related the story of the Horse Sacrifice performed by Rama's father, king Dasharatha. All the details were laid down in the good book: how the rituals were performed by those great sages, Rishyasringa and Vashishta; and how all the rituals strictly followed the steps laid out in the Vedas. On that occasion, there was a uniform sense of triumph for good having overcome evil, and a general celebration across the kingdom.

There was another instance when the Horse Sacrifice was performed in the Ramayana, but under less happy circumstances. As was well known, the exile of the royal brothers and Rama's wife Sita had ended badly. She had been abducted by the king of Lanka, Ravana, and then subsequently rescued by Rama and Lakshmana with the able help of Lord Hanuman. Although Ravana was depicted as a ferocious and cruel king, Rama could not rid himself of the suspicion that Ravana might not have been entirely unattractive to Sita. Had Ravana succeeded in ravishing his queen after all? Sita herself unequivocally refuted his suspicions, but when they persisted, she voluntarily exiled herself back into the forests. There, unknown to Rama, she bore him two sons – the twins, Lava and Kusha. As she was raising her children in the ashram of the sage Valmiki, Rama in the capital Ayodhya announced that he would undertake an Ashvamedha, and the horse duly set out on its wandering, accompanied by an army lead by his able commander Hanuman. The horse, in its travels, was stopped by two young boys, who tethered the horse to a tree and challenged Rama's mighty army. According to the rules of engagement, the army was bound to attack the young boys but found to their amazement that the boys could not be defeated. It was then that Hanuman realized that these were no ordinary foe: they must be king Rama's sons. Of course, Rama was overjoyed at having word of this remarkable discovery and immediately had his children brought to the capital so that they may be united with him. He magnanimously offered to take Sita back as well, but she would have none of it. She preferred to return to her mother – Earth – and was never seen again. Legend had it that on that occasion and many times subsequently when Rama performed the Horse Sacrifice, he conducted the rituals with a golden statue of Sita at his side.

At the vihara, Krishna Rao found everything in order. Vaman Bhat and his colleagues had the situation well under control. Sixteen priests were in attendance, and all the other necessary officials were already in place. The sacrificer and the officiant; the cantor and the carver; the invoker – all these were present and accounted for. They had all been coached in the rituals, and knew their parts exactly. Hopefully they would not fumble when their big moment came.

They were all alerted to the schedule, and asked to adjourn to the front entrance where the initial ceremonies were to take place. Krishna Rao himself set off briskly in that direction. When he reached there, the procession had completed it first round of the temple, and the crowds were preparing themselves for viewing the magnificent sight for a second time. A great cheer erupted again when the triumphant procession appeared for the second time, and this time it came to a halt in front of the entrance to the temple complex. Leading out from the entrance and into the huge clearing outside the front entrance was a strange sight. A massive tent had been erected, with the flaps on all four sides let down. All the spectators wondered what it contained, but had been told that they would have to wait until the king and his chief queen arrived. Their impatient anticipation was soon rewarded. Another cheer – possibly the loudest yet – went up, and the grand chariot bearing the royal couple entered the clearing and swung to a halt. The king and queen alighted, waving to their subjects, and as they turned towards the temple, the flaps on the tent were drawn up.

The sight of the interior was greeted with awed silence. Inside, a tall stake had been driven into the ground, and an assortment of animals had been tethered to it. Krishna Rao knew there were supposed to be six hundred and nine animals in all, but it had been deemed sensible by the priests to have only about ten token animals here, with the others held in a pen on the grounds of the palace some distance away. The logistics of having even these ten animals tethered here had been mind-boggling. The tame ones, the cows and sheep, were no trouble. But the wild goat, the wild ox and the black buck – it had been a horrendous task keeping them under control.

The royal couple entered the tent, the sign for the ceremonies to begin. The horse was brought forward, and the queen ceremonially poured water over it several times from a golden jug. Next came a huge jar of clarified butter, which was then poured over the horse, and rubbed all over into its hide by the queen and her assistants. A third set of people came up bearing a heavy tray. It was weighted down with gold and precious jewels. These were entwined around the horse's head and neck and its tail. Finally, the sacrificer stepped up and offered the horse its final meal – a plateful of grain that had been blessed by the gods.

All this took a while, and the crowd watched in silence. After the horse had eaten its fill, it was led into the tent, and tied to the stake along with the other animals. At this point, the officiant gave a sign, and the flaps of the tent were dropped down again. Outside, the guards began dispersing the crowds. "The show is over! All other ceremonies will take place inside the temple! Please go to the food tents and eat your fill. The king has made all arrangements for your comfort and entertainment. Please enjoy yourselves! Go quickly, while supplies are plentiful!"

Although there was some groaning at this abrupt halt to the entertainment, most of the spectators were hungry and tired and quite looking forward to the hot meal that had been promised. The group inside the tent was barely aware of their existence, so grisly was the scene that was unfolding before them now. The sacrifice was making short work of all the sundry animals that had been tied up, and soon there was a mass of bloody carcasses heaped up in a pile, ready to be eaten in the ceremonial meal that was to follow. The crush of people inside the tent, the rising crescendo of chanting led by the cantor, the cries of the frightened animals and the overpowering smell of blood – was this really a celebration? Of what?

## ii

At the first aid tent, as Devi had predicted, business was picking up at an amazing pace. While the procession was underway, and during the aftermath, the tent had been completely deserted. Even the girls had run off to watch the proceedings, and Nagi had followed them, scolding under her breath. When they returned, flushed with excitement, and with words tumbling from their lips in their hurry to be the first to describe all that they had seen, they were followed by the first of what turned out to be a veritable flood of clients. Most of the cases were of minor injuries sustained during the long trip here. There were some cases of extreme exhaustion, particularly with some of the older people. There was one dramatic moment when it looked like a young woman was going to deliver her baby in the tent, but it was a false alarm, and what had seemed like labor pains were just the natural aches and pains resulting from a rather long trek to the city. Nagi had ticked the girl off roundly. "Seeing this circus is more important to you than your own health and the health of your child?" she had berated her, before turning to her husband and giving him a piece of her mind. "Take better care of her in future, this is no way to strain the body so close to the birthing time. What if the baby had come when you were on the road? Now get a horse cart and take her home safely – don't make her walk any more. Have you got money to hire a cart? Tell me, otherwise I will get it for you." The young man, suitably cowed, humbly admitted to having enough money to take his wife home, and went off in search of a horse cart.

Sometime in the afternoon when they were all more than ready for it, Devi's mother appeared with their lunch. Nagi helped to unload all the baskets of food from the cart.

"A fine lot we all are!" she berated herself along with the others. "Poor aunt Sita has been slaving over a hot fire all morning, cooking up all this delicious food. I hope we have saved some lives, to justify all this effort she has put in!"

They assured her that they fully deserved to be rewarded for their day's work so far. Then they all fell upon the food with ravenous appetites, and Sita laughed as she watched them eat. "It is a good thing I had a premonition of this! Poor things, you must have had hardly anything to eat before you left home, ages and ages ago. Eat well, you will need to keep your strength up. This is going to go on late into the night, I am sure. Once people come to town, they will not leave until they have got their money's worth. I believe all kinds of arrangements have been made for their entertainment – street plays and performers, food and drink, lighting of lamps after sunset – what more could they ask for? This is more entertainment than they have had in all their lives, I am sure!"

"What about father?" Devi asked her. "Will he be done any time soon?"

"Oh no! He has asked me not to wait up for him. The ceremonies will go on all night, you know. It is a very complicated affair, and your father and his team will have to be on hand to give advice and clarifications right through the process. Your father has been completely preoccupied for the past several weeks with the preparations," she confided in her children. "Today, of course, I don't expect to see him at all. Krishna Rao has asked him specifically to stay at his side. He needs his moral support! Something is going on, something behind the scenes."

"Like what?" Udaya asked curiously. "Father also hinted at something like that the other day when we were talking, but do they know what it is and who is behind it?"

"That is just it," Sita sounded anxious. "Nobody knows, and your father is very perturbed about it. Some people, like Siddayya, are suddenly becoming very influential, while others who were so respected until now are being sidelined. It is all being managed so quietly that it is done even before anyone realizes it. It looks like the king is being misled, but the source of all this is a mystery. I hope this doesn't mean that some ill will befall the poor king – he is a good man, and he has brought so much stability and prosperity to the kingdom. Unfortunately this Horse Sacrifice and the military campaign that came before it has sowed the seeds of discontent among both the nobles and the common people. I hope he doesn't pay too high a price for it."

"Well, anyway, this celebration seems to have gone off well," Devi remarked. "Such a huge undertaking. All kinds of things could have gone wrong. The organization has been superb; it must have cost a fortune."

"That it did," Udaya said with a grimace. "What a waste of resources, when there are so many needy people around. This much money could have fed them all for a year, if not more."

"Yes," Nagi snorted, listening closely to the exchange. "But it would not have fed the king's ego, would it? That is what this is all about, after all. And the people are so foolish too. No one remembers the feeding of the poor, but they do remember a ridiculous spectacle like this one. People deserve what they get. Let them starve for a year. They will have the memory of this day to warm their stomachs!"

Seeing that this was riling Nagi up unnecessarily, Devi got up and started clearing away the remnants of the lunch. There were hardly any leftovers, and at her mother's prompting, she kept what was left for a snack later in the day. Then Sita left, wishing them luck with the rest of the day, and offering further sustenance should they need it.

# Chapter 8

Jayadeva sat in the doorway of a small temple in a quiet side street. He was unfamiliar with this part of town, which was why he had chosen to seek shelter there. There was far less chance of being recognized here. In any case, he had taken the precaution of shaving his head and draping himself in the robes of a Buddhist monk. This was a disguise as effective as it was innocuous, and nobody spared him a second glance. It was several days since he had come into town, and now the long-awaited Ashvamedha celebrations were to start in a few hours. He reflected on the past few days, and had to admit that all the people that he had been watching so assiduously had behaved with extreme circumspection. Perhaps word had got around that the king had made his own private arrangement to gather information? That would explain the lack of anything to report. Or maybe they were gathering their forces for a big push later today or tomorrow? That was possible too. Whatever the reason, business had been slow, and Jayadeva was waiting for this phase to be over so that he could get back to doing what he loved best – leading his men into battle.

Time was passing, and Jayadeva knew that he should be elsewhere now. He had risen early and got himself ready so that he could leap into action at a moment's notice. So what was he wasting his time for, dawdling here thinking about life? Shaking himself out of his reverie, Jayadeva got up and hurried down the street.

He knew today was going to be a busy day for him, although he was not participating in the parade, and nor was he going to be watching it, except for whatever glimpses he caught from a great distance. He needed to have all his senses about him today, for if there was any plot afoot, today was probably going to be the day that it would be put into motion. Quickly grabbing a bite to eat at a wayside stall, Jayadeva set out towards the palace. The time had passed quickly, and the parade would start at any moment now. The crowds were already gathering restlessly, and their numbers were swelling by the minute. Jayadeva dodged through the marketplace, trying not to trip over his robes. His objective was clear – he had to get into the palace and keep a watch on the comings and goings within. With everyone preoccupied with the events unfolding in the temple complex, the palace wore an abandoned look. It was a perfect opportunity for anyone with mischief on their mind. With the king and all his senior officials off the premises, and with all the spectacle of the parade distantly visible from the palace balconies, even the skeleton force of guards that had been left behind was thoroughly distracted. Jayadeva had no trouble gaining entry into the building, and was even able to wend his way to the corridor outside the king's chamber without being challenged. Where were all the palace guards? Cosnpicuous by their absence! There should have been at least four stationed in this stretch of corridor and he had been all set to dodge their notice. Had the Commandant of the palace guards actually given them the day off? It seemed highly unlikely, but then what could be the explanation? Whatever it was, it certainly made his job a lot easier.

Standing hidden behind one of the massive pillars at the end of the corridor, Jayadeva commanded a clear view of the entire area around the king's chamber, as well as the adjoining chambers of all the senior officers. He had no idea what he was waiting for, nor how long he would have to wait, but this was his task for the day. When he was growing up, if he had been told that one day he might spy for the king, he would have been hugely excited, he was sure. It all sounded so glamorous and cloak-and-dagger. The reality of it was just plain dull and tedious! Waiting around for something to happen or for someone to do something....

Today was more dull and tedious than usual. The usual hustle and bustle of the palace was down to almost nothing. All there was to observe hour after hour was an occasional passing servant desultorily sweeping the floor. Jayadeva lounged in his corner getting slowly more bored and sleepy. And hungry! He realized now that he should have prepared himself better for the vigil. He did not have so much as a handful of nuts or a fruit to eat. He was used to going hungry for long periods of time, but that was in company and in times of war, when lack of regular meals was the least of their problems. But now, with little else on his mind, his thoughts seemed to be focusing exclusively on food or rather, the lack of it.

So he contented himself with dreaming about meals he had eaten in the past, cooked either by his mother, or at weddings that he had attended. This only made him hungrier, but on the other hand, it distracted him from his boredom, so that was at least one objective satisfied! In this manner, he managed to idle away a surprising number of hours, and resigned himself to do so for several more. He was determined to spend the entire day on the premises, because that was his assignment for the day. The excitement out on the street was dying down, and he guessed that the parade had come to an end, and the crowd was dispersing. Perhaps now the action inside here would pick up! The thought roused him, and he sat up straighter, and craned his neck this way and that to see if he could spot anyone or anything amiss. About half an hour after things had quietened down somewhat, his vigilance was finally rewarded. Clearly, it was not for nothing that the king had asked him to be stationed within the palace premises today – something was afoot, and it was imminent!

At first, he heard a confused sound, as if a large group of people was tramping into the corridor, but when he was finally able to get a glimpse, it turned out to be a small group of three people. It appeared that two of them were addressing the man in between, who was the oldest of the three. The two younger men were strangers to Jayadeva, but he thought he had seen the older man in the middle before, although he could not immediately recollect where. Their conversation was not fully audible, but he could hear snatches of it. It appeared to be about the recently concluded celebrations.

"Everyone is saying the celebration is fantastic, but frankly I was expecting something more," one of the men was saying.

The other man made some indistinct reply. The first one addressed the older man in the middle. "What do you think, sir? Has it come up to your expectations? You should have been given much more importance today. As the person who supplied the Ashvamedha horse, you are the main hero of the day! Your horse is the one that has given the king so much success, yet I felt they had not done enough to appreciate your contribution."

Now Jayadeva recalled where he had seen the man before. At the time when the king had been picking his army of soldiers, this man had been present, and he seemed to recall his father even introducing the man to him, although he could not at the moment recall his name. The man was responding to the younger man's charge. He was denying that he had been mistreated in any way. "No, no, I have received a very fair compensation for my contribution," he was saying. "The king very properly offered me his fourth wife, as is the custom. But I of course refused. Another wife is just another source of trouble, as far as I am concerned! Besides, my current wife holds most of the purse strings – if I had turned up at home with another wife, I can picture the scene! So I accepted the king's very proper offer of an alternative reward. It was very generous, I can assure you, very generous indeed!" He then lowered his voice so that Jayadeva could no longer hear him, but he seemed to be describing all the gifts the king had bestowed upon him in lieu of an additinal wife.

One of the younger men stepped back and said loudly, "Oh sir! You are too easily pleased! You should have held out for much much more!" Then he too lowered his voice, and said something to which the older man was vehemently shaking his head.

"No, no, whatever you say, I still feel that everything went very well, and it has been a grand success," the older man declared. "I am very satisfied, and you young people should learn to have realistic expectations! What you are saying is preposterous, and I never wanted any such thing! You had said this to me before also, and even then I had given you the same answer. To be governor of a province is a politician's or a soldier's job, not the job for a simple businessman like me! I raise and trade horses, how on earth would I have been able to administer a province? Even with all the help that you so kindly promised me, I would never have managed, and I have no desire to rule. I would never have dreamed of making such a demand, even though I know the king was bound to accede to any demands I made on this day!"

So the men were hectoring him for not being ambitious enough in his demands of the king! Jayadeva supposed that they had tried to influence him previously, no doubt offering to be his right and left hands when he got the governorship. They must have been seriously disappointed not to have been successful. However, one of them clapped the older man on the back heartily, and said laughingly, "Don't worry sir! What is done is done! You are happy with your reward, and that is the important thing. Today is your day, after all, and you deserve the best. Why don't we go into the room and have some refreshments, and then we can go on our way? We have to return to our village this evening itself, so come, let us together raise a toast to a successful day."

The men then led the older man into the Prime Minister's chamber. Jayadeva watched curiously. He had checked all the doors before retreating into hiding; they had all been firmly locked. Yet now the men entered smoothly, without using a key. Evidently the door had been opened. But how? Jayadeva had been watching the corridor and the actions of everyone who had enetered it since the morning, and nobody had approached the door, nor opened it! Surely he had not dozed off? No, he was certain that he had not. So how could this be? He crept out from behind his pillar and went stealthily up to the room. There were no windows looking out onto the corridor, and the door was of solid wood. He held his ear to the door for some moments, but could hear absolutely nothing. He went back to his vantage point behind the pillar again, so as not to be spotted by any passerby.

A considerable period elapsed, perhaps about half an hour. Jayadeva was still puzzling over how the men had entered a locked room without using a key. It could be that the lock had been operated from inside. In that case, somebody had been locked inside that room all this while, waiting for these men to arrive. Jayadeva was positive that nobody had entered after his arrival. Suddenly the door burst open again, and this time the two men came stumbling out, holding the older man up between them. The man appeared to be having some type of fit. His face was convulsed, and he was gasping for breath. The men were dragging him out forcefully down the corridor towards the main entrance. Jayadeva emerged again from behind the pillar and raced silently in their wake. He peered around the corner to see where they had gone, and got a surprise. They had abandoned the older man at the entrance, and both the younger men were nowhere to be seen! Jayadeva went quickly to the entrance and looked out. There was no evidence of either of the men anywhere in the vicinity. He went back to the older man and knelt at his side. He felt for his breath: there was none. He was lying completely inert, and Jayadeva was quite convinced that he was dead, although there was no sign of any external injury.

Just then, he heard the sound of someone approaching. Jayadeva raced towards concealment in one of the many niches along the corridor. He peered cautiously out from his hiding place just in time to see a large man come in through the main entrance. The man saw what was lying there and came to a dead halt. He went closer, and then fell to his knees next to the body of the older man. "Uncle! Uncle!" Jayadeva heard him cry urgently. He was shaking the older man, trying to wake him up. But there was no response. The man looked around to see if there was any one about, but saw only the deserted corridor. He appeared to be quite distraught, and was now sobbing, as he began to realize that something was seriously wrong with his uncle. He bodily lifted the older man over his shoulder and strode purposefully out onto the street.

Jayadeva ran back towards the Prime Minister's room to see if there was anyone inside. But the door was locked again! He looked closely at the lock; it was as he had suspected – the handle could not be operated from the outside without a key. He had not seen either of the men lock the door as they left the room. So how could the door now be locked? Was there someone inside the room still? Who could that be, and how had he gotten in there? Jayadeva had been watching the room all day, and no one had entered save the trio that had gone in a short while ago. Dashing out and turning the corner, he saw that the window on the external wall of the room was slightly ajar. That had not been the case earlier in the day. He had checked all the windows in the morning. Was that how someone had entered and exited the room without his knowledge? Deciding to return later to examine the premises more closely, Jayadeva quickly turned back to follow the man and his uncle and see what transpired there. As he did so, he saw a figure detach itself from the shadows ahead of him and move stealthily in the direction that the large man had taken. Jayadeva stepped back, surprised. This was a new element! Who could this person be? There was only one way to find out.

Jayadeva realized that he now had two people to follow, and luckily they were both on the same mission. The first man had a few minutes lead time, but given the heavy burden he was carrying, he could not have gone far. Sure enough, Jayadeva caught up with him as he was making his way down the passage on the South side of the temple complex. He was hurrying as fast as he could, and he seemed to know where he was going. Now Jayadeva saw his objective: it was the first aid tent. The first aid tent and its healer had been the talk of the town for the past many days. Everyone had been completely taken by the concept, and the novelty of it. The location of the tent had been widely publicized so that those in need would be able to find it with ease. This, then, was the man's destination, and a logical one.

Jayadeva followed the man closely, and watched as he shouldered his way through the crowd and entered the first aid tent. The second shadowy figure was a little ahead of him, also keeping the man with the body slung on his shoulder well within his view. The open flap revealed the interior of the tent clearly to Jayadeva's watchful eyes. There seemed to be several people inside, and it was hard to tell who the patients were and who the healer. All Jayadeva knew was that the healer was a woman – that too had been the talk of the town. It was most unusual that the king had picked a woman to be the healer, most unusual for a woman to be a healer in the first place! Jayadeva was curious to see this woman, and to see also how she was going to handle this situation. God knew how the next few moments were going to play out, but this was for sure. Things were going to get difficult. Even before he laid eyes on the healer, Jayadeva thought to himself that he would help her through this difficulty if he could.

## ii

After lunch, the team in the tent settled down once again to tending to their patients. The girls were busy with putting together potions and dressing wounds, and the stream of patients did not let up. Devi and Udaya took breaks in turn so that they did not exhaust themselves too much. "This is a total success!" Udaya remarked to her at one point; and even Devi, with all her skepticism, had to agree that the response was better than she had expected. Her fears of sitting there twiddling her thumbs and having Siddayya or one of his henchmen coming by to jeer at her were completely unfounded. On the contrary, if Siddayya had deigned to visit the tent, he could not fail to have been impressed by the turnout. Whether he would have reported it to the king or not was a different matter, but he would have known that she had pulled off the challenge in spades.

As the evening wore on, there were brief respites when the whole team could stop to draw a breath. "Looks like people are beginning to return home," Devi remarked during one of the lulls. With the setting sun, people were beginning to be reminded of the need to head home before the night became pitch dark, multiplying the dangers on the road. Slowly the crowds were melting away, and hopefully soon the town would be back to normal. Inside the temple complex, the ceremonies were still being conducted, uninterrupted; but the townspeople and visitors were oblivious to this, not being party to the ceremonies any more. "Maybe we can start packing up," Devi suggested to Nagi. Nagi got up and looked around, trying to decide what to tackle first. She was just beginning to draw up the roster of tasks for the girls when there was a commotion at the entrance to the tent.

"Out of my way, out of my way at once!" a stentorian voice was shouting at some stragglers who were lingering near the entrance. They scattered helter skelter, and a large man made an impressive entrance into the tent. Tall and well built, he was sporting a luxuriant black mustache, a bright pink turban edged with gold thread, and flashing diamond earrings. But most riveting was the burden that he carried slung over his shoulder. It was the body of a man hanging like a sack of potatoes.

He strode purposefully towards one of the mats on the floor and unceremoniously dumped his burden on the ground. He glared at Udaya. "You! Are you the healer? Do something, and hurry! This is my uncle, he is a very important man, especially today. You better save him!"

Udaya stood aside and pointed to Devi, who quickly went forward and knelt by the unconscious man on the floor. She had a bad feeling about it even before she touched him. She lifted his arm to feel his pulse, and her worst fears were confirmed. The man was already dead, there was nothing that could be done for him.

Devi got up and stepped back from the body. "What is it?" the man shouted. "Why aren't you doing anything? Look at him lying there unconscious! Give him some medicine or massage him or something! Why are you just standing there like a dummy?"

Nagi went to Devi's side protectively. The man was not only being offensive, he was also towering over Devi in a threatening manner. It was clear that all was not well, and the man's behavior was likely to become even more aggressive very shortly.

"There is nothing I can do for him," Devi told him quietly. "He was already dead when you brought him here."

Given the man's behavior so far, his reaction to this news was no surprise. "You incompetent fool! You killed him! Do you know who he is? Do you know what bad luck you have caused this kingdom by your stupidity?" He was beside himself.

Udaya tried to pacify him. "Come sir, you can hardly blame my sister for this sad event. There was nothing to be done for him by the time you arrived! I do not know what happened, or where you found him, but he was dead when you brought him here. There was nothing to be done for him." But his words fell on deaf ears.

"Shut up! Who are you to address me? Who are you to defend this murderess? Passing herself off as a healer – you should call her a killer, that would be more appropriate! You wait, I will let everyone know of her true nature! I will tell the king! Everyone shall hear of her callous treatment of my poor uncle, and how she caused his untimely death."

Devi was incredulous. The man was twisting events around, and creating a fiction. "But he has hardly been in the tent for five minutes!" she protested. "What are you talking about? When he came in, he was dead! Everyone here can vouch for that. What were the circumstances that made you bring him here? Did he have some sort of attack, or collapse, or what? Whatever it was, it was serious enough that it caused his death immediately. There was no way anybody could have saved him. He was brought here too late!"

"Oh ho! So that's the way you're going to play it, is it?" the man sneered. "You people are going to gang up on me, is it? You will get all your friends and servants to testify that my uncle was dead when he came here, trying to blame me for bringing him too late! Let me tell you I have strained every muscle in my body to bring him here as fast as I could. Nobody else would have been able to bring him here in as short a time as I did! And now you say I slowed down so that my revered uncle could die!"

"No, sir," Devi tried desperately to calm him down. "You have misunderstood me. It was not my intention to imply that you delayed bringing him here, deliberately or otherwise. I only said that it was too late even when you started. It looks like he had a severe attack, and was dead even when you left the place where you found him."

"No, no," the man was adamant. "You cannot get away with that! Do you know that he was the owner of today's sacred horse? He was an important man! His death is very bad luck, and you have caused it! When the king finds out it will be bad very for you, I can tell you."

Devi's blood ran cold at this. She looked at Udaya, who was also looking grim now. This was a very grave charge the man was laying at their door, and if indeed the dead man was the owner of the sacrificial horse, then it would turn out badly. The owner of the sacrificial horse was a revered figure, and would have been eligible for all sorts of rewards and preferment. Now, despite all the evidence to the contrary, this man was leveling the false charge of negligence – or worse, murder – at them, and they would have a hard time defending themselves. At best, they could try and do some damage control by trying to get the man to see reason. While they were trying to come to terms with this disastrous turn of events and devise some reasonable response, there was a further commotion. A large crowd had gathered at the entrance, the better to observe the drama unfolding within. Now they were being summarily thrust aside to allow another figure to enter.

Why was she not surprised to see Siddayya elbowing his way in? Devi had somehow had the premonition that this would have something to do with him. She took a deep breath to steel herself against the inevitable onslaught. Next to her, she felt Udaya tensing up. Neither of them had any hope of anything good coming from this encounter. They could not even count on the protective presence of their father, who even now would be deeply embroiled in directing the rituals within the temple complex.

Siddayya stood surveying the scene in the tent. The large men dashed forward and fell at his feet and clutched at them. "Sir, sir, my revered uncle is gone, sir! You saw him today, sir – he was so full of life, in such a jolly mood! And now look at him – just a shell." Suddenly he ceased his groveling and, leaping up, he turned viciously on Devi and Udaya and pointed an accusing finger. "It is all her fault, sir! She did not know how to save him! She calls herself a healer, but she is a murderess, sir! And her so-called brother is trying to stage a cover-up operation so that she can be spared the due punishment for her crime! Please give me justice, sir! I cannot get my beloved uncle back, but I must have justice!"

Siddayya looked sardonically at Devi. "What do you have to say for yourself, young lady? I knew this was bad idea from the start, except the king was so set on it. Now the worst has happened, and your esteemed father is not here to protect and defend you as he usually does. What has happened here, and how are you going to explain away this body? You are aware that this man is an extremely important figure, especially today. His death will not be easy to conceal. The king will have to be told, and right away. It will not sit well with him. I cannot answer for the consequences. You better have a good defense ready!"

"The man was dead when he was brought here, sir." Devi knew it was no use appealing to the man's better nature or his sense of justice. He had neither. There was nothing to be done but to state the facts and stick to them.

After a pause Siddayya said "And is that all you have to say? Just a bald statement like that? And am I supposed to just believe it because you have said so? No explanation, no excuses, no mitigating circumstances?"

"What explanation do you want us to give, sir?" Udaya questioned him. "The plain truth is that when this man laid his uncle down on the mat, he was already dead. We have no idea in what circumstances he was taken ill, but most likely he had a massive attack which must have caused his heart to stop beating. When my sister examined him, she found he no longer had a pulse, which means that his soul had already departed his body."

"I see. And am I to understand I have only your word for this?"

"Well, we were all here, sir," Devi clarified. "Udaya was here, and Nagi and my whole team. They all saw what had happened."

"Your brother, your childhood nurse and three girls you have rescued from an orphanage! Yes, they are highly reliable witnesses alright! I should take their word for it, why not? Completely objective and unbiased, I am sure!" Siddayya gave vent to all the sarcasm that came naturally to his sour nature. "Alright, if you claim he was dead when he was brought here, what is your best guess as to why he died?"

"I have not been able to examine the body closely, sir. This man has been obstructing us, and creating a disturbance. If he moved aside, maybe we can take a closer look and see if we can get any hints as to the cause of death."

"Well, well, you must excuse Ranga for his excess of emotion, he is overcome with grief. But now he will allow you to do your job. Go ahead. I am also interested in observing the process you use to arrive at your conclusions."

Devi once again knelt down beside the lifeless body of Ranga's uncle. She first made a close examination of all four limbs, running her hands carefully down the length of each. Then she moved aside his top cloth and examined his chest and stomach. Removing his dhoti she examined his lower abdomen as discreetly as she could with her audience watching closely. She examined his head and face carefully. She first ran her fingers all over the skull, probing both the front and back. She lifted the eyelids and looked closely at the eyeballs and pupils. There was a popular superstition that in cases of wrongful death, the image of the killer was sometimes preserved in the dead person's pupils. No such thing had happened in this case. She opened up the oral cavity and checked inside for any foreign substances lodged there. Then, with Udaya's help, the body was turned over and she was able to examine the back and buttocks. Finally, she rose and faced Siddayya, ready to make her report.

"This man died a natural death from the look of it. There are no bruises or contusions on his body. None of his limbs is broken, and his skull is completely intact. There are no cuts anywhere on the body and no signs of external bleeding. He has not choked on any material, whether edible or not. There is a slight blue tinge on the lips, which is an indication of the heart having stopped. That is all I can glean from the body. I could take the body back to my clinic and cut open the abdomen to examine it more closely for further clues, if you like."

Ranga immediately started forward with protests, which Siddayya silenced with a raised hand. "That will not be necessary. Your external examination is sufficient. I think we are done here. We will remove the body so that we can get on with organizing the appropriate obsequies. I have noted your version of the events that transpired within this tent. But I must tell you that I have also noted Ranga's serious charges against you. We will have to undertake an inquiry into this matter. I am sure the king will demand it! And rightly so. This is all very murky and suspicious."

There was no point in protesting, and Devi and Udaya watched silently as Ranga stooped to pick up his uncle's body. As he walked out, he deliberately stepped towards Nagi and shoved her roughly aside as he walked out of the tent. Nagi, taken by surprise, went sprawling. Before she could collect her wits, both Ranga and Siddayya had left the tent. Udaya helped her up, and advised her earnestly to leave it alone and refrain from running out behind Ranga to wreak revenge, richly though he may deserve it. "Don't, Nagi. We are already in enough trouble! I'm not sure how we will come out of this. How I wish father were here. He would have thought of something to do immediately. As it is, by the time we are able to tell him our side of the story, the king would already have been told the distorted version that Ranga is putting about. Good god! I just thought of something! Maybe father will be with the king when this news is broken to him! After all, they are all in there, conducting the Ashvamedha rites."

It was a very different team that wended its way home that evening than the one that had set out in the morning. They had been all happy anticipation and excitement then. Now they were somber, dreading what the morning would bring.

# Chapter 9

The next day was a confused blur of comings and goings. Vaman Bhat was, of course, their first visitor. He had indeed, as Udaya had suspected, first got wind of the calamities being visited upon his children within the temple complex, in the midst of the rituals. He had been completely stunned and inclined to drop everything and rush to Devi's side. But he had been prevailed upon by Krishna Rao, who had advised him not to compound his problems by abandoning the king in the midst of this, the most important ritual he was likely to perform in his lifetime. "There will be time enough to deal with your problems later, Vaman. I will help you, do not worry. I can smell some mischief here, and I can almost lay my life on it that the author of it is you-know-who. I will start the groundwork now – as soon as the king is alone, I will speak to him and represent to him the foolishness of suspecting your daughter of foul play."

Vaman Bhat was thankful for his support, but was still filled with a deep sense of foreboding. He had been having these flashes of bad feeling ever since Krishna Rao had told him that it had been at Siddayya's behest that the king had asked Devi to set up the first aid tent. He said as much to Krishna Rao now. It stopped him in his tracks. Glancing around quickly, Krishna Rao grasped Vaman Bhat by the arm and pulled him abruptly aside into the shadow of a temple pillar. "Do not mention that to anyone else," he said sharply in a low voice. "The fewer the people who know about Siddayya's machinations the better. We will work this out between ourselves and discreetly. Understood?"

Vaman Bhat, though surprised by the sudden change in Krishna Rao's normally dignified demeanor, had readily agreed. He was not by nature a conspirator, and he rarely had the need or the opportunity to do so. How would he know the best course to take when it came to palace intrigue? Krishna Rao was a seasoned operator, naturally he knew best. He would follow his lead in this matter absolutely.

Vaman Bhat, Devi and Udaya had been closeted together for a long while, and Nagi was not privy to what went on behind closed doors. The first thing Vaman Bhat did when he met his children was to walk them through the events of the previous day in meticulous detail. When had they reached the venue? Who was there to meet them? What materials had they received? Who had delivered the materials? Had Udaya noticed anything unusual at the time? What happened after Devi and the girls arrived? Who was in the tent when the procession was passing by? What could they tell him about the patients who had come in? What types of ailments had they come for? And so on and on, Vaman Bhat questioned them on each point and listened carefully to their replies. Eventually, they arrived at the most critical part of the day, the part when the crowds had dispersed and the day was beginning to wind down.

"What time was it when Ranga entered the tent? Who all were present at the time inside the tent? What were they doing? What happened as soon as he came in?"

Udaya thought for a moment and replied. "It was getting to be dusk when Ranga entered, father. In fact, we were wondering whether we should pack up, because the numbers of patients was dwindling, and most people were heading back to their homes. Then Ranga burst in, carrying this load on his shoulder. We were all there. The girls were cleaning up the materials, and waiting for Nagi's packing instructions. Devi and I were standing just inside the entrance, organizing the wrap-up."

"I see. And what was your first impression of Ranga, as he entered?"

"At first, he sounded like a mad man! He was shouting and I thought he was going to attack us. Then he dumped his uncle's body on the ground and started threatening us with dire consequences if we did not revive him immediately. But he was already dead!"

"You could see that?" Vaman Bhat asked keenly. "This is important. How did you conclude that the man was already dead?"

Devi said, "The way the body fell to the ground showed that the man was definitely unconscious. His limbs had no strength in them, and he himself was insensible – eyes closed, immobile. Then I bent down to examine him, and I immediately realized that he was already dead. There was no breath in him, and no pulse. His heart had already stopped!"

"I see. And you told this to the man Ranga?"

"Yes, of course! But when I told him that, he became abusive, and started demanding that we revive his uncle because he was an important man and so on. But there was nothing to be done for his uncle any more. He was long gone!"

"And then what happened?"

"Then we were in the middle of this altercation, because the man was already accusing Devi of being incompetent and even a murderess, when Siddayya came in."

"Siddayya!" Vaman Bhat was astounded by this. "Why was he there? What had prompted him to come there?"

"This is what we do not know, father," Devi said dejectedly. "What prompted Sidayya to show up at just that moment? Perhaps he had followed the man Ranga for some reason? Or perhaps he really came to see how our day had gone, as he said? Whatever it was, he had a chance to see us at our lowest point of the day, and to reinforce his complete lack of faith in me and my abilities."

"No, daughter, it is important to find out why Siddayya came there at all, and why at that juncture. In some ways, his arrival could actually have helped you, you know. I am beginning to feel that his arrival was definitely connected with Ranga and his uncle. Somehow Siddayya knew that Ranga was on his way there, and was going to make trouble, and he came actually to rescue you. At least that is my theory. Why he should have wanted to help you out is still a mystery, but his presence definitely defused what could have been an extremely ugly situation for you."

Both Udaya and Devi were thoughtfully silent at this. They had so far been thinking of Siddayya as the villain, but this threw a new light on the matter. "You know, father is right," Udaya said slowly. "That Ranga was working himself up into a lather, and he was getting ready to start an all out fight. I don't know where it would have ended if Siddayya had not entered at that moment and taken charge of the situation. Once he arrived, Ranga calmed down, and matters proceeded more rationally, even though Siddayya managed to make some sarcastic comments at your expense. But he did allow you to make a thorough examination, and he did take your diagnosis at face value. I mean, even though he made some threatening noises as he left, he did not dispute anything you said, and he did get Ranga out of the tent and away from us!"

Devi could not entirely agree with her father and brother on Siddayya's role, but she did not want to argue the matter. Anyway, Vaman Bhat was moving on, questioning her about the findings of the physical examination of the body. And this was when Devi had to make the revelation that she had held close to her chest all this while.

"Father, there is something…..I am not sure what it means. I examined the body closely, father, and everything was as expected, except the eyes! The pupils were unnaturally dilated, as if the man had consumed a large quantity of some drug. I think the man had consumed something that caused his death. There are drugs that can do that, as you know."

Vaman Bhat was not expecting this. He could see the implications of such a finding, and they were not simple. Such an allegation would have to be investigated thoroughly. He went over and over the details of the physical examination, questioning Devi closely on her assessment of each vital organ. All of her findings seemed to him to be in order, the only anomaly being her observation on the size of the pupils.

"Are you sure, my child?" he asked for the nth time. He wanted her to be absolutely sure of her facts before taking this forward. The charge that Devi was making was extremely serious. If the man had been administered some harmful drug that had caused his death, then a full-fledged investigation would be required. If he were to take Devi's suspicions to the king, he would certainly take it seriously. The dead man was, after all, a member of the king's inner circle. If it later transpired that the suspicions were not well-founded, it would be extremely embarrassing and politically damaging to the king, at a time when he was already vulnerable. Devi and Vaman Bhat himself would be open to allegations of treason or worse. A mis-step now could cost them all dearly.

"Yes, father, yes. I am sure!" Devi reiterated, understanding her father's need for reassurance and the caution with which he was approaching the issue.

"I too have heard of the effects of drugs being discernible even after a person has died, but I had never heard of this before," Vaman Bhat said thoughtfully.

"But it is true, father – I do not know where I heard it, or who gave me this knowledge, but I know it. When the pupils of the eyes are dilated, it is because of a drug that also causes the heart to stop beating."

"What sort of drug is that?" Udaya asked curiously.

"You are familiar with it, Udaya! It is from a plant that grows everywhere. I have heard you praise the flower so many times. It is the hatapatri – the purple flower that you see by the roadside. It is a common medication that is prescribed for treating weakness and fatigue. The usual prescription consists of eating a few of the leaves. The problem arises when you eat too many. Then it can cause the heart to stop beating. And one of the indications that a person has consumed an excess of hatapatri is that the pupils of their eyes are dilated."

"But why do you suspect that he could have been administered hatapatri by someone else? Maybe he had already been prescribed hatapatri by his healer for some heart condition? Couldn't he have taken an excess dose by mistake? Maybe he was distracted with all the excitement of the day, and took a second dose?"

"No, Udaya, that doesn't seem plausible. For one thing, Ranga never mentioned that his uncle had any medical problem. And when I examined him he showed no other indication of heart disease. He was not fat, nor was his face unduly red or flushed. Besides, it takes massive doses of hatapatri to kill a man. He could not have taken it by mistake. It had to be administered to him, either by force or through trickery. Since he bore no bruises or other injuries on his body, my guess is that he was administered the leaf in his food by someone he trusted. It could easily have been ground up and mixed with his food or drink, and he might not have noticed the bitterness too much if it had been mixed with a dish of bitter gourd or spinach."

"Maybe Ranga did not mention his uncle's prior condition because he wanted to get you into trouble," Udaya suggested.

"Yes," Vaman Bhat added. "What if this whole incident was a ploy to slander you? Perhaps Ranga's uncle died of natural causes, and they used that unfortunate event to their advantage. I don't put anything past Siddayya and his gang."

"I do not see the logic of that, father," Devi said thoughtfully. "Alright, suppose there was an accident and the excitement of the moment caused him to die of natural causes, would Ranga actually allow his uncle's body to be used in that way? He seemed genuinely distressed by his death – it seems too cold blooded and calculating to use such a tragedy to serve Siddayya's purposes. Would even Siddayya sink so low? If he had wanted so desperately to discredit me, he could have picked something less dramatic, surely. And remember what you yourself pointed out - in the end, when he did show up, he did not aggressively denounce me. If he had really wanted to milk the situation for everything that it was worth, he could have created a much bigger ruckus. Instead he conciliated Ranga and actually defused the situation."

"There is one thing you do not know, child," Vaman Bhat said quietly. "It was Siddayya apparently who suggested that you manage the first aid tent in the first place."

Both Udaya and Devi were stunned by this revelation. "What are you saying, father? Who told you this? All this time I had thought it was a direct decree from the king! I wouldn't have taken on this accursed project at all if I had known it was Siddayya's brainchild!" Devi cried.

Vaman Bhat looked uncomfortable. "I should not have revealed this to you. In fact, I have been specifically asked not to mention it to anyone, so I must ask you to maintain the utmost secrecy in this matter. But it was Krishna Rao himself who told me this. He was actually present at the meeting where Siddayya made the suggestion and persuaded the king to entrust the responsibility to you. Krishna Rao feared that he had done it for some nefarious purpose of his own. But could he be as evil as this? Could he be so bent on teaching you a lesson and bringing about your downfall that he was willing to be party to such a heinous crime? Now I am torn between these two completely opposite views! On the one hand, it could be that his appearance in the tent was a god send and that he rescued you from an extremely difficult situation. On the other hand, it is remotely possible that he himself was the author of that crisis, carefully designed to discredit you. I am not sure what to think," Vaman Bhat ended somberly.

"But in a way what you are saying proves my theory, father!" Devi exclaimed excitedly. "Siddayya must have planned the old man's death, he must have engineered it! He could not have counted on him dying that day, how could he? If he did indeed have problems with his heart, he could have lasted for years! People can live for many years even if they have heart pains or other such troubles. Siddayya could only have guaranteed his death on a particular day and time if he had actually caused it. It was cleverly timed, you must admit – just as the day was waning and the crowds were thinning. At any other time, we could have easily blamed the crowds for the poor man's death, and Ranga would have found it harder to allege negligence. After all, it would have taken them forever to force their way through the huge throng and actually show up at the tent. As it was, they picked a time when that excuse was much harder to make, because there was not so much of a delay caused by excessive crowding."

Vaman Bhat frowned. "No, daughter," he cautioned her. "Listen to yourself. Don't you think it sounds far-fetched? Here is a man who is one of the most powerful in the land.

He has the king's ear, he has been the architect of the events of the past several weeks. Can we really imagine that he has to resort to so much subterfuge just to squash a young healer, to prove a point? He has the power to simply poison the king's mind and get him to issue a decree shutting down your clinic! Why would he go to such lengths, you tell me that. And we are not talking about something small, we are talking about murder! A man does not commit murder for a reason such as this!"

His heart ached for Devi. Why did children have to make life decisions that were so hard and fraught with dangers? He supposed that was the way of children – of his children, at any rate. The easy route would have been to settle down with a nice man, produce a son and a daughter in quick succession, and dedicate oneself to the home and family. He had long ago realized that this was not to be; and he was proud of the independence and determination of both his children. But there was a downside to all that independence and determination, especially in their essentially conservative society.

"We must not jump to conclusions," Udaya agreed slowly, reflecting on all that Devi and his father had just said. "For instance, Siddayya might have suggested Devi's name thinking that she would make a mess of things, since he genuinely believes that women are not capable of doing anything beyond the four walls of the home. It could be that all he was trying to do was to establish what he thinks is an immutable truth. He may have been dismayed that no disaster occurred all day to prove his point; but so disappointed that he was willing to commit murder? I agree with father – that is a bit of a leap! Is Devi's downfall really so crucial to Siddayya – particularly at this point of time, with so much political turmoil associated with the aftermath of the Ashvamedha – that he would jeopardize his own freedom for it? After all, he must realize that we would not take such a charge lying down, and that we would have some kind of investigation done. So I am a bit skeptical about that theory."

"Then what do you suggest?" Devi challenged him. "You are suggesting that I am biased against Siddayya – well, fair enough. Perhaps I am. And I do admit that I am such small fry that it's a bit arrogant to think that Siddayya would make me a target for the full power of his evil designs. I'm open to other theories, believe me. I know we did nothing wrong! I refuse to sweep this under the carpet and carry on with the rest of my life. If we do not clear this up, it will be like a dirty secret I have to live with forever."

Vaman Bhat patted his daughter's shoulder soothingly. "Calm down, my child. I will do my level best to clear this up. And even if we never get to the bottom of this mystery, I will ensure that Ranga or Siddayya or whoever is concerned tells the truth. They have to be made to admit that the man was dead before he arrived at the tent! If only Ranga would see reason, he could be made to face the consequences of his lies. Perhaps he doesn't realize that the charge he has made will have a serious impact on your professional integrity. I will talk to him. He will see the rationale of our case, and the passage of time will also make him less emotional. You will see, it will all get ironed out."

He got up and picked up his upper cloth. "Now I will go to the king's guard and see if he can spare a man to conduct this investigation. The first hurdle is to convince them that a criminal case exists and needs to be looked into. Right now everyone is convinced that it is a tragedy caused by negligence, and if I try to convince them of anything else, they will accuse me of acting in self-interest. I will consult with Krishna Rao and see what he advises me to do next. I will have to share your suspicions with him, as well as this medical evidence that you have reported to me. Let's see how he responds to that."

So saying, Vaman Bhat left the clinic. Udaya and Devi glanced anxiously at each other. It was going to be a long wait spent wondering how all this would eventually turn out.

# Chapter 10

Jayadeva strode purposefully towards the king's chamber. Now that the celebrations were over, the king would have time to discuss last evening's untoward incident. He would not be pleased, Jayadeva knew. And he would be even less pleased to hear what Jayadeva had to tell him. Murder within the four walls of the palace! That meant the enemies were close. If they had gathered this much courage, either they had a very powerful sponsor, or they were very sure of their victory. Either way, it did not bode well for the king.

He was stopped at the door by his old friend Mada, the King's personal valet. He was also the one who conveyed messages between Jayadeva and the king, perhaps the only other person who knew that he was still alive. The king trusted him with his life and well he should. Mada put his own life on the line every day for his health and safety. Apart from being his personal valet, he was also the king's food taster – and in these dangerous times, that was a risky occupation indeed. But Mada was glad to do it. He wouldn't have trusted such a critical task to anyone else, and he would happily give his life in protecting his beloved king.

"He is there," Mada said quietly, "but he is not happy."

Jayadeva sighed. He was not surprised. "Should I come back later? I have to see him today though. I have something very important to tell him."

"What about?" Mada could always judge the urgency of any errand.

"About the death of the old man, you must have heard of it? The old man who supplied the Ashvamedha horse came to a sticky end yesterday evening."

"Of course I have heard of it! Is there anyone in the kingdom who has not?" Mada exclaimed.

"The news has spread like wildfire, I am sure it has even reached the provinces by now. Well, if you are here to tell the king something about that, you will be very welcome! You had better go inside at once." So saying, Mada opened the door to the king's chamber so that Jayadeva could enter.

Entering through a private side door, he found himself in the inner sanctum of the royal quarters. The room was simple but exceedingly elegant. It was also extremely large, and flanked by several smaller chambers that led off from it, for the king's personal attendants and his guards. The king's own chamber had a large bed in the very center, heavily carved and draped with some richly patterned silk. There was a profusion of cushions and bolsters arranged on it for his comfort. However, he did not often recline there, and used it only for sleeping. Most of his meetings took place towards one side of the room, where a more modest divan had been placed, where the king would sit and meet his visitors, look over documents and generally conduct business. Apart from this furniture, there were many woven mats sprinkled about the room, as well as a large number of oil lamps, which lit up every nook and cranny brightly. No chance of any marauder hiding in a dark corner!

In private, the king was a simple man, of average size, and given more to intellectual than physical pursuits. Of necessity he was physically fit and and an expert horseman and swordsman, but these things he did because he had to. It would be a poor king who could not keep up with his courtiers and warriors in the battlefield or when out on a hunt. But he was also a thoughtful man, deeply concerned for the well-being of his subjects, and willing to listen to good advice on all matters. Since he was of a liberal and philosophical turn of mind, he often met with philosophers and intellectuals of different persuasions, and he encouraged this type of discussion and debate amongst his inner circle as well.

But for all his intellectual leanings, he was no dreamer. It was his native pragmatism that had led to his employing private sources for information on the goings on at his court in this time of political upheaval. The recent military campaigns had been the trigger for unrest. People were happy to be on the side of the victorious army, but they did not want to pay the price. As he well knew, he had no choice. It was the king's duty to expand his dominions if he could, and that could only be done by waging war. In order to win a war, one had to be better equipped and better trained and have a larger army than the enemy – and all that cost money. There were those who wanted to call a halt to war, and they had all kinds of reasons for it. For the most part it had to do with petty jealousies – someone felt they should get more of the spoils of war than their neighbor, or they felt somebody else was getting an unfair share, or both. But for some with a more philosophical bent of mind, the king's on-going expansionist campaign was a challenge to their sense of what was right and good. The king's role should be to ensure the safety, security and happiness of his subjects, not to be continually engaging in wasteful wars!

This had led to a huge increase in the prevailing paranoia at court, and the king could not afford to be immune to it. He was well aware that many of his senior advisors and courtiers were engaging in espionage of a very sophisticated kind. Some were in favor of taking matters into their own hands, and that could not be tolerated at any cost. It was hard to know who to trust, and he knew that some members of his own inner circle had betrayed him. There were times when he felt alone, isolated – did no one understand that lasting peace would come, but only after the price had been paid!

The king was seated in a deep and comfortable chair, staring bleakly into the middle distance. He looked up as Jayadeva entered and nodded tiredly. "Come in, son. What brings you here? Did I call for you?"

Jayadeva was surprised at how dispirited the king sounded. He himself seemed to realize it, because he rose with a short laugh and said, "You are surprised by my questions! I don't blame you Jayadeva. You find me very tired this morning. The ceremonies yesterday took their toll! Interminable hours spent in front of a fire, with all that smoke and the heat! Give me a battlefield anyday! Those Brahmins had a field day yesterday, I can tell you. Every scripture, every ritual, every tortuous detail – I don't think they missed a single trick in the book. But I can't blame them, it was my idea after all! I just didn't know what I had let myself in for."

Jayadeva had not expected this outburst. The king sounded almost bitter! From all that he had heard, the ceremony had been a triumph, with every detail meticulously observed. Surely that was a good thing?

"But the whole court was satisfied," the king continued, as he seated himself once more. "The queen was satisfied, that was a wonder in itself! I should call the Council of Ministers and thank them for having made all the arrangements – Mada! Please make a note. I will have an audience with my ministers this afternoon." Mada bowed low and indicated that he would do whatever was required.

"Now, tell me. What is it you have come for? You surely have something on your mind, or else you would not have come unbidden," the king commanded Jayadeva.

Jayadeva came to attention and marshaled his thoughts. He needed to be absolutely accurate in his narration of events, leaving out no detail. "It is about the death of the old man yesterday, sire," he began.

"There's another thing!" the king interrupted. He got up again agitated, and strode about the room. "Why did that man not just sit quietly at the ceremony? He was an honored guest, after all. We had come to an amicable understanding on his reward for supplying me that magnificent horse. He did the right and proper thing by refusing the fourth queen and took instead a handsome cash settlement. After that, why should he go wandering about, offering himself up as an easy target for bandits and scoundrels? In fact, at some point during the ceremonies, I did notice that he was missing, but little did I realize that he would turn up dead!

It is most aggravating, and now I will have to bring this up with the Council for some elaborate damage control measures, I suppose," he ended resentfully.

"Actually, sire, the story is a little different. With your leave, I will try and explain." The king again seated himself and watched Jayadeva narrowly.

"Tell me," he said quietly. "All I have been told so far is that he is dead. I am yet to be told how and by whose hand."

"Yesterday, sire, as you had instructed me, I kept watch over the palace all day. I maintained a watch on the premises from a vantage point in the corridor outside your chamber, sire. What I saw from there will tell you that Thimmappayya was killed by neither a bandit nor a scoundrel, sire, but something much more mysterious." With that, Jayadeva described in detail all the events that he had witnessed in the palace the evening before – the locked room, the three men and their conversation, their unceremonious exit and the collapse of Thimmappayya on the steps outside.

The king had risen again, and stood at the window, listening intently to everyting Jayadeva said. "So, let me understand this. You are telling me that whatever the foul deed was, it was committed in Krishna Rao's room? By whom?"

"That is the thing we do not know, sire. As I said, the door was being opened and locked by some mysterious hand within the room, but I did not catch a glimpse of that person. Whoever it was had entered and exited from the window on the outside wall of the room, and there was no way I could see them from where I was hidden."

"Hmmm, so Thimmappayya was found lying on the steps, is it? Who found him? Where were all the palace guards when all this was going on? Do you tell me that not one of them challenged these men and stopped them?" the king wanted to know.

"That is the peculiar thing, sire. There were no guards in that entire wing! I wondered at it myself. Perhaps they had all left to see the celebrations? That also puzzled me."

"It is more than puzzling. It is a scandal! If we find out who gave them leave to abscond for the day, I think we will learn a lot about this death! But carry on. Who found Thimmappayya?" the king returned to the story.

"His nephew Ranga, sire. He suddenly appeared out of nowhere, and then he lifted him bodily and carried him away."

"The fellow always was as strong as an ox," the king commented drily. "And carried him home, is it? That is a fair distance, as I recall!"

"No, sire, not home," Jayadeva clarified. "He took him to the first aid tent. To the healer, sire, to seek her help."

At this the king stood up again. "Really! So the tent was up and functioning, was it? It was a success, then?"

"Oh yes, sire, they had been busy all day, people were streaming in with all kinds of maladies, I understand. From what I hear, they did a marvelous job. But then, in the evening, they had this disaster, with Ranga descending on them with his uncle on his shoulders. I was outside, sire, having followed Ranga all the way, so I could not hear the details. But the bystanders told me later that a regular scene ensued, with Ranga almost attacking the healer and her helpers."

The king was astonished. "Attacking the healer? Why would he do that?"

"He held her responsible for the death of his uncle, sire. Apparently she tried to explain that he was dead on arrival, but he would not listen to her. He kept insisting that she had killed him through her negligence. Luckily, Lord Siddayya arrived to save the day."

"This is a day of surprises, indeed!" the king exclaimed. "Siddayya! And what pray was he doing there?"

"He had also followed Ranga from the palace grounds, sire. I saw him. He had been waiting outside in the palace gardens, I am not sure why. He went into the tent, and then the noise died down somewhat. I am told by the eyewitnesses that he questioned the healer and got her to physically examine the dead man to determine the cause of death. After a while he and Ranga emerged with the body and left for home."

"And they left for home…." the king repeated softly to himself. "There is obviously a lot of catching up I need to do! Your account of the events raises more questions than it answers….at least now I know where Thimmappayya came to his death. But why? And by whose hand? We need to get to the bottom of all this."

Jayadeva interjected. "Sire, from what I hear, when Ranga was accusing the healer of killing his uncle, Lord Siddayya did not refute it. Perhaps he also held her responsible? But then he did not see what I saw, so one cannot blame him."

"Siddayya can be a cussed old so-and-so. I can guess why he might not have refuted Ranga, but that is not what we need to discuss right now. Tell Mada to send in the Commandant of the palace guard on your way out. And stay close, I might need you again later today."

Dismissed, Jayadeva went out and gave Mada the message. He hurried off to fetch the Commandant, and Jayadeva slipped quietly out and wended his way back to his rooms, there to await his further instructions.

Meanwhile, the Commandant of the palace guards was having an uncomfortable interview with the king. Why had the palace guards been absent from their post yesterday? That was the question, and the Commandant had no response, He had not been aware that the guards were missing. As far as he knew, their strict instructions had been to maintain their positions and stick to their usual roster. He had given them no command to the contrary, not verbally nor in writing. The king did not upbraid him, but made it abundantly clear that if he wanted to remain in his post, he would have to come back to him with a reasonable explanation for this incredible lapse in security in very short order. Luckily for him, the king was not quick to anger. Any other monarch would have had his badge long before now. He was giving him a chance to redeem himself and the Commandant emerged with swift and furious instructions to his lieutenant to gather the guards in question immediately for interrogation.

This did not take long, for he ran a tight and disciplined ship. It was therefore all the more galling for him to be accused of having slipped up and that too on such a critical occasion! When all eyes were on the palace and anything untoward could have happened, how could there have been such a gaping hole in his ranks? He rained his wrath down upon the soldiers – where had they been? Why were they not at their posts? On whose orders had they dared to step away?

When the guards finally got the chance to speak, they told a curious story. They had reported for duty as usual yesterday morning and taken their posts. Shortly after that, a small troop of soldiers along with their commander had arrived in their wing and informed them that they were relieved for the day, because the king had ordered a military presence in the wing to provide heightened security. The commander had informed them that he was a senior officer in the provincial army, and he was taking over the guardianship of that particular wing for the day. He had then dismissed them and stationed his soldiers in their place. So they had left the palace and joined the festivities, enjoying their unexpected holiday.

Had they checked this so-called commander's credentials? No, sir, they had not. But he was dressed in correct uniform and so were the soldiers.

Had they asked any questions to ascertain which province they had come from, who was their Governor? No, sir, they had not. The man had been very authoritative, and they had no reason to doubt him.

Had they anything to say in mitigation that could save their sorry skins? At this the guards fell silent. They were young men who had been given an unexpected treat, and used it to spend a day out with their families. The Commandant sighed and dismissed them. Then he went back to report to the king.

The king was waiting for him. "Well?" he asked as the Commandant entered.

The Commandant bowed deeply and said, "Sire, I have conducted an enquiry as you ordered. It appears that there was an infiltration, sire. The palace guard was dismissed by a group of soldiers in full military uniform, after which we do not know what happened. We do not know whether these were genuine soldiers from a provincial army as they claimed, or imposters sent by enemy forces for some nefarious purpose. All we know is that the loyal palace guard was not in place in this wing all of yesterday, sire."

"Well, we need to find out who these fellows were and double quick! Because you would have heard by now that there was a death."

"But the death was outside in the city, sire. I understand that it occurred in the First Aid tent."

"It was nothing of the sort!" the king retorted. "My agents tell me that the death occurred here, within the four walls of this palace, within shouting distance of my own chambers. This is how I know that the palace guards were missing." The king then related all the circumstances of the death that Jayadeva had told him, including the infiltration of the palace by persons unknown, the trespass into the Prime Minister's chambers and the dead body on the front steps. "I suggest you make this investigation your first and only priority. I want to know who these people were, and why they chose to kill Thimmappayya. There is more to this than meets the eye. We must settle this swiftly, before we get mired in rumors and intrigue of various sorts. Those are your orders, now go!"

The Commandant needed no second bidding. He had his orders, and he would now execute them.

He had barely left the royal chamber when there was another discreet knock on the door. Mada entered with folded hands. "It is the Council, sire," he announced to the king.

In his wake entered only two people – Siddayya and Krishna Rao. The king looked at them inquiringly. "Where are the rest?" he asked. He had called for a meeting of the full Council, ten members.

Krishna Rao answered. "We discussed it, sire, and thought it best if just the two of us meet with you at first. We are in a situation where we don't know whom to trust any more. I hope you will agree that we two can be trusted to give you good counsel for now; and we can wait to share all of our information with the rest of the ministers. If you insist, however, we can have the others here in no time."

The king considered briefly, and then said, "No, leave it. Maybe it's best that we keep it confined to just the three of us for now. Time enough to bring the others in later. You will have guessed what this is about. A man is dead. Under mysterious circumstances. We need to get to the bottom of it, no question. I have already instructed the Commandant of the guards to start his investigations. Some extremely suspicious activity in and around my own chamber – and actually within your chamber Krishna Rao! – has been reported to me by my agents. We need to have all this carefully looked into."

Krishna Rao looked shaken. "My chamber, my lord? How is this? What activity are we talking about? Who could possibly have told you such a thing?"

The king was not about to reveal his sources, but the others were well aware that the king had his own secret agents. That was standard practice. So without naming any names, the king repeated Jayadeva's story, ending with the curious incident of the palace guards which the Commandant had just related to him.

"The foremost question to my mind is: why were all these arrangements made for the man to die within the palace walls? Was his discovery by Ranga pure accident?" The king was speaking almost to himself. "If he had been found dead inside the palace, there would have been an even bigger furore! A death outside my own chambers, on such an auspicious day! Can you imagine?"

There was a silence after he finished. Both Siddayya and Krishna Rao were thinking through the facts presented to them so far. "It is possible that the man died of natural causes, sire, even if the circumstances appeared suspicious," Krishna Rao ventured.

"Well, if he did, why did the men not take the body home and arrange for the proper obsequies? Why abandon the body like that? Evidently they were acquaintances of his, they were spending the evening together. Why the guilty behavior?" the king demanded. "And let us not forget that the palace guard was tricked into leaving their post. That hardly points to a natural death!" There was no reasonable answer to that.

Krishna Rao responded hesitantly. "Well, sire, I heard something in passing, that there was some supernatural quality to the death. Someone I met had seen Ranga carrying the corpse into the healer's tent, and they claim that the man's face was all twisted, as if he had seen the very devil before he died."

"Supernatural rubbish! I hope you quashed all such nonsense! People who talk like that have some ulterior motive, I can take a bet on that! You must think – what good will come out of alleging that evil powers are responsible for the crime?"

"I have not heard anyone talking about evil powers, my lord. Perhaps Ranga was right. Perhaps Thimmappayya was not dead, but the girl's negligence killed him." Predictably Siddayya suggested his pet theory.

The king laughed without humor. "You would like to put that story about wouldn't you Siddayya? What do you have against the girl? Just because she goes against your old traditional views on what a girl should and should not do, are you really willing to foist a case of manslaughter on her? Perhaps you are even willing to go further and accuse her of actually murdering the man?"

Siddayya drew himself up, insulted. He did not dare retort to the king, but a cold and irrational fury against the girl built up in his heart. Because of her, he was being caricatured by the king!

"Perhaps she had nothing to do with it, sire," he admitted grudgingly.

"I am quite sure of it," the king replied shortly. "I suggest we steer clear of red herrings and try and get to the bottom of this as soon as possible. Take all the resources you need, and keep me updated on your investigation. If we do not resolve this soon, it will foment a lot of trouble, I can feel it in my bones. Whoever planned this has thought it through deeply. We need to outsmart a very smart man."

# Chapter 11

After his discussion with Devi and Udaya at the clinic, Vaman Bhat returned home. He paced up and down the verandah in his anxiety. Not only were both his children currently under a cloud, his daughter was also alleging that a man had been murdered within the palace precincts on one of the holiest of holy days. He was not sure what he should do about the whole situation. To clear both his son and daughter of all suspicion in the death of Thimappayya and then to reinstate them professionally was of course his number one objective. But what was the best course of action? He would have given anything to have some wise counsel on this matter, but there was only one person whom he felt he could trust and that person was not available to him at the moment. Krishna Rao was caught up in a meeting with the king on matters of state; grave matters, from the look of it, because they had been closeted together for the entire day, and still no signs of any of them emerging from the king's chambers. Vaman Bhat knew that these were difficult times, and there were many more earth shattering problems facing the realm than the accidental death, perhaps murder, of a businessman and the consequent shaming of a young healer. But what to do? To each person, his or her own problems were paramount, even if they were insignificant in the grand scale of things.

Sita watched her husband as he paced about the veranda. She wished she could offer him some comfort, but she was afraid of saying the wrong thing. She herself was convinced that her children would be completely vindicated since they had done no wrong. But if someone had asked her how that would happen, she would have had no response. It was just a feeling she had – maybe even just her hope – that this would all end well. Her husband would be impatient with such an argument. He would point out to her that things did not just turn out alright by chance, they had to be worked at. They would have to pursue a careful strategy to reveal the truth and that may or may not end with Devi and Udaya being vindicated. Whoever had got them into this jam in the first place was obviously bent on creating trouble for them – had, in fact, gone to some lengths to do so. Had, in fact, committed murder to do so, if Devi was to be believed. In such circumstances, Vaman Bhat considered it sheer folly to sit around with baseless convictions, which were all that Sita could offer him at the moment.

"I'll be back," he suddenly called out to her and stepped out of the veranda towards the gate. Sita understood his need for action, and was not surprised at all that he should set off at a rapid pace towards the center of town. She had no idea whom he had gone to meet. Perhaps no one! But it was better than sitting around doing nothing at home.

Vaman Bhat strode down the road without much idea of which direction he was going in nor whom he intended to meet. He did intend eventually to meet Krishna Rao, no matter how late he had to sit up in order to do so, but at the moment that was not an option. He decided to walk towards the temple and be distracted by the crowds and activity. Anything was better than the continual brooding that he had been doing for all this while!

As he looked around, he suddenly realized that he was at the very spot where all the trouble had started. Yes, this was the very spot where the first aid tent had been erected that day. The scene looked very different today, of course. All the stands around the temple had been dismantled and carried away, and although there were plenty of people about, it was as nothing compared to the crowds that had thronged the temple complex on the day of the sacrifice. Vaman Bhat stood still and observed the surroundings. He stood there for a while, reflecting on all the events of the past few weeks. He wondered now whether he had done the right thing that day. Should he have requested the king to give him leave from the task of supervising the rituals so that he could have been here to support his daughter? Had it been selfish of him to stay close to the king, to desire to be noticed for his erudition and special knowledge of the scriptures? Now in retrospect the outcome was such a bitter pill for Vaman Bhat to swallow that he felt he would have given up all thought of self had he known what the day would bring. But then hindsight is always perfect.

Lost in his own thoughts, Vaman Bhat did not at first pay attention to the snatches of conversation that could be heard around him. But slowly he became aware of a particularly insistent set of voices engaged in a heated debate at quite close quarters.

"Sir, I tell you, all this is bad luck! You tell me, isn't it a bad omen when such an important man dies on such an auspicious day? I have heard that his face was horribly twisted, and his eyes were staring wildly, as if he had seen the devil! It is the work of the devil only, to bring bad luck to the Horse Sacrifice." Vaman Bhat turned around to see a large, impressively mustachio-ed man, wearing a bright red turban and a face to match, stating his facts heatedly. His companion was an equally tall but less impressive man, thin and looking rather washed out in comparison with his florid friend.

"But how can you say that, sir?" the thin man was asking, almost pleadingly. "I know Ranga, and he says that his uncle died only because they did not take good care of him inside the tent. It was that young girl, you know. She had no experience, probably she got confused and did not know what to do."

"No!" the florid man was getting more agitated. "There are two problems with what you are saying! One is, I know that girl. Her clinic is close to my village and I tell you, she is a very good healer. I know many people whom she has healed even from very serious conditions. So you cannot say that she did not know what she was doing or that she was confused. Second, I saw Ranga arrive with his uncle on his shoulder. I tell you, I saw that uncle's face. He looked like he had seen the devil! It was terrible – I am a strong man, but remembering his eyes I am getting nightmares nowadays!"

The thin man seemed to be impressed by this line of argument. He was no expert on what happened to people's eyes when they had seen the devil, but the florid man seemed to know, and his was a forceful personality.

"I am just repeating what Ranga told me," he said again, but with much less conviction. "But now that you say so, I remembered something else," he resumed with a slight return of the old combative manner. "You remember just a few days ago that young man also disappeared – they didn't find even a trace of him, he just vanished into this air! Maybe the devil took him also?"

The other man was irritated at this appropriation of his theory. "What are you talking about?" He demanded of his friend.

"Do you remember that boy Jayadeva? He also disappeared mysteriously! I think it is all bad luck, that's all I can say. What is the use of all this Ashvamedha and celebrations when the devil is walking amongst us? Carrying away young men, important men, and all the time the king wants to flaunt his wealth and boast about his accomplishments. It's a pox on him, I tell you – he is being taught a lesson for becoming too big for his boots!"

Several members of his audience nodded their heads vigorously in agreement. Yes, yes, they seemed to feel. The king's hubris was bringing about its own downfall. All the successful conquests had gone to his head and now the fates were exacting their revenge! If the king didn't watch out, even worse things might befall him. What worse things, some enquiring minds wanted to know? This was left open to each person's active imagination but the message was clear – bad luck was beginning to visit the kingdom, this was amply demonstrated by these untimely deaths. And unless the king adopted greater humility and moderation, the trend would continue. Military success was not all it was cut out to be. It had attracted the evil eye, and there was no telling how to propitiate it…..

Vaman Bhat could feel his bile rising as the conversation proceeded. This same crowd, that had cheered every new conquest while the going was good, that had enjoyed the celebrations of the Horse Sacrifice to the hilt, how quickly had they changed their empty minds! This was the way of the mob, he supposed. A couple of untoward occurrences could be so easily twisted around to mean something completely different. Had this been the intention of the criminals, after all? Vaman Bhat was confused. He had been wracking his brains to come up with a motive for the murder of Thimappayya, and now he had a glimmer of an idea. Whipping up public opinion against an otherwise successful and popular king – how else could it be done, other than by invoking the supernatural? Mysterious deaths, evil lurking in the shadows – such was the stuff that ignorant minds reveled in. Such rumors caught the imagination of the riffraff that gathered in street corners and town squares in the evenings, and they would spread like wildfire. If this was indeed the intention of those who had orchestrated the crime, how happy they would be now!

The argument was now proceeding on more common ground. The third man was chipping in, "Say what you like, this is bad luck. After all that grand celebration to end the Ashvamedha campaign, for such an inauspicious thing to happen! Everybody is saying that is a bad omen. That Ranga's uncle, Thimmappayya, was the owner of the horse, you know! Can it be good luck if he dies on this important day?"

Vaman Bhat turned away and decided to go back home. He had no stomach for further investigation at the moment. He would approach Krishna Rao later in the day, when his mind was less jaded with this idle gossip.

Unknown to him, another man had also heard the idle chatter in the marketplace. He was a young man currently disguised as a monk. He was also amused to find that he was suspected of being finished off by the devil! But the amusement was shortlived. He too realized the danger of this kind of gossip and rumor-mongering. He would need to report it to the king forthwith.

## ii

Early that morning Vaman Bhat had left purposefully for his daughter's clinic to discover the truth of what had transpired in the first aid tent the evening before. He now got up purposefully for the second time that day. "Alright, now I will go and see Krishna Rao. And I will try not to get distracted in the marketplace again!"

"But why are you going to see Krishna Rao, husband?" Sita asked, a worried frown marring the smoothness of her brow. "He will no doubt tell you something that will trouble you even more. I know he is a good man, but somehow in the past few days, he has done nothing but give you sleepless nights."

"What do you mean, Sita?" Vaman Bhat questioned her sharply. "Krishna Rao is a friend of longstanding and a valued advisor. Do not speak dismissively of him! If he can, I know he will help us. I go to him seeking his opinion, that is all. He is a wise man, experienced in the ways of the world.

I am sure he will have a new point of view to offer. Plus, he did say he would do his best to sort out this mess, and I want to inquire whether he has been able to make any progress."

Sita looked a bit put out at being rebuked by her husband, but did not give up. "I do not deny any of what you just said. But remember, he is the one who told you that giving Devi this heavy responsibility was Siddayya's work, and ever since then I know you have been restless. It would have been better if you had never known that. Sometimes fearing the worst can actually bring it on, you know!"

Vaman Bhat realized that his wife was as much under stress as he was, and was only voicing her concerns and not criticizing his actions. "Don't worry, wife," he said comfortingly as he took his leave. "It will all work out for the best, you will see! That has always been my philosophy in life. Everything happens for the best. And it has not failed me yet. Even you know the umpteen times that it has been true in our own lives. So leave it to god, and he will take care of it."

"All very well for you to say!" she called to his retreating back. "I don't see you heeding your own advice!"

Vaman Bhat walked away from his home with a lighter heart. His mind felt fresher now. There was no point seeing Krishna Rao in a heated frame of mind; he was glad that he now had a much cooler head.

The first order of business was to tell Krishna Rao about the medical evidence that Devi had revealed to him. That appeared to be crucial, and pointed clearly to some violence having been done. The dilated pupils and other signs of the man having been poisoned – surely that was important information that he ought to tell Krishna Rao? Vaman

Bhat hoped that Krishna Rao would be free even for a few minutes, so that he could have a private word with him.

After a brief exchange with the guards on duty - who were now taking their duties very seriously indeed! - Vaman Bhat entered the palace and went straight to Krishna Rao's chamber. The guard at the door informed him that Krishna Rao was not in, he was at a meeting. At a meeting – that could be any where in the palace.

But by one of those strange quirks of fate, as he turned into the main corridor, he suddenly ran into the man himself! Krishna Rao was equally taken aback, and quite unaware that he was the man that Vaman Bhat had been hoping to meet.

"Vaman!" he exclaimed with pleasure. "What are you doing here? If you are hoping for an audience with the king today, I'm afraid you are out of luck. He is completely absorbed by the aftermath of the Ashvamedha, and will not be able to see anyone today."

"No, no, actually it was you I was hoping to see," Vaman Bhat assured him. "I am aware that king has many matters of state on his mind, and in any case I have nothing to do with him. But if you have a few moments to spare…"

Krishna Rao hesitated, and then said, "Come, let us step into my chamber. Talking in the hallway is fraught with risks these days, no matter how innocuous the topic. Things get twisted around and reported back to the powers that be in unrecognizable ways! Come." So saying, Krishna Rao led him quickly down the corridor to his room, a spacious chamber, quite lavishly appointed, although care had been taken not to appear garish or extravagant. There was richly carved sandalwood adorning the doors and window frames;

thickly woven silk fabric shades shielded the room from the heat of the sun. The floors were of smooth polished granite in a golden color, on which were placed comfortable mattresses and pillows on which Krishna Rao and his visitors could sit and conduct their business.

Krishna Rao himself usually sat behind a large low desk, embossed with the king's emblem – the two headed eagle. But today someone else was already sitting there – Siddayya. It was an unpleasant surprise, both for Vaman Bhat and Krishna Rao himself, who physically started at the sight of the interloper. "Lord Siddayya!" he exclaimed, with forced geniality. "I thought you were in an all-day meeting with the king!"

"I was in a meeting with the king, but it was only for an hour or so. Why, Krishna Rao, you sound almost unhappy to see me? Am I so unwelcome in your chambers now?"

Krishna Rao quickly recovered himself and laughed lightly. "Not at all, sir, why would you even think that? It's just that I did not expect you, that is all. As long time colleagues, and I like to think friends, surely we are always welcome in each other's chambers!"

"Good, good," Siddayya retorted, managing to sound oily even in that simple utterance. "And I see that you have your friend and admirer Vaman Bhat with you."

Vaman Bhat shifted uncomfortably. This was the last thing he had expected or indeed wanted. At the best of times Siddayya was a man he was wary of, and today he had wanted to have a private word with Krishna Rao. Now he had no choice but to say his piece in Siddayya's presence. Trying to pass off this visit with just small talk was not an option, since he had already hinted to Krishna Rao that he had something important to say. But having Siddayya there made it awkward, there was no denying it.

"Greetings, sir! I wanted a word with Krishna Rao, if you will give me leave." Before Siddayya could respond with a characteristically sarcastic jibe, Krishna Rao himself interjected.

"Tell me," Krishna Rao said, and although the command sounded brusque, it was probably only an indication of the shortness of time available to him and the need to be succinct.

"Sir, it is about this business of the death in the first aid tent – of Thimmappayya. The repercussions of that are going to be grave for my daughter, sir. You had said, if you recall, that you would see if something could be done."

"Yes, yes, Vaman, of course, this matter must be foremost in your mind. I am sorry, but you see, there are more pressing matters at hand at the moment. But you may rest assured that when the opportunity arises, I will try and prevail upon the king to take a lenient view. He is upset, though, I can tell you that much. It is a bad omen, because of Thimmappayya being the owner of the horse, you know. People are talking."

"Yes, sir, I am also unhappily aware of that," Vaman Bhat could still hear that conversation in the marketplace ringing in his ears. "If only we could establish the facts, then the talk would also die down. For example, there are some people who can attest to the fact that Thimmappayya was dead before he came to the tent."

"Really?" Krishna Rao queried sharply. "Who are these people? If you can give me some names, then when I get a chance I can have someone follow up with them."

"I don't know names and details like that, sir, but I can find out. I can set my son the task of interviewing some people and getting their stories down correctly. It is only what I heard today in the marketplace," Vaman Bhat clarified.

"Vaman, don't let your hopes lead you astray," Krishna Rao said kindly. "All kinds of stories and rumors are going around. None of these stories will stand up in a court of law. They will not tell the same story twice! So although you maybe tempted to clutch at straws, I advise you to take your time and look into the matter with a cool head while putting together your case. Being emotional will not help."

Siddayya burst out as if he could bear this no longer. "Your transparent attempt to shield your daughter will do you no good, Vaman Bhat! I was very close at hand that day, don't you forget it! I walked into that tent a few minutes behind Ranga. It is by no means certain that the man was dead, and you will not convince me or any other sensible person with the word of some riffraff hanging about gossiping in the market place! The facts will need to speak for themselves, and there is an investigation already underway, looking into some circumstances surrounding the death that need not be shared with you. That investigation will reveal whether or not your daughter was to blame, I cannot say any more."

Vaman Bhat turned white with anger. It was rarely that he was roused to anger, but this man seemed to have a natural talent for pushing him to the limit. But he had the deepest respect for Krishna Rao, and did not want to insult him by losing his temper in his presence. Mastering his emotions with an effort, he responded with as much civility as he could muster. "I will keep that in mind, sir. I am sure whatever the investigation is, it will exonerate my daughter completely."

"Besides," Krishna Rao added, sensing the tension in the air and perhaps wanting to lighten the mood, "it is being put about every where that it is the handiwork of the devil! People are alleging that it is the king's bad karma that is being visited upon the land. Mysterious deaths, disappearances – yes, yes, I go around the market place too, you know. I have also heard that loose talk. And in these disturbing times, who knows what the truth is? Let us face it, a man did die in mysterious ciscumstances, and there is a young man who has disappeared without a trace! How many more such incidents will take place, I wonder? And then maybe we will have to admit that there is a supernatural force at work after all!"

Siddayya turned on him with a sneer. "Supernatural forces, indeed! I am vilified by you and many others for being conservative and traditional, but at least I am not superstitious! I leave that to the ignorant rabble. The only problem is that the same rabble can become a powerful force, and that is something people like us should work on reining in, Krishna Rao! Not adding fuel to the fire by actually giving credence to such foolish talk!"

"Calm down, Siddayya," Krishna Rao said quietly. "I am not giving credence to anything. I am merely pointing out that there are rumors abounding in the four corners of this kingdom which are alleging that supernatural elements are ranged against the king. They want to discredit him, bring him down from the heights to which he has risen after the successful military campaign. How have these rumors spread with such rapidity and taken such strong hold of the popular imagination? Obviously, someone is making it their business to spread these stories. I completely agree with you that we must nip it in the bud, the question is how?"

Krishna Rao made to stand and end the interview, but Vaman Bhat stopped him, and said, "One more thing, sir." Caught in the wrangle between Siddayya and Krishna Rao, he had not had a chance yet to communicate the crucial piece of information.

"Yes, what is it?" Krishna Rao said with a hint of impatience. Siddayya had riled him up and Vaman Bhat had already taken up more time than he could spare today, but he liked the man and did not want to dismiss him abruptly.

"Sir, my daughter revealed something about her medical examination of the body which I have not told anyone at all. I wonder if you have a minute, so I can tell you something."

Krishna Rao sat down again, watching Vaman Bhat closely. "Go on."

Siddayya interrupted rudely. "What are you saying now? I asked your daughter to examine the body closely and tell me everything she saw. She did quite a thorough job of it, too," he added grudgingly. "Are you telling me she did not give me all the facts? This is intolerable!"

Vaman Bhat chose his words carefully. "Actually sir, the thing is like this: when she was examining the body, she noticed that the pupils were unnaturally dilated. According to her, such a thing can only happen if some drugs have been administered in large doses. Considering that the drugs could not have been consumed in such large quantities by accident, it is possible that they were given to

Thimmappayya by trickery or by force. In which case, we must conclude that there has been some foul play, sir."

Both Siddayya and Krishna Rao sat silently for a moment. "Your daughter is well trained to have observed all this. And very clever to have concealed this from me. What could she have meant by it?" Siddayya was furious.

There was no point trying to cover up the facts. "She was afraid, sir. She could see that there was something untoward, but she did not want to raise any alarm for fear of making a mistake. She waited until she saw me and voiced her concerns. I was able to confirm that indeed what she had observed was a suspicious circumstance. And I have come as soon as I could to report the matter to Krishna Rao, and as luck would have it, to you too, sir."

Krishna Rao stepped in to defend Vaman Bhat against Siddayya's aggression. "Yes, very good, Vaman. This is indeed an important piece of evidence, and one we must bring to the notice of those who are conducting an investigation into the matter."

Vaman Bhat was relieved that he had not rubbished his story, and that he was actually willing to discuss it. "Sir, she would not have said such a thing unless it was based on facts. She is not one to invent stories. So I believe her, and I believe too that it could have been caused by massive doses of the drug hatapatri, which can stop the heart in a matter of minutes. But who gave it to Thimmappayya, and when and why, I have no idea. Perhaps if we had cut open the stomach, we could have been more certain – but Ranga would not allow it."

"I see," Krishna Rao continued to be thoughtful. "So you give credence to this theory then? And you have told no one else?"

"No sir, you are the only person I would have trusted with a suspicion of so grave a nature. And of course, Lord Siddayya, who is also a loyal member of the king's inner circle. You may know what to do with such information. With your intimate knowledge of palace politics, you may guess at who would want to engineer a bad omen for the king on the day of the Ashvamedha celebration. I thought I should tell you this, sir, for what it is worth."

At this Krishna Rao got up and walked across to Vaman Bhat. Putting his arm around his shoulder, he led him to the door. "You did the right thing, Vaman, and you are also very right not to reveal this to anyone else. Keep it to yourself, and tell your children to keep it to themselves. This is not something we want to speculate wildly about. The matter will be investigated along with all the other circumstances surrounding this death. I know you would rather I did it soon, since it will then put your daughter in the clear, and don't think I don't sympathize with you there! But there is a right time for everything, as you know, particularly in matters relating to the king. So leave it to me, and I will do what is necessary."

With this, Krishna Rao saw him off at the door, and went back in to confer with Siddayya. Vaman Bhat felt light and hopeful. He had left his problem in able hands, and he had a feeling that things would start taking a turn for the better very soon.

Back inside the room, a heated exchange had broken out between Krishna Rao and Siddayya. It was gloves off when it was just the two of them together. Siddayya took the first swing.

"You had to go and promise to save his daughter! We have no idea what the investigation will reveal. How can you make such promises?"

Krishna Rao pooh-poohed his accusation. "I am confident that the girl will be fully exonerated! There is something eerie about this death, there is much more than meets the eye. The man was in the healer's tent for a mere few minutes, how could she possibly be responsible for his death. Use your common sense, man! Your judgement is completely clouded by your prejudice against the girl."

These were fighting words. Siddayya took a menacing step forward, but it would have taken more than that to make Krishna Rao quail. "Watch yourself, Siddayya," was all he said, as he stepped away towards his desk.

"I am going to the king with this information," Siddayya declared.

Krishna Rao had known this was coming, he was prepared for it. "And how will that help," he asked him impatiently. "The king already knows there was some foul play, his agents had already informed him of that. It appears my chambers have been used for some dark purpose, I have no idea how or why. This piece of information is merely a confirmation of what he already knows. I hardly think there is a reason to go rushing to him like an eager schoolboy!"

"There is a reason, and there is no question of being an 'eager schoolboy' as you put it!" said Siddayya, further incensed. "It is called due diligence, something you are constantly being so pious and holier-than-thou about! We know something that could benefit an on-going investigation, surely it is our duty to go and report it. I do not know about you, but I am going to do it, and immediately. You are very clever, I am sure you have some convoluted justification for delaying or even withholding the information, but that is up to you." With this, Siddayya made for the door.

"Oh no, you are not going alone to give the king some biased and garbled account of what you just heard. The girl noticed something odd and confirmed it with her father, who then immediately came and reported it to us. So do not try to cook up any conspiracy theories where you have the girl concealing evidence and trying to obstruct justice. I will come with you, if only to ensure that the story is told correctly."

"To ensure that you can provide the girl with adequate protection, you mean," Siddayya sneered nastily.

And on that acrimonious note, the two old colleagues marched out of the room in search of their king.

# Chapter 12

Two days had passed since that horrendous evening. It was gathering dusk when Devi started getting her paraphernalia together. After the events of the last few days, she was looking forward eagerly to returning to her normal schedule, and doing the things she loved. She desperately needed to get her mind off the immediate anxieties and get back in touch with her sense of purpose. The preparations for her evening outing were so cloak and dagger that an observer might have mistakenly suspected her of setting out for a clandestine rendezvous. It might as well have been. If anyone got wind of what she was about to do, the repercussions would be severe.

Devi quickly started filling up a hamper with supplies. Her experience through the last few months had taught her what the bare minimum ought to be. Hearing a sound at the door, she quickly looked around. It was Udaya, removing his slippers at the door. She smiled warmly at him, and they exchanged their usual greetings. "Alright, now let's get going," Udaya got business-like, perhaps guessing something of what was going through her mind. "Have you got everything? I can start loading the cart. Remember to pack enough holy basil tea and turmeric paste. What with the cold weather coming on, there will be plenty of demand for those."

Devi had already thought of that. They set out into the darkness with just a small flare to light the way. They dare not take a torch, for fear that it would be seen and followed by someone. In that rural area, most people went to bed when it turned dark. But there were always miscreants around who lurked in the dark to see what mischief they could get away with. Neither Devi nor Udaya had a fear of being robbed. They were well known and respected enough to be generally confident that criminal elements would steer clear of them. Besides, they really had nothing worth stealing – a handful of herbs and a pot of medicated oil, not particularly valuable by any reckoning.

They usually went silently through the night. They both already knew the destination. They did a monthly rotation of eight locations, two every week. But today's silence seemed charged to Devi. Was it just her imagination, or was Udaya a little different today? She was so used to him keeping his emotions under tight control, and behaving as if everything was as usual. But somehow today she sensed something different, and tread warily. She had no desire to precipitate something – a declaration perhaps? – for which she had not yet prepared a response.

She need not have worried. Udaya was preoccupied, but his thoughts were very far from being romantic in nature. He had much on his mind, and his thoughts were about Devi, yes. But they were entirely to do with her current predicament, and possibilities for getting through it. Deeply immersed in his thoughts, Udaya barely noticed that they were making rapid progress through the night. Before he knew it, they saw the lights of the village. On a normal night, such a village would be plunged in darkness. But tonight was different. In the past few months, they had gotten used to a small but life-changing alteration to their accustomed schedule. On the first Tuesday of every month, they could now count on a visit from the goddess. That was the way they saw her and thought it only fitting that she had a name to suit her nature. No one had ever done anything for them before. They were the lowest of the low, the untouched, the untouchables. They were not allowed to live within the main village. Their hamlets were set apart, and no one from the main village ever ventured close to them for any reason. If an upper caste even laid eyes on them, they would be cursed roundly for having crossed their path, and the upper caste would flee to the river for an emergency ritual bath to cleanse himself of the impurity of having seen such a creature.

So when this young woman first came with her bagful of promises, she was met with nothing but suspicion. It had to be a plot, only they could not figure out for what. She could be a witch – reports of those were common enough. Let them into your home and they would suck your blood and swallow your soul so that there was no re-birth and no after-life. Just all eternity as a ghost, haunting the cemeteries in the hope of inhabiting an abandoned body.

That first time, they did not open the door to her, although they could hear her as she stumbled in the darkness, trying to get her bearings. Since it had been an early spring night, there was bright moonlight to guide her as she had stumbled from door to door, saying "Please, I am a healer.

156

I want to help you. I have some medicines here with me, if you have a cold or a fever or stomach trouble, you don't have to suffer. I can help."

Why had she picked this village? Because she had heard of it that day. One of her patients at the clinic had presented with a high fever, accompanied by a rash. One look at her and she had told all the other patients to stand back, and quickly had the woman taken into the examining room. She knew that such fevers quickly spread from person to person just by a look or a touch. She asked Raji to hurry out and get a bowl of water and then got some clean cloths and started sponging the woman to bring down the fever. The sponging slowly began to have the desired effect, and the woman's skin was now decidedly cooler to the touch. As the fever slowly abated, the woman's eyes flickered open, and she looked up at the older woman who had come with her, evidently her mother.

"Akka!" the mother cried out. "Look, she has opened her eyes!" Devi reassured her that this was quite expected, and she hoped to give her some medicines that would cure her daughter completely. The mother was overcome. "Thank god, akka. It is all due to his blessings and your good karma that my daughter will be well. When I saw her this morning I thought this is the end – three small children she has at home, you know. I will always look after them, of course, no matter what happens, but a mother is a mother."

There was no arguing with that.

"But when did this start? When did she begin the fever?" Devi had tried to get some details so that she could figure out the right course of treatment.

"Yesterday afternoon!" the mother spat out. "That she-devil Kalli came from her village to tell us that her husband would not come today to collect the night soil because he had a high fever and a rash. I believe everyone in her benighted village has this fever. Why couldn't she have told the servants at the backdoor and gone? No, the filthy whore has to come into the house, polluting the whole place. We should have been at home just now, purifying the house with fresh cow dung, but there was no time. My daughter fell sick as soon as she laid eyes on her, I tell you."

"What village is that?" Devi asked.

"Who cares?" was the mother's reply, but at Devi's insistence she gave her the name – Kanakanpura. "But not the main village, mind," she clarified. "They live with the other sinners outside the village, in their own dirty quarters."

Devi had learned what she wanted to know. Many people in Kalli's village had this same fever right now. They would receive no treatment, Devi knew that. No healer ever ventured into such ghettoes. She decided it was time to put her plan into action. For quite a while now, she had wanted to provide services to these untouchables, the forgotten of humanity. After all, wasn't she supposed to heal all human beings? So she had made up her mind. She would put her idea into action that very night! She would tell Nagi where she was going, but she would not allow her to come. This was her turn to be firm. Only she would expose herself to the dangers of this enterprise, and the social ostracism that was bound to follow if it were ever found out.

Nagi had been vociferous in her protests, even threatening to go at once to tell Vaman Bhat what his precious daughter was planning, but Devi held firm. She called Nagi's bluff. Nagi had never intended to sneak on her to her father after all. Her loyalty to Devi was absolute, and her simple credo was: what Devi wants Devi must have. With her lips tightly pursed and registering disapproval with every fiber of her being, she put together the necessary supplies from the store, and packed them away in the little bag that Devi was going to take with her.

And so Devi had set off on her first night-time adventure, only to find that the people she so desperately wanted to serve wanted none of her. This was unexpected. She did not know what she had anticipated, but she had vaguely pictured being welcomed into sick homes with gratitude. Instead she was met with suspicion and a firmly shut door. After much trial and error, she had finally fetched up outside a hut with a baby crying inside. She knocked. "Let me in, I can help you," she had said with as much authority as she could muster. The baby continued to cry, but the cry was getting weaker, as if the child was giving up.

"Open up," she had said again, urgently. "Open up, I tell you. I can help you. I am a healer. The child will die otherwise."

After an interminable pause, the door opened a crack. A scared little face looked up at her. It was a child, maybe five years old. The baby continued to cry somewhere inside the one-roomed hovel. "Is that your brother?' Devi asked the little face. It was hard to tell in the dark whether the child was a boy or a girl. The child stared for a little longer, then suddenly opened the door and stepped aside so Devi could come in. "It is my brother, he has been crying for two days and he is so hot, like he is catching fire."

Devi quickly went in and took the baby from the mother, who was sitting listlessly on the floor, exhausted with nursing a sick child for two days. He was burning up.

"Get me some water," she said to the older child. Then she unwrapped the baby from all the filthy rags the mother had wound around him. She gasped when she saw the baby naked. He was covered with the rash, as expected, but it was his thinness that struck her so forcefully. It was a wonder he had withstood the fever for two days, being so undernourished and weak. The older child had returned with the water. Not bothering to ask for a clean cloth – her quick glance around told her that such a thing was not available on the premises – she took one of the rags lying on the floor, soaked it in the water and started sponging the child down. The mother watched, too tired to care. After a while, the crying stopped and the child was relatively cooler to the touch. She handed the baby to the mother. "Feed him," she said. "He needs some energy to fight the disease."

"He hasn't drunk any milk for two days," the mother finally spoke. "He has just been crying. I thought he would die tonight."

"Feed him now," Devi said again, urgently. The mother put the child to her breast, and he sucked hungrily, while the mother watched in some wonder. "He didn't drink for two days," she said again, looking at Devi, her eyes glistening with tears. Devi patted her arm, then gave her the medicine she had already prepared and brought with her, knowing that she would encounter this fever in the village. She instructed the woman on when to give the medicine and to continue the sponging with cold water. "Have you understood what I told you?" she asked the woman anxiously, but was reassured when she nodded eagerly and said "yes akka, don't worry. I understood, I will do as you told me."

Devi got up and shook out her saree, making ready to leave. That was when she noticed the gathering at the door. She had been so absorbed with the baby that she had not realized that she had an audience. Thirty or forty people were gathered outside and peering through the doorway, watching what she was doing in the meager light of her flare. As she came out, the crowd parted to let her through. But she did not get far. A voice said, "Akka, can you come to my house? My husband also has the same sickness." Soon the voice was joined by others. Devi had never looked back since then. Word had spread from the village to others around the area, so that she was eagerly welcomed wherever she went from that day on.

Today she had Udaya at her side. He had winkled her secret out of her after Nagi had dropped broad hints to him of his sister's doings. She too felt it was reasonable to have someone in the family know about her activities. If something untoward were to happen, this whole chapter of her life should not come as a rude shock to everyone. He had been quite angry with her at first, but only because she had taken all these risks by herself. His religion did not recognize these divisions of caste, anyway, and he was as exercised by the injustice of human beings living in such conditions as she was herself. He immediately offered himself as her assistant, and she did not hesitate to accept. These trips were admittedly lonely and scary, and having him for company would not only make it more fun but also literally lighten her load. He took over the task of hauling the medicines, and he had the stamina to push the cart long distances.

Their arrival now was greeted with much shouting out of greetings and clapping of hands. Devi and Udaya laughed at the enthusiasm with which they were welcomed. The headman of the village himself came up with folded hands and thanked them for being there. "By god's grace, we have not had people dying due to any disease, akka. But we have the usual problems - some fever, some cough and cold, everybody has some small problem or the other."

"Don't worry, sir, we will deal with them as we have been doing before. That is why we are here."

These formalities over, Devi and Udaya sat down by the lighted lamps, and started their work. One by one, the villagers came to the mat to be examined. As Devi had suspected, most of the conditions today were related to the season, and they had carried sufficient quantities of the necessary medicines to go around. They had almost gone through the entire line of patients when there was a sudden eruption of sound, like a massive raid, rapidly bursting upon the orderly scene of the makeshift clinic.

Both Devi and Udaya leapt back from their mats, unable to fathom the source of the confusion or its nature. What seemed like hundreds of people were pouring in from nowhere, and the villagers raised the alarm to fend off the intruders. Several of the younger men went running back to their huts to fetch their spears and other weaponry. It looked as if an all-out war was about to break out.

And then there was a remarkable turn of events. A loud and authoritative voice spoke out. "Wait! Wait, you villagers of Kanakanpura. Put away your arms! We are not here with any evil intent. We are here to rid ourselves of evil! Where is the healer? Take us to the healer!"

Devi congealed in her place. The healer? That was her. What did they want with her?

As she stood there, a prey to the worst fears, a figure threaded its way through the crowd. Devi had never seen such a creature before. It was hard to tell whether it was man or woman. The face was a painted mask. The torso was covered only with bead necklaces bearing all sorts of colorful talismans. Only the loincloth below seemed to indicate that the figure was masculine. He was dragging behind him a pathetic apology for a human being, grasping her cruelly by the hair. She was wearing not a stitch, and was screaming and whimpering alternately. She was unbelievably filthy, her hair matted with dirt, her body covered in all kinds of muck. There was blood oozing from fresh wounds, either because she had been beaten or due to the rough manner in which she had been dragged here.

This unlikely pair stopped in the small clearing in front of Devi and Udaya. For a long moment nobody said a word, and then the figure burst out with: "This woman is possessed by the devil! You must do something! Look at her! She is covered in filth and she is just as filthy on the inside! She spreads evil wherever she goes. Either you cure her or we kill her! If it is the devil inside her, then get it out! Or we burn her and she can take the devil with her!"

Devi's blood ran cold. She glanced at Udaya, who looked like he was carved out of stone. What did one do in such a situation? She was at a complete loss. Suddenly Udaya came to life and said, "We try to cure the body of its ills. Let us look at her. Maybe she is sick. If so, we can try and help her."

The figure spat in the dust. "She is not ill in the body. Her body is fine. It is her soul that is tainted. She has sold it to the devil. Oh, my good sir, if you could see her when she is possessed by the spirit, you would not be able to sleep for many nights. She shrieks like a banshee, she is like a wild animal. She has bitten and maimed so many of the good people in our village. The children are the most scared. She has told them she will eat them if she catches them alone anywhere. She will, I believe it. She is capable of anything when she is possessed by the devil."

"What do we do, Udaya?" Devi muttered to her brother under her breath.

"I do not know! We must do something, though…. or else they will burn her right here, with us watching! We cannot stand by and let that happen. Let us stall for time, and we can think of something in the meanwhile."

Devi agreed with the general principle of stalling, although she was not sure the delay would yield any results. "Tell us, sir, who are you?" she asked, hoping to get a clearer picture.

"I am the greatest shaman that you are ever likely to see, little lady! I am the great shaman Shambhu Maharaj. I have lived long in the great mountains many leagues north of here, and there I have meditated for many years so as to gain superhuman powers. I can tell your fortune, I can predict the future. I can even change your future! I can control the earth and the sky and the wind and the rain. On a good day I can control the heavens themselves. I speak regularly to all the great gods – Shiva, Vishnu, even Brahma!"

So the creature was a man. Devi interrupted him here, since it was obvious that he could go on in this vein for a while. "Shambhu Maharaj, we are honored to have you here with us today. Now could you please tell us something more about this poor girl?"

The poor girl was at the moment snarling at some of the village children who had ventured near to look more closely at her, at which they screamed and ran away as fast as they could. They would have nightmares about this for weeks to come.

"What is there to tell, sister? Such a sad story. Look at her, like an animal! It is no wonder people are afraid of her and call her a she-devil. She was found wandering in the forest many years ago, when she was a young child. Who knows? Her parents must have left her there. Or maybe she has no human parents. Maybe she was born through the evil coupling of the devil with some forest animal. Anything is possible! But the villagers here are kind and simple people. They brought her to the village and they have all been looking after her ever since. And look at the gratitude she shows! Attacking them viciously, biting them, eating their animals. Yes, she tears up the chickens and goats with her bare hands and eats them raw, you have to see it to believe it! And now she is threatening to eat the children too. It is too much! Something has to be done!"

Devi and Udaya exchanged glances. Then Udaya turned to address the crowd. "My sister and I need to discuss this case for some moments. Please give us time, we will be back shortly. I would like you all to be calm, and do not aggravate the situation. It is very possible that you all are right and that she is possessed by the devil. We have no choice but to try and exorcise her. Let us take the girl inside one of the huts, so that she can be prepared for the exorcism. Remember!

Exorcism is a serious procedure, there must be no children present, it is not a fit thing for them to witness. I suggest all the women and children go back to your homes and lock the doors firmly, so that any evil spirits released by the exorcism do not come and lodge in your homes or in your bodies. Get away now! And leave us in peace!"

This speech effectively cleared most of the crowd. Nobody wanted to be present when evil spirits were released, and the women and children hastened away, many accompanied by the men of the house as well. Only Shambhu Maharaj remained, and along with him, some of the more curious and bold youths who did not want it to be put about the next day that they had chickened out of watching an exorcism.

After the crowd had thinned, Udaya and Devi looked around for the village headman. He had retreated into the background. After all, this was not his problem, and he wanted no part of it. Unfortunately, he would have to be involved, since all the resources at hand were at his disposal. "Sir, is there some place safe where we can keep the girl for a little while?" Udaya asked him quietly. The headman was reluctant to endanger the sanctity of any dwelling in his village with evil spirits, but finally they persuaded him to let them use of a small empty room a few hundred yards away from the clearing.

The girl seemed to have quieted down after the crowd dispersed, and went quite docilely along with Devi into the room. "Just sit here quietly for a while, alright? We need to plan what to do next." The girl did not give any indication that she had understood what had been said to her. She sat down on her haunches in a corner and started to hum tunelessly to herself.

Devi turned to Udaya. "What next?" she asked him nervously.

"I am thinking….what if we sedate her and then cart her away from here? If we leave her here, these people will lynch her, or worse, they will torture her. We cannot risk that. I suggest we give her a powerful draft of opium that will knock her out. We have the handcart. Hopefully it will take her weight, and it is not that much of a distance. You better think of some mumbo-jumbo to chant that will fool that old fraud Shambhu. Make it last fifteen or twenty minutes. It will take that long for the opium to take effect."

"Do you think they will let us take her away?" Devi was doubtful.

"Why not?" Udaya asked. "It is not as if there is any love for her among these people. They kept her this long for their own amusement and because they could not give her away. If we tell them that we will take her far away and rid them of the devil, I am sure they will not object."

They put their plan into action. Taking a large opium ball out of the medicine bag, Udaya mixed it into a thick paste with some honey. Approaching the girl would be tricky, given how jumpy she seemed to be. But all the excitement of the evening seemed to have tired her out, because she allowed Devi to come up to her without any protest. When Devi held out the betel leaf with the opium paste on it, she sat up and took it from her curiously and then quickly put it into her mouth, leaf and all. She swallowed the mixture and then sank back onto her haunches again.

"Now, we must get going, quick!" Udaya commanded. "She needs to be awake when the procedure starts. If she falls asleep halfway through, that will look convincing, as if the departure of the devil has exhausted her and put her into a trance."

Both Devi and Udaya emerged from the room and declared themselves to be ready to start the exorcism. What was left of the crowd gathered again in the clearing. Devi asked for a small fire to be lit, and several of the young men quickly gathered together twigs and dry leaves that were lying around and got a fire started. Meanwhile, Devi took Udaya's shawl and wrapped the girl in it. The large amount of opium on an empty stomach had made her very passive, submitting without protest to Devi's handling of her. Devi almost had to hold her nose when she did it, the poor girl smelled so foul.

Working quickly, since the girl was almost asleep, they went back to the clearing and placed the girl next to the fire. Devi searched wildly through her memory for any chant that would remotely suit her purpose and drew a blank. Surely there must be something that was not a prayer that everyone was likely to know, that sounded suitably esoteric and ominous! Suddenly she had a brain wave, and she started a slow sonorous chant:

"Om Agnidevatheya Namah!" She first invoked the fire god. She followed this with the impromptu chant.

| Shudha Abhrak Bhasma | Jayfal churna | Shatavari Churna |
| Sudha parad | Vidharabij Churna | Nagbala Churna |
| Shudh gandhak | Shudha Dhaturbij | Atibala Churna |
| Karpur Churna | Churna | Gokshurbeej churna |

| | | |
|---|---|---|
| Javitri | Vidhari Kand Churna | Hijjal bij churna |
| Tambul patra swaras | Galo Ghan | Tribhuvan kirti rasa |
| Suvarna vasant malati | Svarna Makshik Bhasma | Guduchi ghansar |
| Talispatra | Vasaka Ghan | Godanti hartal |
| Ashwagandha | Maha sudarshan churna | bhasma |
| Dugdha Pashan Bhed | ghansar | |

With each phrase, she threw some dhoop or incense powder from her bag into the fire. This generated an impressive amount of smoke. Looking down she realized the girl was now sound asleep. Time to end this charade!

"Om Shree Sarvebhyo Devebhyo Swaha!" She shouted out suddenly.

The she pointed dramatically at the girl.

"Look! The girl has lost her senses! The devil has left her! Oh god be praised, the exorcism has been successful! Quick, quick, let us take her away from this place!"

Udaya had the cart handy, and they prepared to bundle the girl into it. The headman and villagers stood by mutely and watched. After all, it was no skin off their nose. They had never laid eyes on the girl before, and did not care what became of her. But Shambhu Maharaj had an intimate interest in the girl's fate and was not about to let her go so lightly.

"Wait, sister, wait! Where may you be taking the girl? We have looked after her for so many years, we cannot simply let her go."

It was all Devi could do not to give the man a piece of her mind. Their years of looking after her were what had reduced the poor girl to this wretched state, and she wanted to tell him exactly what he thought of him and his precious villagers. But she had to bite her tongue. It would not profit her and certainly not profit the girl to have a heated exchange with Shambhu Maharaj at this point.

"Maharaj, we are taking her away somewhere safe, as a precaution. We do not know what her condition will be when she comes out of this trance. We hope that we have chased away the devil, but what if we have been unsuccessful? Then it will be a terrible thing to see her when she wakes. The devil will have grown and will be enraged by what we tried to do to him through our exorcism. We do not want to endanger your dear simple villagers by unleashing such a monster on them if such is the case. Surely you too want the safety of your people to be ensured?"

Surrounded by his people, Shambhu Maharaj saw the wisdom of agreeing with this logic. "Yes, sister, you are right," he said reluctantly. He sensed that there was something fishy going on here, but he could not put his finger on it. A past master himself at pulling fast ones, he recognized sleight of hand when he saw it. But even he could see that there was no immediate advantage in insisting on the girl being left behind. Besides, what did he want her for? If he got rid of her, as well as the devil that possessed her, so much the better. He could put an advantageous spin on it the next day when the event was rehashed back in his village.

So he stepped aside graciously, and seeing their only impediment out of the way, Devi and Udaya quickly trundled their cart onto the road back home. They were almost halfway back when Udaya suddenly asked her, "What was that stuff that you chanted?"

Devi blanked out for a moment. Then, remembering, she said, "Oh that! Just the Sanskrit names of various ayurvedic herbs. I was counting on no one knowing them."

After a moment, Udaya started to laugh. Hearing him, she began to laugh too. And that is how Nagi received them at the door, where she waited anxiously. "What on earth are you two laughing about?" she inquired crossly. "I've been worried half out of my mind over you!"

# Chapter 13

The next morning, Devi sat quietly contemplating her garden. At times like this, it was an activity that offered her immense solace. Thinking back on the events of the last few days, she couldn't help feeling that somehow the fates had been conspiring against her.

Devi sighed….it was all too complicated and unfair. It was all because of her own greed. If she had only turned down that offer of being heroine for the day, she would have been fine. Life would have proceeded uneventfully along its previous trajectory, and that had not been so bad, after all! She had been doing her work and finding fulfillment within her small clinic and the neighboring communities she was serving. The thought of expanding and being renowned across the kingdom had never even occurred to her as a possibility. It was that devilish suggestion of Narayanachar and Siddayya that had lead to all this…she felt a surge of pure anger against them both, particularly against Siddayya, who had probably wanted her to fail from the start. And how she had failed! Spectacularly! She had outdone all his expectations, she thought bitterly. To be branded as incompetent, probably criminally negligent – it was a heavy cross to bear.

Her thoughts moved on to the events of last night. Now there was another tangle! She had not really given much thought to what should be done with the girl. The last thing she needed was some irate parent showing up at the clinic, accusing her of kidnapping! It did not seem likely, from the story Shambhu Maharaj had narrated last night, but it was within the realm of possibility. There were people who would jump at the chance of benefiting from blackmail, and right now she was vulnerable enough already without that sword hanging over her head.

Shaking her head to clear away all the negative thoughts, she turned back to her garden. She had taken great care when planning the garden, keeping in mind both the aesthetic and the utilitarian roles that it would play. She had chosen to plant a formal garden, laid in a series of beds, forming a wide area of concentric squares. Although the area was not vast – perhaps an acre and a half – it was sufficient for her purposes. Between each bed she had had a stone path laid, both to enhance the geometric order of the garden and for ease of access to all the plants. In the center of the concentric squares she had placed a comfortable bench, which was where she now sat and contemplated her handiwork. The central portion of the garden was devoted to the basic medicinal herbs that she commonly used at the clinic. As she looked around today, her eyes lit upon a soothing patch halfway to the periphery – lavender. Today she needed the balm the lavender could give her, both the color and the smell soothing to her jangling nerves.

Her peaceful reverie was soon interrupted, as she knew it would be. Nagi came marching up to her, breathing fire and brimstone. Since this was not an unusual phenomenon, Devi was not overly perturbed. She looked up at her expectantly, waiting for the outburst to begin. Sure enough, Nagi started with a snort, "A fine specimen you brought with you last night! You couldn't find anyone filthier or with a meaner temper, is it? She almost bit Raji just now – the bite would probably have killed her, so foul are that girl's teeth and breath."

"Oh, I'm sorry to hear it," Devi said soothingly, for she was genuinely concerned about the health and well-being of her staff. It was all very well to set out to do a good deed, but the recipient of her pity appeared to be least grateful or appreciative of the favor! "How is Raji? Should I come and look at her wound?"

"By the grace of god, Raji has survived," Nagi admitted grudgingly. "No thanks to that little she-devil you have brought in! What ails that girl anyway? She seems quite fit, and she's as strong as a horse, I can tell you that! It took all my strength to hold her down when she was rampaging about attacking all and sundry. I almost called out to the gardener boys to come and help, can you imagine that?"

Devi could not, in fact, imagine that. The idea that Nagi needed help in physically quelling anyone boggled the mind. She was the one who was generally acknowledged to be as strong as a horse!

"Anyway, finally I pushed her into the small room in your clinic and locked her in," Nagi continued. "But we cannot leave her there forever! She has to be cleaned up, for one thing. Immediately! She is absolutely filthy, smeared all over with muck and goodness knows what else. She smells to high heaven. She has not eaten anything so far either. But that may have been Jaya's fault," Nagi ended with a mumble.

"Jaya's fault? How come?" Devi wondered what was making Nagi so uncharacteristically shamefaced.

"Well, I was in the kitchen putting away the vessels, and asked Jaya to go give the creature the food that I had set out on the plate. That was a mistake…I should have gone with her, I realize that now. Anyway, the minute Jaya caught sight of the girl, she let out a shriek that could have been heard a mile away and dropped the plate and ran for her life. Didn't you hear the commotion about an hour ago? Things went from bad to worse. When I saw the state Jaya was in, I tried to give the girl a fresh plate of food myself, but she would have none of it. The creature's feelings were hurt, I think! But what does she expect? Look at her condition! Does she really expect people to embrace her with open arms? She should hardly be surprised if people are frightened or repelled by her appearance."

Devi was disturbed by this account of recent events. She had been loitering in her garden when she ought to have been taking responsibility for her new charge and ensuring her comfort. "But Nagi, Udaya and I told you about the circumstances in which we found her. She is not an ordinary girl. Poor thing, she has been through experiences that no human being ought to endure. I think we all agreed last night that she needed special treatment, and a great deal of sympathy and understanding. I'm sorry I was not there this morning to conduct the proper introductions, but I did hope that everyone would behave in a sensitive manner."

"We would have behaved in a more sensitive manner if the girl was not a wild cat," Nagi was stung by the implied criticism. "She refuses to listen to reason or to cooperate with any of the suggestions I make. I mean, is it a crime to ask her to have a bath? And, mind you, I was fully prepared to take her to the pond myself, and to scrub her down if necessary. But her response was to try to take a chunk out of Raji! Don't expect me to be sympathetic with that kind of behavior! I don't tolerate nonsense from anybody, no matter how cruelly they have been treated in the past!"

Devi could see that this would not be an easy battle to win. Her break was over, she needed to return with a bang to reality. She got up and walked around to where Nagi stood, stiff with indignation and hurt pride. Putting an arm around her shoulder, she gave her a quick hug and said, "Don't worry Nagi. You will not be troubled by the girl much longer. I will take care of her myself. It's not fair of me to ask this of you."

At this, Nagi bridled again. "Don't imagine that I don't want to do this! You don't have to spare me any tasks. It is my job to spare you from tasks. I have tried my best to do it for all these years, and I intend to do it for many more. I saw you sitting there, thinking, and I didn't want to disturb you, but finally I had no choice. We have to decide what to do with the girl, the sooner the better!"

Devi walked towards the house with a sigh. Clearly, Nagi was determined to take offense, no matter what she said. The house was in a quiet uproar. None of the day's work had been done. Even the gardener's boys had abandoned their posts and all were in a huddle in the kitchen. They quickly broke up when they saw her enter, eyeing her guiltily and waiting for a dressing down for having neglected their chores. But Devi was not in the mood for it – she knew that the situation was too novel for the household to be functioning normally.

Devi addressed the group calmly. "I know this situation has come as a shock to all of you. You must realize that my brother and I had no choice but to rescue this poor girl. She was being treated like an animal, and has been the victim of unspeakable cruelty. We should all have some sympathy for her. Any questions? Feel free to ask me whatever you like."

The group regarded her wide-eyed, trying to take in what she was saying. They had plenty of questions, but did not want to inadvertently offend Devi by asking the wrong one. So she was greeted with silence, and was about to turn away towards the clinic, when Jaya ventured shyly, "What is her name?"

Devi stopped short. "You know, Jaya, that is a very good question! I don't know. And you're absolutely right, we cannot go on referring to her as "the creature" or "the girl" – that's very de-humanizing! Since I don't have a name for her, why don't we come up with one? Any suggestions?'

This was greeted with further silence, but it was a thoughtful silence. After a few minutes, Raji said, "How about Shani? She looks like a she-devil, just like a shani."

Devi had to hide a smile as she said, "Well, Raji, I can understand why you would want to call her that, after she almost bit your finger off. But maybe Shani is not a kind name, no? Let's think of something a bit more complimentary."

"But we don't know anything nice about her!" one of the gardener's boys burst out.

"True," Devi agreed. "So what do we know about her?"

"Well," Jaya said, "the only thing we know for sure about her is that she is a girl. How about we call her Kumari?"

And so it was that the girl came to be known as Kumari.

Devi unlocked Kumari's room. The first thing that hit her was the foul odor. The girl desperately needed a bath! Devi wondered how they would ever get around to giving her one. Unless….. the simplest thing would be to repeat the trick of yesterday, and feed her some opium. It would calm her down and sufficiently sap her will to resist so that they could quickly clean her up. But how to give her the opium? Yesterday Udaya had been there, and between the two of them they had been able to administer it to her successfully.

As if in answer to her prayers, Udaya was at her side again.

"I hear you have had some trouble with our new ward?" he asked her in a low voice.

Devi turned with a start. "Oh Udaya! Thank goodness you're here!" she exclaimed, also in a whisper. "Yes, lots of trouble. We may have to calm her with the opium again, at least until she learns to trust us a little and stops resisting us so violently."

There was a stirring in the room, which was in semi-darkness. As her eyes adjusted to the dark, Devi saw Kumari crouching in a corner of the room, watching. "Kumari, don't worry, it's just me. My name is Devi. Do you remember me? Look, this is my brother Udaya. All of us have decided to call you Kumari. Does that suit you? If you want us to call you by some other name, you can tell us." There was no response to this. Devi thrust Udaya a bit further into the room. If Kumari was going to get violent again, Udaya was better equipped to handle it!

Still no response. In the stillness of the room, they could hear her harsh breathing, but she made no movement. Devi stepped slowly into the room, careful not to make any abrupt movements that might alarm Kumari. "Come here, Kumari," she urged her gently. "Come, eat something. See! I have something nice here for you to eat."

Kumari did not move. Devi glanced at Udaya. "What do we do?" she asked him, anxiously. "She hasn't eaten anything. I don't think she has drunk anything either. She could get really sick if she persists like this. We have to persuade her to eat something and then to get her into clean fresh clothes!"

"Not much hope of that right now," Udaya said grimly. He stepped further into the room, and then walked towards the crouching figure. "Come, Kumari, you must listen to us. We are your friends. Come and eat something, and you will feel much better." He spoke firmly and clearly, his tone brooking no refusal. He walked right up to Kumari, standing over her, then reaching down to take her arm.

That was his mistake. At the first inkling that he was going to touch her, Kumari reacted in a flash. She flew up and would have scratched Udaya's face with her talon-like nails if Udaya had not jumped back instinctively and grabbed her hands in a tight hold. Devi started forward, wanting to grab Kumari and pull her back, but Udaya stopped her with a shake of his head. "Don't worry, Devi, I can handle this. Kumari, look, I am not going to do anything to you. See, I am going to let go of your hands. I will not hurt you. I was only going to help you to stand up, that's all. You don't have to fear me or Devi. We are your friends. We want to help you to get better. We want you to be with us, we will never send you back to Shambhu Maharaj and all those other people. If you like this house, you can live here. It is your choice. You can do whatever you want."

Udaya kept talking to her in a low firm voice, which seemed to have some effect on the girl. Slowly, some of the tension left her body, and Udaya gradually released her hands, watching her closely for any fresh attacks. But the fight seemed to have gone out of Kumari, and she slowly sank back onto her haunches and crept back to her corner. Devi's heart went out to the girl. She looked so young and lost and alone. Just the thought of all that she had gone through in her young life made Devi want to weep. She sat down next to her, and unmindful of her smell and filth, she took her in her arms and held her close. Encouragingly, Kumari did not resist, although she did not respond either. Udaya brought the plate of food close, and bit by bit, Devi fed the girl about half of the food that Nagi had set out for her. "Some water," Devi requested Udaya, and he quickly stepped out and came back with a brass jug full of water. Kumari drank it down thirstily, spilling some down her face and neck in the process.

After Kumari had settled down a bit, she took her arm and said, "Come, let us go down to the pool. It is clean there and refreshing. You can have a nice swim - the water is warm and comfortable. You will enjoy that, won't you? I will swim with you. Let's see which of us is the better swimmer!" Surprisingly, Devi found that her tactic seemed to be working. Kumari took her hand and allowed herself to be led out of the room quite docilely. As they walked out towards the pool, they went past the other members of the household, all watching the proceedings with great curiosity.

Nagi followed Devi and Kumari down the stone stairway to the pool. Kumari continued to be extremely quiescent, and did not protest when Nagi started stripping away the pathetic scraps of her clothing, what there was of it. It was impossible to see even a patch of skin under all the dirt. Nagi had kept all her tools ready to give the girl a thorough cleaning. There was a bowl full of shikakai, a natural soap that Nagi planned to use to scrub her body and wash her hair, and some coconut husk with which to scrub away the more stubborn dirt.

"Do not let her get into the pool just now!" she ordered Devi sharply. "Better get the worst dirt off her first. Otherwise we will not be able to use the pool for weeks!"

Nagi had kept a large brass vessel full of water ready to complete the first stage of the cleaning operation. Devi lead Kumari to a stone ledge and helped her to sit down on it, while Nagi dipped a smaller vessel into the water and started pouring it over her. Although she started violently and shied away from the water at first, she made no move to actually get up and run away. As long as Devi stood by her and held her hand, she seemed to be resigned to her fate. Taking advantage of this unusual submissiveness, Nagi set about her task with gusto. She scrubbed and she rubbed and she splashed water about to her heart's content, and after a while, she turned to Devi in a voice filled with awe and said, "Akka! Look!"

Looking down, Devi saw what it was that had surprised Nagi. She had made quite impressive progress with her cleaning, and now that she had gotten rid of most of the dirt, and Kumari's skin was showing through, they were faced with an amazing revelation. The girl's skin was like a patchwork quilt! Some of the patches were the palest pink, while other patches were from very light to a slightly darker brown. It was most surprising! Devi in all her experience had never encountered such a thing.

"Is it the effect of the light in here?" Nagi asked doubtfully.

Devi shook her head. She knew it had nothing to do with the dappled light down near the pool. It was something else, and she would have to consult Vaman Bhat to find out more about it. She ran her fingers over the skin – it was perfectly smooth and soft. It was only the coloring that was unusual. She asked Nagi to finish up, but here again Nagi had an objection.

"I cannot wash her hair," she declared. "It is completely matted, and full of lice. It will have to come off."

Devi readily agreed. It did make sense, given the condition of Kumari's hair, to shave her head and make a clean start. But would she allow it, was the question. The strangely lethargic state she was currently in could wear off any minute and then they would have a real battle on their hands all over again.

"Well, if we must, we must. But make it quick! Run upstairs and get the razor, and let's finish it before she realizes what is going on."

Nagi needed no further prompting. She went swiftly up the stairs, and ran all the way to the house for the razor. Devi had meanwhile gathered all of Kumari's hair into a bundle at the nape of the neck, and kept the hairline clear so that Nagi could begin shaving easily. Briskly stropping the razor on a nearby stone, Nagi set to work and soon the filthy strands of matted hair fell away to reveal a clean shiny scalp. The scalp was pink all over, not mottled like the skin on her body. While she was at it, Nagi used the razor to trim the nails on her hands and feet as well. Then rinsing her from head to foot again, both the women dried Kumari off and wrapped her in a brand new pink saree that Devi had just taken out of her cupboard.

What with the sense of urgency with which they had been working all this while, neither of them had actually stopped to take a look at Kumari. Now, as she stood, still heavy eyed and quiet, they looked at her for the first time. She was quite pretty! If it had not been for the strange discoloration of the skin – which Devi was hoping would be a curable condition – she might have been very pretty. Her features were sharp, and her eyes a deep grey. It was those grey eyes that had increased her resemblance to a cat, and possibly provided fodder for the children's teasing. When her hair grew back, it would be thick and black, and frame her small rounded face quite nicely.

"Well!" Nagi gave voice to the sense of satisfaction both felt at the transformation. "She cleaned up nicely, didn't she? At least she is presentable now." She leaned down and gave Kumari a shake. "Aren't you feeling a lot better?" she demanded of her, but got no reply. "You should see yourself now," she continued to address the girl, who seemed least interested in her appearance. Not to be discouraged by this, Nagi pulled her down to the water's edge. "Here! Look at yourself!" She thrust Kumari's face a little forward so that it was reflected in the water. This seemed to have some impact. Kumari did not pull herself away and step back, as Devi had expected, but stood for a long moment looking at herself. She raised her hand and passed it over her face, as if to confirm that it was indeed her own reflection in the water. She looked once more, with interest. Then she looked up, and was it just wishful thinking, or was there the shadow of an impish smile in her eyes when she looked at Devi? It was the first reaction of any sort that they had had from her since she arrived here that was not violent or aggressive, and Devi sent up a silent prayer at having crossed this first hurdle relatively easily. Maybe the rest of the road to Kumari's rehabilitation would not be as tough as she had anticipated.

"Alright, enough of admiring yourself!" Nagi picked up her cleaning paraphernalia and made for the stone steps. Kumari followed hesitantly, and Devi put an encouraging hand under her elbow. The girl looked exhausted and in need of some rest. They made their way slowly up the stairs and there encountered the impatient Udaya, who was by now quite beside himself with curiosity. "Where is she?" he demanded of Nagi.

"Goodness, so jumpy! She is right behind me. If you step aside and let me pass, you will be able to see her sooner!"

Udaya hurriedly allowed her to go by, and watched while a strange figure emerged from the depths. His mouth fell open as he saw who it was and how different she looked now. Devi came up from behind her, and looked at her brother expectantly. "What do you think?" she asked, a bit breathless with the excitement of it all.

"Unbelievable," Udaya said simply. "It is incredible. I would not have thought it possible. Nagi and you have pulled off a miracle."

Devi smiled. "Yes, but she has a strange skin condition, Udaya. Maybe you have seen this before, or perhaps we will have to refer her to father, Look!" Devi pushed the saree away from Kumari's arm to show Udaya the strange patches on her skin. Udaya stepped closer and reached out his arm to touch the discolored area. "I don't think I have ever…" he was beginning to say, when it happened again!

Suddenly, the quiet and lethargic Kumari sprang back to life and went straight for his throat!

Udaya stumbled backward and fell heavily, but luckily managed to evade her curling fingers. Devi was shocked! Just when she had been congratulating herself on having crossed the first hurdle, it was a rude awakening to realize that they had done nothing of the sort. She grabbed Kumari in a firm hold, although she knew she was no match if Kumari decided to really get violent. "Had you given her some sedative earlier?" she breathlessly asked Udaya, who was slowly pulling himself up off the ground. "Yes," he said, with a groan. "A little something in the water I gave her."

"Well, looks like it is wearing off," Devi said grimly, pulling her ward back towards the house. Kumari followed, seemingly quiet again, although watching Udaya like a hawk all the time. Devi caught her eye as she looked back again towards the house. Again, she saw that strange look in her eye. Had she imagined it, or was that shadow of an impish smile back in those mysterious cats' eyes.

# Chapter 14

It was with a relatively light heart that Vaman Bhat walked to Devi's clinic a few days later. He had put all the facts before Krishna Rao as soon as he could, and now that weight was lifted from his shoulders. It was up to the proper authorities to take up the case if they wished and deal with it as appropriate. As an upstanding citizen he had done his job, and as a father he had tried to protect his daughter in the best way he knew how. Now he felt he was justified in pursuing his simple pleasures! It had been several days since news of the addition to Devi's household had reached him, and he felt it was time to make her acquaintance.

"How is your protégé this morning?" Vaman Bhat asked as he walked into the clinic.

"Not too bad, father. I want you to meet her right away. I think she will be of great interest to you."

"Why so?" Vaman Bhat cocked an eyebrow. This sounded intriguing!

"You will see for yourself," Devi said, as she led her father towards Kumari's room. For the last few days now, the small room adjoining the clinic had been converted into "Kumari's room". There was no way yet that she could be integrated into the household. Through the week, she had continued to be extremely aggressive and difficult, and although her routine activities were now less tricky, the worst was far from over. She was regularly polishing off the meals being provided to her, and she went quite eagerly with Devi for her daily swim. But she was impossible to approach for any other reason, and all the girls left her severely alone. Nagi's overtures had been largely ignored by Kumari, and she seemed to take a perverse pleasure in antagonizing Udaya when he came to visit, which he did, every evening. She would then turn her back on him, or laugh uncontrollably when he tried to talk to her, or start humming or jabbering to herself. She had not attacked him physically again, although that threat was by no means laid to rest. It was different with Devi, who spent long hours with her in the room, either just sitting still, or conducting a one-sided conversation, speaking about a range of topics, sometimes personal, sometimes professional, whatever was uppermost in her mind at the time. She had even spoken about all the troubles currently besetting them, proposing the pros and cons of various theories that could explain all the circumstances. Kumari had not uttered a word to her in all that time, nor to anyone else, at least nothing intelligible. Did she even know how to speak? It was hard to tell. She did seem to understand what others were saying to her, so there was reason to believe that she knew the words and could probably articulate them.

Devi opened the door to Kumari's room slowly. It was no longer locked, and Kumari would shut it herself. There was no latch on the inside that she could lock it with thankfully. Devi could well imagine the girl locking herself into the room for days at the slightest pretext! As always, it was a bit dark inside, since Kumari preferred to keep all the windows firmly shut, but now there was no stench. Having thoroughly cleaned out the room after Kumari's first bath, Nagi had burned incense inside for several hours to sweeten the air. The lingering fragrance was pleasant, and Kumari was now meticulous in her ablutions. In fact, she appeared to be taking some pride in her appearance. She would carefully choose from the selection of sarees that Nagi set out for her in the morning, and a fair bit of her time at the pool was spent regarding her reflection in the water. She would sometimes summon Devi closer and look at their reflections, side by side, and compare each feature by touching her eyes or her nose or her mouth first and then touching Devi's in turn. This would afford her a lot of amusement, and Devi too would join in her infectious giggles as they contemplated one another's faces in the water. Her hair was growing back in a stiff stubble, and she had taken to thoroughly massaging her scalp with coconut oil after her morning bath.

"Kumari, come here," Devi called to her. As usual, she was sitting on her haunches in a corner of the room. "Come, don't keep sitting there in the dark. I have someone here to meet you, someone who has come a long way. See, my father is here to see you." Devi tended to speak to her as if she was a small child, although she clearly was well into her adolescence, maybe even older.

Maybe the idea of meeting Devi's father aroused her curiosity, or perhaps she was bored of sitting around in the dark day after day doing nothing, but for whatever reason, Kumari rose quite readily from her corner and came towards the door. As she emerged into the light, the patches on her skin showed quite obviously. Vaman Bhat stepped forward and greeted her with folded hands. "Good morning," he said to her, gentle as always. "I am Vaman Bhat, Devi's father. You can call me 'appa' if you like. I am very happy to meet you. Both Devi and Udaya have told me much about you."

Kumari regarded him seriously. She carefully surveyed him from head to foot, taking in each feature of his face, his clothes, the shape of his hands and feet. Then, as she perhaps always would, she took both of them completely by surprise. Bending down, she touched Vaman Bhat's feet, and said, "Appa".

## ii

Vaman Bhat completed his examination of Kumari and sat back. They had moved to the clinic and she was sitting on one of the mats reserved for examining patients. "This is extraordinary. It is something I have never seen before, and I am not sure what to make of it. The skin is perfectly smooth and even, and there is no sign of infection or putrefaction. It appears it is only the color of the skin that is affected, and the patchy appearance is spread all over the body, on her torso and limbs and face. It is definitely not the dreaded kushta roga, because although the skin is patchy she has no loss of sensation. Mind you, some people could well mistake it for that, especially those who are ignorant or not properly trained in diagnosis. I will have to consult my texts and see if there is a reference to this condition, and whether there is any suggested treatment for it."

"I hope she can still be treated…" Devi was afraid that it may have been left too late. Sometimes, when diseases were allowed to settle in and become deep-seated, they tended to be impossible to treat.

"I hope so too. Usually, skin conditions do respond to treatment, even chronic conditions. And there are usually two ways to treat them – both internally through tablets and potions and externally through ointments and packs. So it may not be too late. I wish she had been shown to a doctor earlier, then the prognosis would have been much better. The one comfort is that it is not life threatening. In fact, it need not impede her day to day functioning at all! It is literally only skin deep."

"Yes, it does not affect her health, but it does affect her sense of well-being," Devi reminded her father. "Everyone stares at her, and she was the butt of a lot of cruelty before we brought her here. Even here, after all the counseling I have given Raji and Laxmi and Jaya, they still cannot look at her without staring. That must be terrible for her."

Kumari was listening closely to this exchange. After uttering that one word that had left Devi flabbergasted, she had again resumed her silence, and not another sound had escaped her.

"I will try my best, my child, both for her sake and for yours. I am sure there will be something in the texts that will help. You know, it is uncanny, but she reminds me of someone, although I can't quite put my finger on it…." He regarded Kumari thoughtfully for a minute, then shook his head. "Hmmm, I can't think who it could be…..Now, if you have some moments to spare, I would like to talk to you about the other matter."

"Please, father, tell me what is new! Has there been any development on that front?"

"Not yet. But I have spoken to Krishna Rao, and I have told him of your suspicions. He gave me a careful hearing, even though he was completely immersed in affairs of state. He was very interested to know of your theory that Thimmappayya had been forcibly administered some poisonous drug, but he wants us to be very careful, and very discreet. He has exhorted us not to talk to anyone about this, not even here in the clinic. Try not to mention it to anyone, even Nagi, if you can help it."

"Of course, father! I have not told anyone except you and Udaya."

After receiving this assurance, Vaman Bhat got up. "I think I will take my leave now. But I am glad to see you in good spirits, daughter. I had thought you might be brooding on this sad matter. But rest assured, if Krishna Rao has said so, he will take care of it. Anyway, your patients will be gathering outside soon, I imagine, so I will leave you to it."

Looking outside, Devi saw that her patients had indeed gathered outside. She had been so immersed in her father's examination of Kumari that she had not noticed. Time to get back to her normal routine!

### iii

The man goes whistling down the country road. He has already walked a mile or more from his village and has another couple of miles to go – not very far at all. On the way he enjoys the fresh crispness of the air, the shrill chirping of the birds, the fragrance of jasmine. He knows all these sights and sounds will soon give way to the busy streets of the town, although this early in the morning, it might still be quite peaceful. He hated going into town normally, the country life suited him best. Plus he had the best of both worlds – he enjoyed the advantages of being in the country while being just a short walk from the town. In his father's time, it had not been such a short walk, their farm had been quite far from the town center. But things had changed – the town had grown, he himself had sold off most of the farm and built a house on the plot closest to the town.

But this was not what he was thinking about as he walked. He was thinking about his errand today. Finally, his cousin had come through! When he had come asking for a small loan all those years ago, the man had thought the loan would be repaid within the year. At least, that is what the cousin had told him. This had turned out to be a vain hope, and year after year had gone by with no sign of his money. The man had been getting angrier and more frustrated as time went by. His cousin seemed to be prospering reasonably, if the improvements to his house and his wife's wardrobe were anything to go by, and yet there was no mention of returning his money. How many times to ask? After a while, he had started avoiding his cousin so that he didn't have to look at that cheating face. But his blood had been boiling.

And then, lo and behold! Yesterday, the cousin's son had appeared at his door. His first instinct had been to speak to the boy harshly, but his better self prevailed. After all, it was not the boy's fault if his father was a thieving hypocrite! So he had invited the boy into the house and offered him some water. The boy had refused, and only delivered a brief message – if his uncle would come tomorrow morning into town, his father would repay his debt. But at no cost should he come home. They would meet along the western wall of the palace.

All this had sounded quite cryptic and mysterious to the man, but his not to reason why. He was mainly relieved that he was going to get his money back, not an insignificant amount either. So as he swings along, it is with a happy tune on his lips. He speculates idly that perhaps his cousin has never told his wife about the loan and that's why he had not invited him home. Yes, he thinks, that's the best explanation, the fellow is terrified of his wife.

He has now reached the outskirts of town, and in the distance can see the palace walls looming over the town's central district. He takes the short cut through the narrow gullies of the inner city. The shops are still shut, but people are already milling around, standing at the roadside exchanging gossip, buying flowers from the streetside vendors for the morning puja, drinking hot milk flavored with almonds or cardamom at small ramshackle stalls. He walks past them without a second glance, and soon emerges in the square outside the western gate of the palace. The palace guards are standing at attention, keeping a watchful lookout, but the area is otherwise deserted. The man goes past the gate along the western perimeter wall, a lonely stretch. He wonders why his cousin has picked this lonely spot. He would make sure and ask him when they met.

He walks along a short distance, and then he spies some signs of life. There is a horse tethered to a tree stump about two hundred yards ahead. It is a tall handsome beast, and he wonders if it belongs to his cousin – the fellow had prospered even more than I had imagined, he thinks bitterly. As he gets a bit closer, he notices that there is some kind of bundle across the saddle of the horse. He wonders what it can be and picks up his pace. As he gets closer, he sees that it is not just a bundle, there are limbs sticking out of it. Now he is beginning to get wary, but still curious, get goes up close to get a better look.

What he sees is that a man has been slung over the saddle of the horse, and his legs are sticking out of a wrapping of clothes and a dirty blanket. Was he drunk? Or ill? The man walks cautiously around the back of the horse to see the face of the man who is so unceremoniously lying across the animal's body. And what he sees on the other side causes him to let out a bloodcurdling yell!

The man is neither drunk nor ill, but very dead. And what a death! It has left his face black and mottled, his eyes staring wildly into the black nothingness, his tongue red and distended. He looks like the devil incarnate. The man goes on yelling without even knowing it.

# Chapter 15

Devi was restless that night, tossing and turning, and muttering in her sleep. Towards early morning, she was visited by one of her dreams, vivid and disturbing as always.

As always, she is a quiet observer, a little girl unnoticed in a corner. They are all crowded in a dark room, gloomy and oppressive. The teacher is there, bending over a woman who is writhing and moaning on a rush mat spread on the floor. She is sweating profusely, and the air in the room is rank with the smell of it. A young man – a student perhaps – is kneeling by her and wiping her face and neck with a wet cloth. The teacher is speaking to her soothingly. "Your time will soon be over, and the pain will be forgotten. I can sense that the moment is coming closer, take courage! Just a short while more." He keeps talking to her in this vein, trying to distract the woman, to no avail. Her cries are reaching a crescendo, and the teacher and all his students gather close around the woman.

The little girl can no longer see what is going on, but she can hear the agonizing moans and the exhortations of the teacher. He is telling the woman to stay strong, to keep her knees drawn back, to push. The little girl doesn't understand what this is all about but there is a growing sense of urgency within the room. Suddenly the woman lets out a strangled yell, followed by an appreciative gasp from the teacher and his students. A lusty cry follows, and the little girl realizes that it is the sound of a newborn baby. She wants to see it, but dares not push her way to the front of the tight knit group.

"Let me see my boy, let me see the baby," she hears the woman ask softly.

"It's not a boy, lady – it's a beautiful girl!" the teacher tells her smilingly. "Lovely black hair and big eyes – just like you!"

The little girl hears the woman's heartbreaking weeping. "What is it? Why do you cry?" the teacher asks her. The woman does not answer, but continues to weep as if she will never stop. Then she says, "Take her away sir, please take her away. Take her away with you, don't leave her here. Whatever you do, don't leave her here, sir."

The teacher does not understand. "Why not, my dear? Why are you so distressed? Tell me."

"Go away before my husband comes, sir. When he sees her, he will take her away from me like he did all the rest. I don't know where he takes them or what becomes of them. All I know is that I never see them again. I want this one to go with someone I know, sir, someone who will treat her well. So please take her with you, sir, I beg of you."

The oppressive room and the weeping woman fill the little girl with sorrow. She wants to get away, but she cannot find the door. She is whimpering in despair – why can she not find the way out of this place?

She felt herself being shaken, and woke up with a start. She sat up, wide-eyed, expecting to have Nagi scolding her again for crying in her sleep, for sure enough her face was wet with tears. But it was Kumari, and she was wiping her face gently with the edge of her saree. "Don't cry, akka," she was saying softly, "don't cry."

## ii

Devi had managed to fall back asleep after her dream, but not for long. She got up, not feeling in the least bit refreshed. She was looking forward to her dip in the pool before the start of another busy day. She gathered up her clothes and walked down to the water, splashing herself liberally with its coolness before stepping in and immersing herself fully. By the time she emerged and got dressed, she felt a good deal better. Her incipient headache was almost gone, and she was no longer feeling fuzzy headed and bleary eyed. Enough of enjoying herself! She reprimanded herself sternly, well aware that the line of patients would already be a long and winding one, and the sooner she got started with seeing them the sooner she would finish.

But when she got back to the house, she sensed that something was very wrong. Nagi was waiting for her in the doorway, and the girls were lined up behind her, practically wringing their hands in distress. She hardly knew what to make of it. Even Kumari was standing behind Nagi, watchfully waiting for her to return from her bath.

"What is it?" she asked Nagi, wondering what to expect.

"Something strange…." Nagi replied slowly. Then she added in a rush, "There is someone here to see you, akka. There is man…."

"What man?" Devi asked impatiently as Nagi petered out again. She started walking towards the clinic, but Nagi stepped in her way. "No, wait, listen to me," she said. "Compose yourself first. And remember, whatever happens now, it will all turn out alright in the end….don't lose heart, akka."

"Alright, so let me go speak to him then," Devi tried to walk past Nagi, but was stopped again. This was getting to be ridiculous! What was the matter with the lot of them?

"He is saying that you are going against the will of god," Nagi said finally.

"What? The will of god? What is he talking about? Who is this man? Let me go, Nagi!" So saying, Devi pushed past Nagi and strode into her clinic.

She stopped short in shock. The person waiting inside was Siddayya. It brought her up short. What was she to make of this? It was a week since the events in the tent, and she had thought she was free from any sort of victimization from the one person who loved to hate her.

"How can I help you, sir?" she asked, sounding breathless from a mixture of anger and fear.

"How can you help me?" Siddayya mimicked her insultingly. "You cannot help me at all, young lady. Let's see if you can help yourself! Surely you cannot be surprised to see me here."

Devi took a steadying breath. She did not want to give him the satisfaction of knowing that he was getting under her skin. Slowly her fear was ebbing and fury was taking hold of her. That was not good either, but it was preferable to standing quaking in front of the man. This was her clinic, she must stand her ground!

"Well?" she challenged him. "What is it?"

"Oh ho, is this what I am to expect then? A fine upbringing your father has given you! Apparently he has taught you a lot about herbs and medicines, but not enough about how to speak to your elders and betters!"

"You are older then me, sir, perhaps you are even older than my father. I am duty bound to offer you my respect, but that does not mean I have to bear your threats and insults silently. You have come here for a reason. Please could you state it and then we can understand each other better."

As if he had not heard her at all, Siddayya moved to the window and looked out. After that, he walked back into the room and did a slow perambulation of all the stacks of books and shelves of medicines lining the walls. Softly, he read out the names on the labels of some of the bottles, and the titles of the books. He seemed in no hurry at all to state his business.

Devi could feel the tension mounting unbearably within her. Nagi and the girls were observing the scene in dead silence, crowding in the open door. How long was she supposed to wait while he completed his inspection? She had to physically restrain herself from speaking – every syllable she spoke seemed to irk him. The less she spoke, the better.

Finally, he looked around and said, "This is a very small clinic. From all the reports I had heard, about the crowds of patients and the huge demand for your services, somehow I was picturing a much bigger place. But you seem to have equipped it quite well – I suppose you can thank your father for that! Although the man is completely misguided in many matters – and especially in the matter of how to bring up children! – he does know his medicines, I will grant him that. You seem to have gathered some very rare plants as well, unusual ones that I have not seen in a long time."

"My father and I make it a point to ask our friends to source plants for us on their various travels, sir. That is how we have built up our collection over the years," Devi explained through tight lips. She could not fathom where this conversation was leading.

"Oh, I am sure you have all sorts of methods!" Siddayya managed to make a perfectly innocent collection of medicinal plants sound like a dirty secret. Did he sully everything he touched? "Well, anyway, you will have to leave this behind you for a while, I am afraid. You have been summoned by the king. You will have to leave here with me now, right away. I am not sure for how long you will enjoy the hospitality of the king, but you can bring a change of clothes if you like."

Devi was stunned! This was not at all what she had expected. "But I cannot leave my patients, sir," she blurted out the first thing that came into her head. She knew instantly that she had said the wrong thing. Siddayya almost snarled at her.

"Your patients! Your patients are not as important as the king the realm, young woman! How dare you even think of objecting to a royal summons? Has your arrogance grown to this? When I say women should not be raised too high, people call me old-fashioned. But if they could have witnessed this moment, I don't think too many people would continue to disagree with me. Just because you have some rudimentary healing powers you think you can challenge the highest in the land? You cannot, understand that! The king can squash you like an ant if he so wishes. So get your things together and let us leave at once. You have been enough of a waste of my time already, I don't intend to hang around awaiting your convenience all day! Get moving, girl!"

Devi had no choice. She quickly turned to see an anxious Nagi standing just outside the door, a mute witness to Siddayya's high-handedness. Going into her room, she quickly threw the few things that Nagi handed her into a bag.

"How long?" Nagi asked anxiously.

"You heard the man," Devi replied. "No idea. I don't even know why I have been summoned. Tell my father, make sure my father knows at once that I have been taken away. He will know what to do."

She then went back into the clinic where Siddayya was waiting impatiently for her. He stalked out when he saw her, gesturing for her to follow. Outside there was a horse-drawn cart waitng to take them back to town. Devi climbed into it first, followed by Siddayya who sat opposite her and then commanded the cartman to drive on. They headed out of the compound and started on the road in silence.

After a while, Devi could stay silent no longer. "Sir, can you give me some idea of where we are going and why?" she asked the stony figure sitting before her.

At first, Siddayya did not deign to answer and she thought perhaps he had not heard her over the rattling of the cart – after all, he was not a young man and his hearing might not be so acute any more. She was contemplating whether to repeat her question when he answered. "You are going to meet with the king, who wants to know more about why you suspect Thimmappayya of being poisoned."

Devi's heart sank. So her suspicion had reached the king! No doubt Siddayya himself had conveyed the story to him, after he had heard about it from her father. Well, what had she expected? Once people like Krishna Rao and Siddayya were privy to that type of information, it was hardly surprising that they had taken it to the king. There was, after all, an investigation underway, with the Commandant of the palace guards himself in charge. This was a high profile case, and she was in the middle of it.

"I have nothing more to tell, sir," she offered, after a short pause. "Whatever I told my father is all I know. I was not allowed to do a post-mortem of the body, so I cannot tell you any more."

"You need not tell me anything," Siddayya responded dismissively. "I am personally least interested in your diagnoses. I don't know how well founded they are and whether you are even competent to speak on such matters. But the king seems to think you have something to contribute, so he has asked for you. You had better gather your thoughts as best you can. Don't embarrass yourself even further by babbling in the king's presence."

Hardly words designed to build confidence! But at least he left her alone with her thoughts and did not continue to shake her poise with his constant heckling. The ride seemed interminable, the road through the woods stretching endlessly on. Finally, they came to the outskirts of the town and Devi heaved a sigh of relief – this journey would soon end, she could see the palace walls already. She wanted one last question answered by Siddayya. "Sir, why did you tell me to bring a change of clothes? Why should I have to stay, if I only have to answer a few questions?"

"You will see," was the ominous answer, after which they turned into the imposing main gate of the palace. Devi hardly had the heart to admire the beauty of the Deccan architecture of the palace, the beautiful grounds with the flower beds and lotus ponds, the intricate topiary and the peacocks calling out gutturally among the fragrant greenery. She was dreading this interview, and Siddayya had done nothing to prepare her for it. How she longed for her father's presence! Hopefully, he would get word of her predicament soon, and come to her aid. But until then, she would have to take her courage in her hands and survive the ordeal on her own.

The cart came to a halt, and they both alighted onto the gravel driveway. Without a word, Siddayya led the way in, and Devi followed close behind. She had been inside the palace a few times as a child, accompanying her father on some mundane task, but that had been a long time ago. It looked as magnificent inside as she remembered, with wide expanses of polished marble flooring, ornately carved and inlaid pillars, and an intricately painted ceiling. The sound of their footsteps echoed in the silent halls, punctuated only by the sound of soldiers snapping to attention as Siddayya marched by. Soon they were at a huge carved door, which glided open at a light knock from Siddayya. A kindly looking man looked out, and immediately stepped back respectfully to allow Siddayya and his young companion to enter.

And then they were in the presence of the king. Devi had been so nervous at the prospect that it took her a few minutes to realize that he was looking at her quite kindly and did not appear to be at all intimidating. He beckoned her closer and gestured towards a silken settee. "Come, my dear, sit down," he said. His voice was surprisingly deep and low. She moved forward hesitantly, but did as he asked. When she was comfortably seated, he came close and said, "Do not be afraid. You have nothing to fear. Siddayya must have told you why you are here?"

Devi looked up at him, and felt her spirits recovering somewhat under his benign gaze. "He said you would like to discuss the death of Thimmappayya, sire. He said you wanted to ask me more about the condition of the body."

"Yes, quite right. I believe your father reported your findings to Krishna Rao and Siddayya and they quite rightly came and reported to me. If what you say is true, then it gives us an important new piece of evidence, which we must take into account when trying to find an explanation for this death. So you are going to explain the whole thing again to me, please. Take your time, and give me all the details."

Devi gathered her thoughts. "When the body was brought in, I soon realized that he was already dead, sire. I felt for a pulse and there was none, and there was no breath in the body either. After that, I was not able to observe the body closely for a while......for various reasons." She did not want to dwell on the scene Ranga had created in the tent, it did not seem appropriate to bring it up in front of the king. "Then Lord Siddayya came into the tent, and on his advice, I examined the body in some detail to determine the cause of death, if possible. This is when I observed certain signs that this death may not have been a natural one." Here she paused again, in case there were any queries.

"Proceed," the king commanded. "You interest me strangely."

"Well, sire, there were two rather unusual things that I noticed. One was that the eyes were wide open and the pupils were completely dilated. This is not at all a common occurrence in all the dead bodies that I have seen before. The second thing was that the man's lips were blue. This meant that he had died because his heart had stopped. It raised the possibility that these two signs were linked. Hence I did not make my findings public, for fear I might say something inaccurate and unnecessarily raise the alarm. I waited to see my father and confirm with him that these signs were indeed out of the ordinary."

"Hmm, I see," said the king. "And what did your esteemed father say?"

"Sire, he said that they indicated a suspicious death. By this time I had looked up my medical books, and I think I have a fairly good idea of what could have been the cause of death."

"Well, speak up, girl! Don't draw out the story for its suspense value – tell the king quickly what you know."

The king glanced impatiently at Siddayya, not appreciating his tone of speaking to Devi, but he said nothing. Devi quickly resumed, "It is hatapatri, sire. A weed that grows very commonly all around us, but extremely poisonous, especially when consumed in large quantities. It causes the heart to burst, sire, and before that releases some *dosha* in the body that causes the eyes to bulge and stare. It is well documented in the ancient texts, sire, in the *Caraka Samhita*."

Sarasa Hardy

"So it is your guess that this man was fed a large quantity of this hatapatri? Could he have eaten it by accident?"

"That is unlikely, sire. It is quite a bitter weed, and no one really eats it. Why would this man have eaten it, unless it was forced on him, or been given to him in some other medium which disguised the flavor?"

"And the effect is almost immediate, is it?"

"It is very quick acting, sire. It may not have taken more than fifteen minutes or half an hour."

The king and Siddayya exchanged meaningful glances. "Come," the king beckoned Devi to follow him into one of the ante-chambers. "I will now show you the real reason you are here."

Wondering what he meant by that, Devi followed him inside. There she got a shock. Laid out on the floor was a man, and from what she could make out, he looked dead. His face was black and mottled; and his tongue had been pulled almost out of his head, and was a livid red. He looked like the devil incarnate! Devi gasped on seeing this apparition and stepped sharply back.

"Don't be afraid," the king said kindly. "Here is a man who was found this morning near the palace walls. A farmer came upon the body. He had been thrown on top of a horse and left for some passing stranger to discover."

"Who is he?" Devi asked, overcome with pity for the poor man's fate.

"That is the interesting part! He is the sais who looked after the Ashvamedha horse when it was a foal. And the horse on which he was lying was the brother of the Ashvamedha horse. Which is why this death has not been treated as a regular police case. When the palace guards reached the spot in response to the farmer's cries for help, they took him first to the Commandant of the guards. It was he who determined that this was no ordinary man, found on no ordinary horse. They then transferred the body here. I then recalled that you had examined the previous mysterious dead body, so I thought it would be good if you took a look at this one as well. Maybe there are common features here that may give us some clue as to who the perpetrator is."

Devi moved forward and knelt by the body. She felt for the pulse and breath as a mere formality – both were long silenced. The man's body had grown cold and stiff with the passage of time, it was well over three or four hours since he had come by his untimely death. She moved his head to get a better look at his eyes and got a surprise. Her fingers came away black, taking some of the color from the face. She looked around and looked at Siddayya. "Could I get some water and a clean cloth, please?" She realized he was irritated by her request – was he her messenger boy? – but even he must have seen that her only other option would have been to make the request to the king himself, since there was no one else in the room!

He went out to fulfill her request, and she began a careful examination of the body from the toes upwards. She found nothing untoward anywhere, although there was some bruising of the flesh around the hips and the abdomen, but this could be because of the position in which the body had been left atop the horse. By this time Siddayya returned with a bowl of water and some muslin, and Devi was able to wipe the black soot off the face of the dead man. Not only the soot, but also the red color on the tongue came off. Someone had taken a lot of trouble to deliberately make the man look hideous. As she wiped the face clean, the blueness around the lips showed through, very pronounced. And one look at the staring eyes told her that the pupils were fully dilated.

Covering the face with a clean piece of cloth, she got up. "It is the same, sire," she said with certainty. At that moment, the king's manservant came in and said something to him in a low voice. The king nodded and dismissed him, and in a moment, they were joined by Vaman Bhat.

Devi was overjoyed to see her father. God bless Nagi! She must have sent a messenger across almost immediately after her departure for her father to have reached here so soon. A large part of the tenson left her. It was not that she had been scared, but she had definitely been intimidated, and having her father by her side made it all so much easier.

The king acknowledged Vaman Bhat's entrance into the room with a nod, and he in turn bowed deeply to the king. "Your daughter was just about to display her expertise," he informed Vaman Bhat with a smile. "Go on, child," he said to Devi.

Devi brought her mind back to the investigation at hand. "The cause of death seems to be the same as before, sire. This man also has the same blueness around the lips and the dilation of the pupils. I would venture to guess that he too must have ingested a substantial amount of hatapatri shortly before his death."

Siddayya turned to Vaman Bhat. "We have not brought your daughter here for any nefarious reason, Vaman Bhat. You came rushing here in some anxiety, I think! But as you see, there has been another death." He pointed to the body on the floor, although Vaman Bhat had already observed its presence.

"May I?" he gestured towards the body. The king nodded his permission. Vaman Bhat stepped closer to the body and bent down on one knee. He conducted a careful examination of the extremeties and then looked closely at the face, noting all the obvious features noted by Devi earlier. He stood up and said, "I had not seen the body of Thimmappayya unfortunately. However, it is obvious that this man did not die a natural death. If my daughter says he has been poisoned, then I would agree with her."

"A second death, using the same method! And it is no coincidence that the victim is again connected closely to the Ashvamedha horse. And they have gone to the trouble of stealing that horse's sibling from the stables as an involuntary participant in this dastardly deed. Whoever has done this, as in the previous case, has been meticulous in their planning and in the execution of the crime. We are dealing with a very intelligent mind!" The king summed up what was on all their minds.

"But why are they targeting the Ashvamedha horse?" Devi asked, perplexed by this coincidence.

Siddayya snorted derisively. "That is obvious! They want to discredit the king, they want to cast doubt on his victory, they want to evoke some supernatural signs to spoil a sacred celebration. We will have to get to the root of this and severely punish those responsible for this kind of treason."

Vaman Bhat spoke quietly. "They are already succeeding, sire. When I was walking through the marketplace on my way here, I could already hear the gossiping tongues wagging. They are seeing all sorts of meaning in this coincidence – two deaths, both connected with the Ashvamedha horse, both occurring in a mysterious manner. They are indeed ascribing it to the supernatural, saying that the devil has entered the kingdom and is going to now start wreaking havoc all around because the Ashvamedha has been cursed. These kinds of rumors need to be firmly squashed, sire, because people are foolish and this sort of thing appeals to their feeble imaginations."

"Too true, Vaman," the king agreed. "But the only way to counter this kind of canard is by finding the truth and exposing the real villains. We all know, I think, that both these men have been the victims of a very human agency, nothing supernatural about it! But unless we find the true culprit and can produce him before the mob, they will continue their foolish speculation. So time is of the essence! The sooner we can locate the real culprits, the sooner we can go back to normal. We have big plans for further expansion, Siddayya here and the rest of my Council of Ministers are well aware of this. But while this is hanging over my head I cannot think clearly." The king sounded thoroughly frustrated.

"We will find him, sire," Siddayya assured him soothingly. "We have made an important connection today, with the healer identifying the common cause of death for both the men. Now, the challenge is to find the criminals and bring them before the public. The Commandant of the guards is on the job, and I think we can be confident that we will bring this to a satisfactory resolution. Do we need the healer to stay, sire, or is she now free to go?"

"Stay? Oh, there is no need for that. Now that her father is here, I think we can entrust her to him. Please ensure that they are provided with transportation to return to the clinic. I can assure you, young lady, that you have the gratitude of the king for your valuable service here today. I did not have the chance to thank you also for managing the first aid arrangements during the celebration. I understand they were a grand success, until the unfortunate incident took place."

Mumbling her thanks, Devi quickly left the room, with Siddayya escorting her to the waiting horse cart. Vaman Bhat lingered behind for a moment.

"Sire, I have a request," he said, after ensuring that Siddayya was safely out of hearing. "You may have heard, sire, that there are stories making the rounds in the town that Thimmappayya died because of my daughter's negligence. As we know, this is not the case at all, far from it. The stories are being spread by Ranga, the man's nephew, I am told. I would be grateful, sire, if you could persuade Lord Siddayya to ask him to retract his statements. He has some influence with the man. It maybe that he is in sympathy with Ranga himself, and therefore has not objected to this public campaign against Devi. But I wish you could persuade him that it would be wrong for him to turn a blind eye and allow this injustice to proceed unchecked."

The king said nothing for a minute. Then, "I will speak to Siddayya," he said briefly. Clearly, he did not want to discuss Siddayya's motivations with a third party. Vaman Bhat left it at that – he had done what he could to protect his daughter. So he left after taking formal leave of the king.

They had been gone for barely a few minutes when the king's chamber was overrun by several of his ministers, lead by Krishna Rao. Marching in, they all demanded to know what the king planned to do about the rumors that were making the rounds not only in town but across the land. "The stories are getting wilder and wilder with the telling, sire," Krishna Rao addressed the king with some vehemence. "People are embroidering the stories with all kinds of nonsense – that the bodies were possessed, that they were laughing and shrieking like banshees, that spirits were hovering about them, that red smoke was billowing from their ears!"

"Krishna Rao, what is happening to you?" the king asked, astonished. "You are usually the voice of reason, and yet here you are reporting all this rubbish as if you expect me to take it seriously!"

Krishna Rao collected himself somewhat. "You do need to take it seriously, sire. This could have serious repercussions, that is what we must realize. The more such rumors spread, the more damage to your authority. I am afraid that some unfriendly elements may take advantage of this situation, try to overthrow your rule at a time when the public is panicking in this manner."

"What are you saying, Krishna Rao? That these baseless rumors can cost me my crown? Surely you jest! This is just the idle chatter of the rabble, nobody will mind it. I think you are being overly cautious. In any case, we are making good progress with the investigation, I think we may even be able to catch the criminals soon. In which case, they can be paraded before the mob, and all talk about the devil's hidden hand will die down."

"I am happy if your investigation is progressing well, sire," Krishna Rao replied tonelessly. "Do you already have information enough to name the culprit?"

"No, certainly not! But we are getting closer. Just now the healer was here and she was able to provide us with a fresh piece of the puzzle. In this manner, I am confident we shall soon resolve this situation. In the meantime, it is our duty to maintain order and put paid to these silly stories. If we ourselves start to panic, then it bodes ill for our ability to contain this crisis!"

Krishna Rao looked at the ground with lowered gaze. "I am only concerned that these tragic events and the unpleasant fallout will prevent you from carrying out your military plans, sire. I know you have been keen on seeing those through."

"And I continue to be keen, Krishna Rao! A small thing like this is hardly going to stop me. In any case, as I said, I am certain we will solve this crime very soon. Nothing will stop me from carrying out my plans – it is for the good of all the people, and for the greater glory of the Kadambas!"

"That is the reason we undertook the Ashvamedha, sire, and yet people are wondering when the good will actually accrue to them. So far they have paid the price, but have not been able to taste any benefit. Perhaps it would be good to ensure that people settle down and enjoy the fruits of the previous victories before embarking on a whole new campaign?"

"Spoken again like an old lady, Krishna Rao! Administrators like you are the backbone of the kingdom, no doubt, but you cannot be expected to have the same ambitions and vision as the king! The people will enjoy the fruits of victory, have no fear. Only, it will have to be deferred a little, that's all. The people will understand, I know they will! These so-called ill omens targeting the

Ashvamedha have been thought up by some factions who are trying to foment dissidence and violence as a way of preventing me from pursuing my legitimate ambitions. But I will not cave in to such pressures! What kind of king would that make me? Either I lead the army from strength to strength, or I sit in my palace cowering in a corner, hiding from my enemies! I will always choose the first option, even if I have to pay a price for it, even if my people have to pay a price for it!"

The king was determined to stick to his chosen path, not heeding the warnings of his Prime Minister. Krishna Rao had nothing left to say. He knew the king's choice; now he had to make his own.

# Chapter 16

Vaman Bhat and Devi rattled along in the horsecart, back to Devi's clinic. Unlike the trip there, when Devi had sat in menacing silence with Siddayya, she was now in the comforting company of her father, who was holding her hand in his warm clasp. "That must have been quite frightening for you, my child," he sympathized deeply. "Tell me what happened exactly, how did you come to be in the palace at all this morning?"

"I have no idea, father. All I know is that I was getting ready to start my clinic when Siddayya showed up and in the most offensive manner possible told me that the king had summoned me. He is such a mean-spirited person that he gave no hint that the king was actually seeking my assistance! He definitely wanted me to fear the worst – that somehow the king was holding me culpable for the crime. I was really scared!"

"That's Siddayya for you," Vaman Bhat patted her hand consolingly. "He instinctively does the mean-spirited thing, although he has other good qualities. So then you went with him to the palace?"

"Yes, we went straight to the palace, and to the king's chambers. He was very nice, very kind! I felt much better after meeting him, I can tell you. He asked me in detail about Thimmappayya's case. I think after you spoke to Krishna Rao and Siddayya, they reported to the king, so he seemed to know that there was some reason to suspect that Thimmappayya may have been poisoned. But even he didn't tell me immediately that there was another dead body! That came later, after all the findings on Thimmappayya had been discussed. When they showed me the second body I got a real shock!"

"I can imagine," her father said. "And you found it was the same situation this time too. My own examination also told me that. It is indeed strange."

"But why is this happening, father?" Devi asked anxiously. The people of Banavasi were used to peace and safety. The wars had been waged far away, causing devastation to people in distant lands, nothing to do with them. This spate of violence in their own midst was unnerving.

"It is obviously politically motivated, daughter. Look at the victims they have chosen, whoever is behind this. Each time, it has been to strike at the king's victorious Ashvamedha. There are many people who have been opposed to these military campaigns, but now it looks like they have decided to act. I can guess why. The king is planning another campaign I think, to the north. I have just heard some hints in the corridors, nothing specific. But if I have heard these murmurs, then others who are more politically connected must have heard them too. Perhaps they have decided to take matters into their own hands. This type of violence will take a powerful hold of the popular imagination; it won't take much for vested interests to turn the victory sour! In fact, I suspect it is already happening, you can hear the rumbles of discontent in the marketplace. The same people who a few days ago were wildly celebrating the Horse Sacrifice are now speaking freely of the devil practicing his dark arts in the palace."

Devi felt a cold foreboding grip her heart. It was not supposed to be like this! This was a peaceful and prosperous place, people were supposed to be happy and contented. Instead, political interests were playing havoc with the lives of ordinary people. After all, what had Thimmappayya or the other man done to deserve their untimely deaths? They were just pawns in somebody else's game, somebody else's very deadly game.

"This is an incredibly unpleasant development," Vaman Bhat remarked, with finality. "We must think of some strategy to deal with it, but maybe not right now. I think we are all in a disturbed frame of mind, and need to calm down a bit before we can contemplate this with any equanimity. All I am grateful for is that my worst fears were not fulfilled! You have no idea what was passing through my mind when Nagi's messenger boy came and told me that you had been taken away by Siddayya! I didn't know what to think. My only solace was in knowing that if he had indeed gone to the king, then nothing untoward would happen to you. The king is an innately just and decent man! But until I saw you safe and sound in the king's chamber, I was eating fire! Luckily, your mother has no inkling of all this – she was doing her puja when the messenger arrived and I simply told her I had been summoned by the king on an urgent official matter."

"In the meantime, let us talk about other matters. On a more cheerful note, last night after I left you, I researched the matter thoroughly and I know the recipe for the special medicine that Kumari requires! So as soon as we reach your clinic we can gather the ingredients and her treatment can start right away, which I for one am very happy about."

Devi was also happy to hear this, and even happier to stop thinking about the stressful events of the day so far. She allowed her father to distract her, and for the rest of the way they spoke about the materials required for Kumari's medicine and the mode of their preparation. They were given a hero's welcome upon their arrival at the clinic, and Nagi's usually tough exterior collapsed as she embraced Devi with tears in her eyes. "I am going to teach that Siddayya a lesson one day, you watch," was all she said ominously as she led her beloved friend back into the house.

Devi knew they were all curious to know what had transpired at the palace, and though she did not want to spend any more time talking about the morning's events, she knew she owed them some explanation. So she explained her interview with the king as briefly as possible, leaving out all mention of the second body, since she knew that would open up a whole new can of worms. Nagi sensed that she was hiding something, but did not comment, knowing that Devi would tell her later if she saw fit. With that, Devi closed the session and, as Vaman Bhat had done with her, distracted the girls with the recipe for Kumari's medicine. They were soon bustling about, fetching herbs and oils from the store room and measuring them out in the required quantities. Vaman

Bhat carefully supervised the proceedings, instructing the girls in how to treat each ingredient, until finally a thick paste of the prescribed consistency was arrived at. He called out to Kumari to come close so that her treatment could commence.

Kumari smiled shyly at him, unused to anyone being concerned for her welfare. With everyone else, her behavior was unpredictable at best; but with Vaman Bhat, she was uniformly respectful, almost reverent. Part of it was Vaman Bhat's own personality, supremely dignified and stately, brooking no misbehavior from anyone whatsoever. But partly it was also Kumari's response to him – it was as if she had some instinctive need to venerate him. Devi was thankful for this. Kumari's erratic behavior with all the rest, particularly Udaya, bothered her not at all. But if she had chosen to treat her father in the same way, she would not have had the patience to tolerate it or make any excuses for her behavior. Despite her wild upbringing, if you could call it an "upbringing", Kumari seemed to know her limits, and was becoming more careful not to transgress them. Although she still had no problem showing her claws when she thought she could get away with it!

"Then let's start at once," Devi said seconded her father enthusiastically. This was the moment she had been waiting for, after all! Immediately the scene was transformed into a classroom-like situation, and Vaman Bhat slipped into the familiar role that he was most comfortable in – that of the teacher. Gathering all his 'students' around him he brought Kumari into the center of the circle and commenced his lecture. He had two pots by his side: one contained the medicine they had all just prepared; the other had some seeds that he had gathered from the garden. From the pot closest to him, he poured out a handful of seeds. "Here, Devi," he instructed his daughter. "These are the seeds of the Bakuchi plant, the magic herb that is going to cure Kumari. You already have a plentiful supply of this in your garden, which is just as well, because you will need a lot of it. Hopefully Kumari's case will yield readily to treatment, but if it doesn't, we must be prepared with adequate supplies of these seeds. Nagi, could you get me a glass of drinking water, please. And take a few of these seeds and pound them into a fine powder."

Devi scooped the seeds back into the pot and handed it to Nagi. She went to the pharmacy to do as Vaman Bhat had instructed. Meanwhile, Vaman Bhat was opening the second pot. This contained the light brown paste that they had just made. "This is the paste you all just helped to make. The main ingredient here also is the seed of the Bakuchi plant, powdered finely and then combined with sandalwood powder, special oils and herbs to make this paste. Let me demonstrate how it is to be applied."

Lifting Kumari's arm, he spread a thin film of the ointment on all the affected areas, concentrating on the border between the normal skin and the discolored patch. He then handed the bowl to Kumari and watched while she did one area for herself. "It is as simple as that," he said, stepping back with satisfaction.

Now Nagi returned with the powdered seeds and a glass of water. Vaman Bhat took a small scoop of the powder and mixed it in with the water and handed it to Kumari. She looked at it doubtfully, but dutifully raised the glass to her lips and drank the mixture down. The face she made as she lowered the glass raised a laugh from the girls, and Vaman Bhat looked at her sympathetically. "Bitter?"

Kumari nodded in wholehearted agreement, and then asked, "Can't I eat something sweet to take away the taste?"

Vaman Bhat shook his head. "You have to take this medicine three times a day. You can't be eating something sweet everytime! Eating so much sweet is not good for the health. Get used to the taste – remember, it is for your own good. And I tried it earlier – it is not so bad! A little more bitter than bitter gourd, but some people might find the taste quite pleasant."

The lesson now being over, everyone dispersed and went about their business.

## ii

Ever since he had re-entered Banavasi on the day before the Ashvamedha yagna, disguised as a mendicant, Jayadeva had been lurking about the city both day and night, gathering information where he could. The marketplace had yielded a rich lode of material, but how much of it was just gossip and how much of it was useful? Jayadeva wished he could have had the benefit of his father's guidance, or failing that, someone elder who was in a better position than he to undertake this task. He had been accustomed to think of himself as a warrior, not a spy! He had been trained to be a warrior, not to sneak around in the bushes, listening in at doorways, pretending to be something he was not. Posing as a mendicant had its advantages, though, as he was discovering. He had not realized how amazingly generous people were to beggars! Especially those with a holy calling.

Sometimes he was assailed with doubt. Was any of the information he was relaying to the king useful? He never received any feedback, that was not part of the arrangement. He pictured the king reading through one of his carefully coded letters and consigning it to the flames with a grimace of disgust. It was disheartening to be operating in a vacuum like this, but there was no alternative. And he knew that at least one of the pieces of information he had recently relayed had been interesting to the king. The meeting the day after the Horse Sacrifice when he had told the king about the suspicious activities around the Prime Minister's chambers and the events leading to the death of Thimmappayya had certainly caught the king's attention. Afterwards, from his vantage point, he had observed the flurry of activity, with the Commandant of the palace guards being summoned into the king's presence, the subsequent questioning of the palace guards and the full-scale investigation that had been launched. All that had been his own doing! So in some ways, he felt vindicated.

Now he crouched under the window in the gathering dusk, hidden by the dense foliage carefully cultivated by the palace gardeners. He was not sure what he was likely to hear, but his visits to the palace had always been fruitful. This was the hub of all activity, after all. His job was to report to the king what he saw and heard, and to do it in a way that he would not be discovered. Being thought dead had the advantage that even if he was observed by some old acquaintance, they would put the resemblance down to a trick of the light. He had learned a lot in the process of gathering material for the king. For instance, he now knew that both the dead men had been poisoned and by the same substance – a fact that was not widely known. It had been confirmed by the healer, he knew that also. He had not made Mada a friend for nothing!

Jayadeva had been thinking hard, ever since the second death had come to light. Two deaths, both connected to the sacred horse, and both using the same method. What could he make of that? Marshaling the facts, three things stood out for him. One, someone was trying very hard to cast a shadow over the king's Ashvamedha triumph. Choosing victims closely associated with the horse was a clear indication of that. Who would have the motive to do that? Second, it had to be someone powerful enough to have the run of the palace. Using the Prime Minister's room to commit the first murder, being able to command people who could act as decoys to the palace guards – who would have had the power to pull that off? And finally, it had to be someone with some knowledge of medicinal plants and their uses. To use a plant like hatapatri in enough concentration to cause death, that could not be done by a layman. Did all this point to a single person, or perhaps two people at least? Maybe more?

All he knew was that both deaths had taken place near the palace precincts. Clearly, the objective was to associate the deaths with the king. There must be a reason for that. And whatever it was, he was going to discover it.

And so he crouched under the window, listening closely.

He was back on the other side of the same room which had puzzled him so much that day. The room where doors locked and unlocked with no explanation. Well, he was determined to find an explanation, and the best way to do so was to stay close to the scene of the crime, so to speak.

His wait was not in vain. He heard the sound of a door being opened, his signal to stop his thoughts from wandering. He went very still and listened for any telling sounds, but the shutting of the door was followed by complete silence. More than one person had entered the room, but it was hard to tell how many. Then there was a rustling of some material, but still no talk. Someone was reading through something perhaps, while one or maybe more people stood and waited. There was a soft cough.

Then a voice spoke, one that Jayadeva knew well. What the voice said sent a chill down his spine.

"The governors are getting restless."

"Yes, your honor," It was hard to tell who it was from the mumble. It was most likely someone too junior to matter.

"They need to be given guidance and a proper direction! This material you have brought me shows clearly that their plans are in disarray. We will prepare a fitting reply for them."

"Yes, your honor," A fellow spy, it seemed!

The enemy spy suddenly delivered himself of a long message. "The governors have been discussing the king's plans to undertake additional campaigns, to expand the kingdom further in the north. They were saying that it is well known that the Vakatakas are in a vulnerable state after the passing of queen Prabhavati Devi and the weakening of ties with the Guptas. They say the young king Pravarasena has not yet reached an age and a stature at which he can be considered a great leader. The governor's were of the opinion that this is perhaps why the king seems to feel that this is a good time to attempt an expansion in that direction, especially in the wake of the successful Ashvamedha. The news of its success and of the king's grand celebration have spread far and wide. The realm is echoing with praise for king Kakushtavarman's bravery and accomplishment, your honor."

"I am well aware of that! But there have been disturbing developments since then, have they not heard that? Have they heard of the ill omens? Has anyone heard of the ill omens attendant on the celebrations? The owner of the horse was found dead! The trusted sais of the horse was found dead! These are grave events, they surely signify bad luck!"

"No, your honor, nobody has mentioned that. Is it mentioned in the material I brought you?"

"You are not expected to ask questions, do you understand? You are meant to relay information, and nothing else. Do not step beyond your bounds!"

"Your honor, forgive me! I meant no offense! Forgive me, your honor!"

Jayadeva could picture the man groveling on the floor in front of the big boss. There was a silence, and then the voice said, "Wait there. I will give you a reply to carry back."

No sound was heard for quite a while, and then the familiar voice said again, "Here, take this. Deliver it as usual, and make haste! I advise you to be very very careful. I hear that the palace guard is on high alert. Also, the king has appointed someone to work against us. So we must be on our guard. I will not vouch for you if you are caught, remember that! That is why we compensate you so handsomely – the risk is yours alone."

"I understand, your honor. I will take care."

There was the sound of a door opening and then shutting. Jayadeva extricated himself from his hiding place without a sound. Running swiftly through the darkness, he rounded the corner just in time to see a muffled figure emerging from the side door. He knew what he had to do. He pulled his knife from the waistband of his robes and followed the figure closely in the shadows, until they were almost at the gates. Then he jumped his quarry and wrestled him to the ground, holding the knife to his throat. He fit the stereotype of a spy perfectly – small and slight and easily overlooked everywhere. Jayadeva was twice his size, and controlled him effortlessly. "Give it to me," he said in a low growl. The man struggled furiously, hitting out, aiming for Jayadeva's jugular. But Jayadeva had the advantage – he was not only physically bigger, he was also armed. He pinned the man to the ground in a vicious grip. "Give it to me," he commanded again.

"What? Give you what?"

"You know what I mean!" Jayadeva tightened his grip in his throat. "Give me the document, I know you have it with you." He groped around in the man's clothes, and had no trouble locating the letter tucked into his turban. It was too dark to check if it was what he was looking for, and he needed to get away before the palace guards came around. He tucked his knife back into his waistband and struck his victim a blinding blow, leaving him knocked out on the ground. Keeping a close lookout, he dragged the inert figure as close as he could to the palace door without being observed. With any luck, one of the palace guards would discover the fellow and pull him in for questioning. They would use the necessary methods to drag the truth out of him.

"Had to do that, my friend," he said under his breath as he melted back into the shadows. He took his time working his way around the perimeter of the palace, and emerged sauntering out of the gate on the distant side. He would be up till the wee hours carefully checking the document before passing it on to the king in the morning.

Jayadeva's swift pursuit of the informant had yielded rich results, and he held the letter close to his chest. But if he had stayed, he would have heard a very interesting conversation between two men in the room outside which he was hidden.

"Two men dead, and yet we have not been able to achieve our end! We are going about this the wrong way, I have told you this from the start! I should never have allowed you to convince me of this mad scheme….all this death on my conscience, and all for what?" The voice was of the man who had earlier been speaking to the informant.

Another voice replied, higher, almost shrill. "If you had managed your part as you should have, the deaths would not have been in vain! I did my part, making sure the potion that was fed to the men was potent enough to have the desired effect. I am not a successful physician for nothing! But you! You were supposed to ensure that the rumors and gossip would reach fever pitch, and public sentiment across the land would turn against the king. You have done nothing to accomplish that! So if the deaths were in vain, it is your fault, my friend, not mine. Remember that!"

"I have done my best, I tell you. My agents are everywhere in the market, spreading stories about supernatural events and ill omens. Here in Banavasi they seem to be having some impact. I myself have heard people in the marketplace, speculating about the evil eye and ascribing the deaths to the work of the devil. But this takes time! It's not as easy as poisoning a man – poisoning the minds of people is painstaking work! Unfortunately, we do not have time on our side, all the events are unfolding so rapidly. I had no idea that the king would move forward with his next campaign so soon! A little more time, and we could have had the desired effect, his people would have revolted against any further carnage and waste of public funds. But as it is, they are still basking in the glory of the Ashvamedha. It is devilishly hard to turn the tide of the king's popularity!"

"So what do you suggest?" demanded the other man. "More deaths of innocents? After all, if a few strategic deaths can prevent large scale bloodshed, it might be worthwhile…."

The other voice interrupted sharply. "No! No more senseless deaths. As I said, I should never have agreed to this mad scheme in the first place. This is not the way to achieve our ends. Let us meet the governors again, those who are with us. We will have to carve out a better strategy. Meanwhile, we better lie low and watch our backs. The palace guards are out in force, and the investigation is well underway."

This was followed by silence, after which there was the sound of the door opening and shutting again. The conspirators had left the room.

## iii

Jayadeva set out for the palace early the next morning. He had spent a long time studying the piece of paper that he had confiscated last night. He still did not know who the man was whom he had overpowered in the bushes, but he did know the shocking truth of who had given the letter to him. The source of the letter was not just shocking, it was earth-shaking! When revealed it would cause a major upheaval. Perhaps the king already had some suspicions regarding the ringleaders of the simmering rebellion. But whether or not he did, what Jayadeva had discovered would cause him extreme disquiet.

The contents of the note were extremely interesting. The code used had been complex, and it had taken Jayadeva all night to decode it. He had carefully recorded the exact words – the king was very particular that way, and he did not want to disappoint him.

Early morning was the best time to find the king alone and private. He had strict instructions to ensure that the king was alone in his room before he entered, otherwise his cover would be blown and he would be of no further use to the king. He was not by any means the king's only source of information. He was in fact just one of an army of underground informants, strategically placed all across the kingdom, who reported back regularly to the king himself. Their information was sifted and categorized and examined and interpreted by the king; and none of them had any idea what eventual use the king made of what they conveyed to him. No two of them knew who the other was. They maintained complete incognito and anonymity, and some of them completely disappeared. Those were the terms of their service. Yet, even among this band of informants, Jayadeva thought that the king valued him above the rest. He was the son of a trusted confidant, and he was a fellow warrior – at least on these two counts he was special.

The king greeted Jayadeva warmly. "What do you have for me today?" he asked softly.

Jayadeva cleared his throat before replying, his heart beating uncomfortably loud. It never failed to make him nervous to be in the same room as the king! "Sire, I intercepted a note last night. I have decoded it."

He held out the piece of parchment on which he had recorded the decoded message. The king took it from him and walked towards an oil lamp hanging from the ceiling. He took his time and read it through several times carefully. "It is as I had suspected, then."

Jayadeva bowed deeply and said, "Yes sire, it is as you had suspected. I asked myself three questions based on the evidence, sire – one, who wanted to spoil your triumph? Two, who was powerful enough to pull together the people who could make all the arrangements so neatly? And three, who had the knowledge of poisonous herbs to carry out these murders so successfully? Remembering the the events that had unfolded before my very eyes on the day of the Horse Sacrifice, I felt there was only one answer, but it was unbelievable! Why would such an important man, so highminded as well, want to commit such crimes? But the evidence was clear: a man went into his room alive, but came out barely able to walk and was left for dead only a few yards further. Later, I heard the gossip in the marketplace about important people being unhappy with the money being spent on wars. I started to put two and two together. Here was a person who had both the motive and the means. I think you may have also had your doubts, and perhaps you found it hard to believe that a man of his stature would betray you. But this note confirms it!"

The king turned away and paced about the room, deep in thought. Then he came back to Jayadeva and handed him back the parchment. "We had no evidence earlier, only unhappy conjecture. But this letter spells it out in black and white. It is the evidence we needed to confront him. Make a copy of this and keep it safe. We do not want to risk the only evidence we have going missing. Good work, Jayadeva – but what an unhappy day! With this letter I lose a dear friend."

Jayadeva knew this was the signal for him to withdraw. But he took the liberty of lingering. "Sire, the third question I asked myself remains unanswered. Who has the knowledge of medicinal plants to be able to use them so skillfully? Do you have an idea?"

"I have a rather good idea, Jayadeva," the king replied grimly. "If you had asked me yesterday, I would have said that it was impossible! But today has taught me that even the impossible is possible in these evil times. Leave it to me!"

Jayadeva took the hint. He stepped into the small chamber, and as expected a small desk had been placed there with all the materials he needed to transcribe his note. It was not a very long one; it would not take much time. But even after re-reading it many many times, it still had the power to shock him. The author of the note had addressed it to one of the Governor's of the southern provinces.

*My dear Lakshmana,*

*I am told that the king's forces are gathering again, this time to begin a campaign to the north, at a time when we are yet to recover from the previous bout of adventuring.*

*For those of us who are concerned with the welfare of the people of this land, this additional expense and waste of resources in opportunistic war-mongering is a travesty! The careful planning and execution of the murder of Thimmappayya and subsequently the palace sais will be for nought unless we manage this situation skillfully. The whole point of eliminating the two main figures associated with the Ashvamedha horse was to cast a pall over the celebration of the previous military "victories". But I understand that our agents in the provinces have not spread the word of these inauspicious events widely enough. Our agents here in Banavasi have been more assiduous and therefore more successful. I suggest you motivate the agents to work harder. There needs to be a popular uprising against the king's expansionist and wasteful tendencies, and the best way to do that is to appeal to the people's innate superstitious nature.*

*Let me hear immediately of your plans to bring this about.*

This was followed by the signature and seal of the writer.

*Krishna Rao.*

# Chapter 17

After Jayadeva left, the king paced the room for a long while. It was not simply that he was agitated, he was also deeply saddened. To be betrayed by his own inner circle! He had always thought himself to be a good judge of men, but in this case he had failed miserably. Or perhaps not. He had always thought of Krishna Rao as a profoundly moral man. These recent events proved that this was indeed so. Only, his morals deviated fundamentally from the king's.

Apart from this, he had no idea of how far the rot had spread. Who else had Krishna Rao worked with? At least one other person, and he had a shrewd guess of who that might be. It looked like some of the governors were also implicated. Lakshmana for one – the man addressed in the incriminating letter. Lakshmana was a good friend of his own son, was he also implicated? The king was deeply troubled by this possibility. Times were changing rapidly, and ambitions of the young could brook no delay. Perhaps things had reached this pass that his own son was plotting against him. Delay the distribution of the spoils of war! Why had he done that? Now the logic that had seemed so relentless at the time rang hollow. He should have given the governor's their share immediately, allowed them to also savor some of part of the prize. He had thought he would re-invest the prize and then allow the governors a share of the larger payoff. Had he been so wrong to do that?

Even now, he did not think so. Most of the governors had been able to see the value in his approach. But the disaffected ones had been easy prey for Krishna Rao's subversive tactics! How had he convinced them? He would have had to appeal to their most venal nature. For a man of his moral character, it must have been galling to do so. But the ends justified the means, in this case. Krishna Rao had been willing to play the part of the money-grubbing opportunist so as to win allies for his actual cause – to stop what he termed 'war mongering' in his treacherous letter.

What to do now? Confront the man? Even as resolute a man as the king hesitated at the thought. That noble face, that upright bearing! Was there any chance at all that there could be a mistake somewhere? No, no, there was no chance of that. The evidence of the letter was irrefutable. And Jayadeva had actually heard him in conversation with his agent, and had recognized his voice. So there was no mistake. And a confrontation was inevitable, better gird himself up for it.

He clapped his hands to summon Mada.

"Fetch Siddayya to me," he ordered.

A guard was immediately dispatched to summon Siddayya. He found Siddayya still in his room, looking over some documents. He looked surprised to be summoned to the king's chambers so unceremoniously, but was not unduly perturbed. He had no inkling of what awaited him......

The king greeted him somberly. His ruminations for the past little while had left him feeling low. He beckoned Siddayya into one of the ante-chambers and sat down heavily on a low divan. "What I have to say, I say with a heavy heart, Siddayya. I think our investigation has reached its conclusion."

Siddayya looked at him quickly. "But surely this is good news, sire. If we know who has committed these heinous crimes, then we can immediately bring him to book!"

"It is not so simple, and you will soon understand why. What we have found is this – the murderer is none other than our Prime Minister himself, Krishna Rao. In fact, I should call him worse than a murderer, he is a traitor. He has turned against me, Siddayya! For some reason, one of my most loyal subjects has turned against me. Here, look at this letter." He handed over the piece of parchment that Jayadeva had given him.

Siddayya was aghast. He took the letter wordlessly and read it twice from beginning to end, unable to credit the evidence before his eyes. Nothing had prepared him for this! Not in his wildest dreams could he have imagined that Krishna Rao would turn out to be the culprit. A man whom he had known intimately and worked with on a daily basis – how was it possible that he had not caught even an inkling of such a tendency in him? He had always been dedicated to the kingdom's greater good, and had many times sacrificed his own personal well-being for his king and country. Siddayya was speechless with the horror of it. Not only the fact that his friend and colleague had been capable of this crime, but also the punishment that would now inevitably be meted out to him. Beheading was the punishment for treason, after which the head of the traitor was paraded through the streets for people to jeer and spit at. Siddayya groped for a chair and sat down with a thump. Was this, then, going to be the ignominious end to such a great man? The butt of crude abuse and vicious jibes from the dregs of the city? What had they come to? And why?

The king understood Siddayya's stunned silence. It only echoed his own emotions, after all. But they could not sit silently here forever, so he asked after a while, "What do you think we should do?" It occurred to him that with Krishna Rao gone, Siddayya was probably his closest and most constant confidante.

Siddayya was equally at sea. "He could not have done all this alone, sire?" he questioned, uncertainly. "He must have had some accomplices! We will have to get to the bottom of this!"

"We will, of course, it goes without saying. But the issue is, once we have uncovered the whole cabal, what next? We have no idea who is involved. How many of the governors have been corrupted, how do we ensure that disloyalty is appropriately punished without disturbing the equilibrium completely? This will throw all our plans into complete disarray! How can we move against another kingdom when we ourselves are not united? What if the governors betray me on the battlefield?"

Siddayya knew what the king's real anxiety was – was his own son one of the dissenters? Siddayya personally doubted it, but one had to be certain. And there was only one way. "We will have to bring him in for questioning, sire. Immediately! Before he gets wind that the game is up."

The king knew this was his only choice and yet he dreaded it. To have Krishna Rao taken away in chains, imprisoned, beheaded – it was unthinkable! But it had to be done. He could hardly tolerate treachery within his own inner circle, his own Prime Minister! "Bring him to me. And bring Narayanachar while you are at it," he said, turning away.

"Narayanachar, sire?" Siddayya asked haltingly, not understanding why he was required.

"Just do it, Siddayya," the king commanded.

It did not take long for Siddayya to return, with Krishna Rao and Narayanachar by his side. "Siddayya tells me you need to discuss some political matter, sire?" Krishna Rao inquired politely.

The king stood for a while, his back to Krishna Rao and Narayanachar, staring out of the window. As the moments stretched on, they both knew. They had been discovered. It did not surprise Krishna Rao. In this climate of intrigue, he had expected to be revealed to the king one way or another. It only remained now to figure out who the source had been, and how much he knew. The consequences of discovery worried Krishna Rao not at all. He had known from the start that when it became known – and he had never doubted that it would become known sooner or later – that he would have to pay with his life. He considered this a small price to pay for his cause.

It was quite the contrary for Narayanachar. Never a man of strong character, he crumpled almost at once. Cringing, he approached the king with folded hands. Feeling this was inadequate, he fell at his feet. "My lord, my lord....," he quavered. But even he knew that there was nothing he could say to save himself. The stony coldness of the king's countenance was enough to silence him. Salvaging what he could of his dignity, he rose to his feet again. "It had to be you, Narayanachar. When I heard the peculiarly medical nature of the murders, I suspected you at once. The men could have been bludgeoned to death, they could have been stabbed, they could have been shot with an arrow. But they were not. They were poisoned, and that too with an unusual medical drug that simulated a natural death. Only one person in my acquaintance has the knowhow to do something like that, and that is you. I had not earlier suspected you of working against me Narayanachar, but I began to fear it after these deaths. Your groveling to me now confirms my fears! Take him away," the king commanded Siddayya, who escorted Narayanachar wordlessly into Mada's custody. He did not bother to even look at him. He was no longer his friend.

The king watched Krishna Rao silently. He too stayed silent. He would not volunteer any information. He did not think the king would authorize the use of third degree methods on him, but even if they did, he had no fear. So he stood quietly, waiting for the king to make the first move.

"I have nursed a viper in my bosom, Krishna Rao. That is the hardest thing to bear," the king said, finally turning to face him. His face was drawn with sorrow, his voice heavy. "Why have you done this thing, Krishna Rao? I have raised you to be the highest in the land, you have wielded untold power and influence, you have been my trusted right hand, my closest confidante! Is this the way you repay me? I know you will give me some argument about your principles, your conscientious objection to war. But you are sworn to do the duty of the king! When did you get the idea that you can start using your office to further your own interests, particularly when they were seditious? What have you to say in your defence?"

"I have no defence, sire."

"If you will be intransigent, I cannot help you!"

"You cannot help me anyway, sire. My fate is sealed. I knew it would be this way from the start, I am prepared for it."

"If you tell me who was in this with you, I can make a case for leniency. Nobody will want you to suffer a traitor's end, Krishna Rao. But we need an excuse to make an exception in your case! Give us the names of your accomplices, of the governors who are involved. I will commute your sentence to life in prison."

"You assume that I value my life above the life of my comrades. I do not. You may do with me as you wish. Put me somewhere that I can be alone. I would like to make peace with my maker."

"Krishna Rao! This is no way to reply to the king," Siddayya admonished him. "You have information that has important implications for state policy. You must tell us what you know. Who else was with you? How far has this plot gone? Tell us!"

Krishna Rao laughed drily. "Do you really think I will yield to your exhortations, Siddayya? When I have refused the king? Look on the bright side - maybe with my departure you will finally realize your ambitions! Until now, your preoccupations have been perforce petty, because I had control over the purse strings. But now you can focus your considerable energies on matters more worthy than, for example, waging a war of words on a defenseless girl. Yes, I know what you've been up to Siddayya – sending your agents out into the marketplace to spread stories about that young healer. Could you not find someone your own size to pick on? One day you will see that all your hubris is worth nothing, all it shows is a mind wanting in wisdom. Strive for more wisdom, Siddayya, it will serve you better than spite."

Siddayya's face was by now a mask of hatred. "Like you have striven for wisdom, Krishna Rao? Thanks very much for your advice, but I would rather not be guided on wisdom and maturity by a traitor!"

The king stepped in at this juncture. This was going nowhere. He knew Krishna Rao well enough to know that he would not cave in, no matter how much pressure they put on him. There was nothing to be done but to put him away, and hope that they could discover his accomplices through their network of informants. He clapped his hands, "Mada!"

Mada appeared at once. "Bring me the Commandant of the palace guards," the king instructed him. In a matter of moments, the Commandant appeared. He was dumbfounded by the king's next instruction to him. "Please escort Lord Krishna Rao to the dungeons. Treat him with all due respect. But keep him under heavy guard."

His not to reason why. The Commandant took Krishna Rao into custody, and led him respectfully out of the king's chamber. Outside, he would summon reinforcements, and they would escort the Prime Minister and deposit him in the noisome depths of the palace dungeon. It would be some days before the news became public, and the whole story came out. Until then, this arrest would be treated with the utmost discretion.

After Krishna Rao had been taken away, the king was once again plunged in thought. He was going through challenging times. It would take time before all the circumstances surrounding Krishna Rao's betrayal would become clear to him. He would need to entrust Jayadeva and others with the task of digging up the truth. In the meantime, there was a lot of damage control that needed to be done. And he had an idea on where to start. He knew that he would not only instruct Siddayya to take the lead in the process, but also confront the man with some home truths. If indeed Siddayya was the man to take Krishna Rao's place, then they must start with a clean slate; and Siddayya must realize that the king was not a man to be trifled with. He may speak softly, but he did indeed carry a big stick, and Siddayya should know that he was not afraid to use it.

Starting with the easy part, the king said, "We will need to organize a public meeting, Siddayya. The public need to be told some part of what has transpired in the past few days. Otherwise the rumor mill will proceed unchecked, and we know how that usually ends! Some garbled version of the story will become enshrined as the truth. Instead, I want you to marshall the facts, just the bare minimum, and present them in a public forum. Make the occasion as formal as you like. It should have the ring of authority. You can talk about the two deaths, of the investigation that was launched, and the findings of the investigation. You must stress that there is no question of supernatural forces here; on the contrary, there is every evidence of human agency. It is not the devil we need to fear, but the evil amongst us! Let us make it clear that we are aware of the loose talk that has been going on, and that we are trying to counter such talk by presenting the facts."

"Shall we talk about Krishna Rao and others also, sire?" Siddayya asked.

"No! No, we must not do that yet. That will start another spate of rumors. Let us simply say that the culprits have been apprehended, and their names will be revealed after due process of law, or something like that. You will know how to phrase it."

Siddayya was well pleased with this important role that had been entrusted to him. This would be a difficult public meeting, and the king thought he was the best person to handle it. It was certainly an honour, and Siddayya was fully conscious of it. Which is why what came next hit him like a body blow.

Because now the king started on the awkward part of what he had to say to Siddayya. It was awkward for Siddayya, not so much for the king, who had no problems laying down the law for his officers. "I am told that that young woman Devi's name is still mixed up with that death, Siddayya?"

Siddayya had to admit that the general gossip indicated that it was.

"You need to clear it. She is apparently a promising young woman, and moreover she is the daughter of a respected scholar. We cannot have the riffraff in the streets bandying her name about. I think you are best qualified to make it clear to the opinion-makers that it was no fault of hers that there was a death in the tent that day. In fact, you should make it clear that despite Ranga's wild accusations, the death took place elsewhere altogether. I mean, you know all the facts already, we have discussed it before! There is no need to hint where it actually occurred, I need hardly remind you. But make sure you clear up this matter at the earliest."

"But sire, I have made sure that the girl has been protected from the worst of it – for instance, I have not allowed the guards to proceed against her with criminal charges. Ranga has been pressing for that most strenuously."

"You would do well to remind Ranga that I do not appreciate false accusers. You know and I know that his uncle was dead when Ranga found him. You know and I know who the real culprits are, even if Ranga does not. Why are we then allowing him to persist in spreading this nonsense? I will not stand for it! You will first inform him that he had better cease and desist immediately if he still wants to live in Banavasi. Rusticating him will be a matter of a moment if he does not."

"Yes, sire," Siddayya said humbly. He had better warn Ranga immediately that he was under the king's scrutiny – always a dangerous thing! He had to admit that he had been secretly fanning the flames of Ranga's resentment, and while ostensibly protecting Devi's reputation, also making sure that Ranga's accusations against her persisted. His subtle double game had better stop, he told himself regretfully.

"But I have never allowed anyone to accuse her in my presence, sire." This at least was true. Siddayya had been careful to ensure that he was outwardly on the side of justice. "I have always made it clear at every opportunity that she was innocent of any wrongdoing that day."

"Yes, well, it is not enough, Siddayya! You must be more proactive now, and seek out your contacts. Tell them to spread the word that the girl is innocent."

The king went back to his idea of the public meeting now, having spent as much time as he was willing to on the minor matter of clearing the name of a healer. It was a while before Siddayya was free to go, and when he was, his first stop was the house of Ranga. It did not take him long to communicate the king's message to him. Ranga was taken aback, and shaken to have come to the notice of the king in such an unwelcome manner. "Who has been speaking to the king about this?" he demanded from Siddayya.

"I have no idea, but I will find out. In any case, that need not concern you right now. Your main concern is that you stop your baseless accusations and start quietly enjoying the rather large fortune you have inherited from your uncle! This large house and all this land were his, were they not?"

Siddayya looked about him and keenly observed a rather comfortable house, surrounded by several acres of cultivated land, where Ranga was now looking quite comfortably settled.

"Yes, my uncle had no son of his own. I was like a son to him." Ranga seemed to consider the possibility of trying on some tears, and then decided against it, since his audience was hardly likely to be impressed by such a demonstration of crocodile tears.

Siddayya then delivered a few more words of warning to Ranga and went on his way. He knew what he had to do next, and it was not a visit that he was keen on making. The last time he had been there, at least he had been able to strike terror to her heart with his veiled insinuations.

But today he had to go and see her as a result of the king's direct order. He resented it intensely, but had no choice. To be groveling to that girl! His blood boiled. But he realized that this was a task that he would have to undertake, and the sooner he finished it the better. It was too late now, of course – it was already pitch dark, and the girl had chosen to set herself up in some benighted village several miles out of town. Siddayya sighed regretfully. Much as he would have preferred to have had this interview over and done with, he would have to put it off until the next morning.

ii

The next day dawned bright and early as usual for Devi. Getting ready quickly, she started her clinic, dealing efficiently with the line of patients waiting outside. The morning was well advanced when Devi had the unpleasant experience of having Siddayya in her midst again. His entrance was typical – she had never known Siddayya to be anything but rude. He pushed aside some of the patients standing outside the door and barged into the room where Devi was seated. She started up in surprise at the sight of him. He was the very last person she would have expected to show up at her door! Surely there had not been another death that the king wanted her to investigate!

She stood up to greet him, because no matter how objectionable his manner, he was a senior member of the king's entourage, and as such, she would be well advised to be respectful to him.

"You are a clever girl," Siddayya surveyed her sardonically. "Much cleverer than I ever gave you credit for. Your father made out that all your intelligence and talent lay in your healing abilities, but now I know that you are also both shrewd and calculating. Who did you approach to speak to the king on your behalf?"

Devi was completely taken aback. She had no idea what the man was talking about and was unused to being confronted in this offensive manner. All the patients had crowded around, knowing that some very important person had arrived, and they wanted to watch the excitement first hand.

"If you don't mind, sir, let us withdraw to another room," she said quietly, and walked towards the kitchen.

Nagi marched purposefully behind Devi, not letting her darling out of her sight for a minute. And behind Nagi hurried Kumari, observing the newcomer with wide-eyed keenness. When they were in the relative silence of the kitchen, Devi turned back to her visitor and said, "Sir, I don't know why you are here or in what manner I can help you. Perhaps you have had a wasted trip, because I don't know what you are talking about!"

"Yes, yes, that is what I thought you would say. Naturally that is your response! But I know better. Why would the king himself take up your cause if you had not approached him in some manner? Who was it that you employed to make a case for you with the king? It must be someone quite high placed, because he or she was able to get the ear of the king alright. I doubt it was your father's handiwork – although he did have a few minutes alone with the king the other day, perhaps he used them to his advantage. But if you have employed anyone else in this, you might as well tell me and get it over with – I will find out eventually anyway!"

After overcoming her initial dread of the man, Devi was beginning to get more than a little irritated with him. What on earth was he harping about? She had no idea what he meant by his repeated accusation. Sifting through what he had just said, it seemed clear that the king had in some way taken up her case and asked Siddayya to do something. What was that something? And since she had not come remotely close to the king, who was it who had spoken on her behalf? This was all completely mysterious, and she wished the man would stop hectoring her and leave her alone to try and figure it out for herself.

"Sir, I really have no idea to what you are referring," Devi replied haltingly. "If you say the king has taken up my case, then I am pleased and grateful. But indeed, if you tell me that it was not my father's efforts that have borne fruit, then I have no idea who else it could be! I know no one, and I have met nobody. Nobody has come here. All I have here is my small team of helpers. You can see them, and I assure you none of them has any contacts that could have brought about a change of heart in someone as exalted as the king."

"Then how do you account for it?" Siddayya challenged her. "The king summoned me yesterday and demanded that I do more to clear your good name. I would have thought I had done enough, but no! Apparently I need to do more. I am expected to put myself out for a presumptuous chit of a girl like you! Things have come to a pretty pass!"

"May I ask, sir, what is it that you have done already to help me out of my difficulties? I ask because my difficulties have been quite pronounced. I know there is all manner of cheap gossip being spread about me in the town. So if you have done something, I am grateful, but I wish that the impact had been more obvious."

"Oh ho ho! Getting cheeky eh? This is the result of letting you girls get above yourselves! I blame your mother for this, more than even your father. He is an intellectual, a dreamer. He probably does not realize the incipient evil in allowing girls so much of freedom. But women know these things! Your mother would have known what the result of all this education would be! Why did she not get you married, tell me that? She could have gotten you off her hands readily enough – your appearance is quite comely, and you come from a good family, at least as far as we know. Your true origins remain a mystery, I am told."

Devi was practically reeling from the repeated blows this man was dealing her, seemingly effortlessly. It was Nagi who stepped into the breach to stop the man's incessant bullying. While remaining respectful – barely – she managed to establish that he could not get away with this type of behavior. "Sir, I think you are getting away from the purpose of your visit. I think it will be better if we all keep a civil tongue in our heads. Please just tell us why you are here and then you can be going on your way."

Siddayya eyed her coldly, but decided not to take her on. He looked at Kumari as well, and turned away from her without bothering to disguise his distaste. "People with incurable diseases should not be allowed to mix with normal people," he said angrily to Devi.

"None of us in this room has an incurable disease, sir. Unless you have some problem for which you are under treatment?"

Siddayya glared at her and said, "Don't try me too far, girl. You think that just because you have got someone to twist the king's arm, you can ride roughshod over me? You can think again! I have to do the king's bidding this time, but don't think I won't get my own back sometime. So far I have protected you from any criminal charges arising out of that Thimmappayya's death, but next time you will not get off so easy."

"You did not have to protect me, as you put it, from any criminal charges!" Devi responded hotly. "The king himself knows that I was in no way culpable in that death! And far from protecting me, I have heard it said all over the marketplace that you have been spreading rumors about me, casting aspersions on my competence and my intelligence! My father has heard these rumors himself! Can you deny that?"

Siddayya did not bother to respond to her question. He stared at her for a long moment and then said, "I will do what the king has asked, which is to clear you of any vestige of suspicion in this death. He has also asked me to re-instate your reputation, and I have no choice but to do it. But beware of me in the future! I am not the man you should have chosen to cross. You will have to pay the price for your insolence some day and I will be the one who chooses when and how."

With this veiled threat, he marched out back the way he had come and then out of the clinic altogether. Devi, Nagi and Kumari stood in stunned silence for a few minutes. Then Nagi sniffed scornfully. "Full of bluster, that's all! He didn't have the nerve to confront your father or your brother – he comes all the way here knowing that you will be here on your own! What a coward! He has been firmly ticked off by the king, that's what it is! So this is his tantrum, and he chose to throw it here! Don't worry Devi – he cannot do anything to you. Do not lose any sleep over it!"

Devi was feeling somewhat calmer after a few minutes of reflection. Nagi was right. Siddayya could rant and rave as much as he liked, but it amounted to nothing. She was innocent, she knew it and he knew it. So there was no way that he could get her into trouble, even though he dearly would like to. "I wonder what he's going to do to clear your name, as he puts it?" Nagi asked.

"Do not ask me! He was speaking in riddles as usual. But we should find out soon enough. Whatever it is, I think it will have to be quite public, which is why he is so furious. I'm sure he would have preferred to just have his dirty work done by his agents. They would have gone around the marketplace trying to reverse the damage they have done all these days. But it looks like, for some reason, the king has told him that he must do this himself, personally! This is going to be fun!"

### iii

It was much later that evening that Kumari came and sat next to Devi. They sat in silence for a while, Devi contemplating her eventful morning. Siddayya's visit had definitely preoccupied her for much of the day. What on earth had he thought he would accomplish? Now in retrospect, Devi was a bit amused by the whole tone of the encounter. Had he seemed a bit desperate? She wondered. It was as if he was trying to see if she would let him off scot free. What had he thought she would say, "Don't worry, sir, I will spend the rest of my life under a cloud so that you need not embarrass yourself on my behalf?" How laughable! Why would she do a thing like that, and why did he imagine she would want to save him from his current discomfiture?

She was deeply immersed in these thoughts when Kumari spoke. "I know that man, akka," she said in a low voice. "I think I recognize him."

At first Devi was disoriented. "Which man? There were so many here today," she said, thinking of all the various patients in the clinic that morning.

"That man Siddayya. I know him," she said again.

"Know him?" Devi was puzzled. "You mean you have seen him before?"

Kumari nodded. "Many times," she whispered. "I think I have seen him many many times, akka." A tear rolled down her face.

Devi reached towards her, now really concerned. "Kumari, what is it? Why are you so distressed? Tell me, please."

"Akka, I think that man is my father," Kumari whispered. Devi was stunned.

Kumari gathered herself now. "He is my father, I think, akka. I am almost sure. When he came here the other day to take you away, I got a shock. It was as if I had seen a ghost. That night I had a very vivid dream, and in it I was a small child. There was a figure in it, a mean and evil figure, and that figure was my father. It is many years since I saw him, but I was old enough to remember him well. I could almost swear that he is the man who threw me out of the house, never wanting to see my scarred face again."

Devi was silent, contemplating the horror of what this child had gone through. "What happened, Kumari? Tell me what you remember."

"I do not remember much, akka. I remember the day my parents saw the patches on my skin. I had seen the patches many weeks before, but I had hidden them. Somehow I knew it was something I should hide, I don't know why. I think my mother had also seen them, but she never said anything to me about it, or to my father. Then one day by chance my father saw me playing out in the sun, and he spotted it immediately. He dragged me to the brightest light and examined me closely. My mother was terrified, I could see. She begged my father to take me to a doctor. But he did not listen to her. He decided that I must be sent away or I would shame the family! I don't know what would have happened if my mother had had her way, and we had seen a doctor. He would probably have told them that it was not kushta roga, but just some skin condition that could be cured with the proper treatment. I suppose my life could have been different then."

"You mean your parents abandoned you because of this skin condition? My god, how evil! And you think that this Siddayya is that same father! I would like to go to him and tell him exactly what he did to his daughter! It would have been better if he had killed you!"

"Sometimes I also used to think that, akka. But they drove me out of the house. They handed me over to the scavenger who came to our house every day to collect refuse and told him to take me home with him, and paid him some small amount of money to do that. I remember my mother crying a lot. The scavenger took me to his village, and I stayed with him and his wife for a few months. But the money soon ran out and anyway he had no affection for me. He was a drunkard, and so was his wife. They were used to spending their evenings with their friends, and they didn't want me to be hanging around. Then the man started to say that the disease would spread to the rest of his family and friends, so he just threw me out of the house. After that I just roamed around, coming back to their house for food whenever I got hungry and then taking off again. And then he died of some fever or other, and I do not know what happened to his wife. She left that house and went away somewhere. So even if we want to ask her if this man is actually my father, I don't know where to find her."

Devi hardly knew what to say or do. This was too big for her to handle, she needed some help. She could not go to Nagi – somehow she felt that would be a betrayal of the confidence that Kumari had placed in her. The only person she could tell was Udaya, and she knew that Kumari would find that acceptable too. But it was too late to do anything about it now. This would have to be resolved only in the morning. She explained this to Kumari, to make sure that she was comfortable with the idea. "Yes, it is alright if you tell Udaya, akka. But what will you do after that?"

"I'm not sure yet," Devi replied grimly. "But we must do something. We cannot let that man get away with this evil thing that he has done. Did you see the way he looked at you even this morning? As if it polluted him just to look at you. 'People with incurable diseases should not be allowed to mix with normal people'" Devi mimicked him. "Normal people indeed! Evil people like him should not be allowed to mix with normal people! No, we must confront him with this knowledge, and we must do it soon. He has gone away from here uttering threats against me – well, he will learn that he has spoken too soon. This will neutralize him completely, you mark my words! But I am sorry you have had to face this today, Kumari. I hope you are not too disturbed by it?"

Kumari appeared quite composed however, after her initial show of emotion. But she was withdrawn, and did not seem inclined to say anything more on the topic. Devi let her be, and did not probe any further. She would deal with this startling new development in the morning. Today had been disturbing enough already!

# Chapter 18

The next morning they were all awakened by a loud thumping on the door. It was barely dawn yet. Devi jumped up with a start, not knowing what to think. To her relief, they heard a familiar voice shouting, "Open up! Open up, you lazybones!" It was Udaya, and he came in laughing to see their expressions of alarm. "Are you all still asleep? I thought people kept early hours in the rural districts!"

"It is early," Devi replied crossly. "What on earth are you doing up at this hour anyway? It's barely daybreak."

"As you know, we are up well before daybreak in our household. Father goes to the river when it is still dark, and has to start his prayers before daybreak. Have you forgotten our daily routine so soon? Nagi, get me something hot to drink. I left home before mother could prepare anything to eat. A glass of milk will do for now."

Nagi hurried off to get everyone something hot to drink, and Devi questioned Udaya again. "No, really, why are you here at this hour? Has there been some crisis? Surely you didn't come all this way just to see what people do in rural districts in the wee hours of the morning!"

"No, my dear sister. I came to give you the news, and to take you all back to town with me. The news is…..and I heard this at the river this morning from a very reliable source…..that a town meeting has been called to day. And you will not believe what the meeting is about!"

They were all agog, hanging on to his every word. "It is about you, Devi! Now, aren't you surprised? Yes, Siddayya has called a town meeting to talk about you and to tell everyone what a fine healer you are, without a stain on your character. Isn't that rich?"

Devi could hardly believe her ears. So this was what he had had in mind yesterday! "I knew he was planning something, but this is definitely a surprise," she said to her brother. "He was here yesterday, you know. He says I have used my contacts to put in a good word for me with the king, after which the king has put some pressure on Siddayya to make things right for me. Can you believe that! I mean, imagine me having any contacts at all, let alone of a level who would actually have access to the king! It would be laughable, except Siddayya was completely convinced of it. He kept badgering me to tell him my contact's name. Then he threatened me with dire consequences for having taken such a step and he stomped off!"

Udaya was thunderstruck at this development. "What! I had no idea! When did all this happen? Tell me all the details!"

So Devi quickly told him all about Siddayya's visit on the previous morning, before running into her room to get ready for her trip into town. "Get ready everyone!" she exhorted the girls. "Let's all go to town to hear what the great Siddayya has to say! It will be a treat to listen to, I am sure. Make haste! We need to leave soon so that we are there in time!"

Hurriedly swallowing the hot glass of ragi malt that Nagi had made for everyone, they all congregated in the front yard in record time. Udaya had come on his horse, and Devi's bullock cart was pressed into service to transport the rest of them. They set off as if to a carnival – any trip into town was high entertainment as far as they were concerned!

## ii

The morning found Siddayya in a foul mood. Announcing that the murders had been solved was fine with him – in fact, he would enjoy that duty. But to have to kowtow to that girl, and to have to make a public spectacle of it! But he had no choice and he was mindful of that. The report would have to go back to the king that he, Siddayya, had done something spectacular in her, Devi's, support. There were many unpleasant pills that a man had to swallow in public life, and this was one of them. His entire household was hopping to his command this morning, nobody wanting to be on the receiving end of his wrath. His wife helped him complete his morning prayers and then stood aside while he doled out the holy water to all the men in the household. He ignored her. He had always ignored her, and she was beyond being resentful about it. In fact, it had been many years now that she had completely withdrawn from public life. Her interaction with her husband and others in the household was as minimal as possible. The less she needed to speak, think, interact, the better she liked it. She sought out the peace and silence of her room for the better part of the day. His treatment of her was no worse than the way a lot of men treated their wives. He was not physically abusive. He was not even verbally abusive – he barely addressed her if he could help it.

No, his cruelty towards her was different, something worse than being treated as if she did not exist. That she could have borne with equanimity; there was no love lost between them. Some women compained that their husbands treated them like animals. To her, that would be an improvement on the way her husband treated her! After all, animals were often petted and loved, they were well looked after, people spoke to them, took them out for walks.

In her case, the way her husband had treated her was something she could not bear to think about, let alone speak out loud. She marveled at her own strength of mind that she had managed to retain her sanity after what he had done to her. She wished she could put it completely out of her head, go deliciously insane – but she was not able to do that. So she did the next best thing by isolating herself from all human contact as far as possible. Despite that, it would keep intruding back into her consciousness, most unexpectedly, at least once every day. Every single day, at least once, her thoughts went back to that terrible day, and the terrible thing her husband had done all those years ago …..

Siddayya finished his religious rituals and marched out of the house. No one from the household accompanied him. They all knew that there was some unpleasant task that he needed to complete this morning, and he did not want anyone from his household to witness it. As he walked out into the market street, he saw to his disgust that word had gotten around and the crowds were beginning to gather. He should have guessed, he thought bitterly! All his enemies would gather like vultures around the kill! And they would have invited all their friends, and their friend's friends. The towncriers had also been out since the morning, apparently with some success. People had come out of their homes in droves. It was not everyday that they had an opportunity to witness the humiliation of Siddayya, and there were many who felt that he had it coming. So many years of arrogance, so little goodwill to his fellow man! It was inevitable that people would rejoice at his downfall.

Today was the day, and that girl was the cause. He would not forget this in a hurry. She was sure to be there, along with her family – that holier-than-thou Vaman Bhat, always taking the high road, and that brother of hers, taking up with that new fangled religion. He could never understand a man like Vaman Bhat, a slave to his children! He himself would not have stood for this type of independence of spirit. Children were sent into this world to uniformly satisfy their parent's desires and, in the case of boys, their ambitions. They were not supposed to express their own wishes and explore their own destinies, and any parent who allowed that sort of nonsense within his household was just a weakling! Vaman Bhat was the epitome of parental weakness, and Siddayya heartily despised him for it. All those feeble arguments he kept putting forward to excuse his daughter's wayward behavior – any other father would have whipped her into submission long ago! Instead she had been encouraged to be a free spirit, and it had gone to her head. Even yesterday, what insolence in her tone of voice, and the way she had looked him straight in the eye! If he had a daughter, he would never have allowed her to get away with such behavior.

If he had a daughter......

Siddayya shook his head to clear it of all thought. He did not intend to get distracted from his avowed purpose today. His long determined strides had brought him to his destination. A podium had been set up in the central square of the marketplace, and there was a buzz of sound from the people already gathered there. There was yet a bit of time before he needed to get started. His friends were standing in the sidelines, and he recognized Ranga with a companion, both standing together and chatting in low tones. They spied him as he arrived, and started forward to greet him and commiserate with him on what he had to do.

The sun had risen high in the sky by now, and all the people were gathering around, curious to see what the show was about. Siddayya decided it was about time that he got this over with. He stepped onto the podium and addressed the gathered crowd. As he had guessed, he saw the girl and her family ranged in the back. He saw many other familiar faces as well. "Friends!" he began, although he knew there were not all that many in the crowd whom he could count on as a friend. "Friends! Thank you all for coming here this morning. I have been wanting to speak to all of you for some days now, as I have some important messages for you. I thought this was a good way to bring all of you together in one place at one time."

"Liar! You didn't want to speak to these people at all!" thought Devi to herself, although she maintained silence so that he could continue.

"I do not want to take up much of your time. As you know, in a big city such as ours, many stories, many rumors, get started. Many such rumors are harmless, and can be laughed off or ignored. But there are some rumors which can cause a person grievous harm, and they cannot be laughed off. I do not mean bodily harm, my friends! But even worse, they cause mental and emotional distress, and this cannot be allowed to happen in our great kingdom."

"There have been some instances of this in the recent past, and there is a need to clear the air. Some days ago you all were here to witness the great spectacle of the Horse Sacrifice." An appreciative roar went up from the crowd. "Yes, it was a great spectacle and showed the greatness of our king, the Maharajadhiraja Kakushtavarman, the king of kings, the greatest king in his line, the greatest king we are ever likely to see. His victories are legendary, and it was only right that he celebrates in a fitting manner. I think you will all agree that the celebration was a great success, and that none of you had ever witnessed its like ever before in your lives!" The crowd roared in approval again – they had never before and would probably never again witness that type of pomp and grandeur.

"Yet, on that day of great celebration, there were some evil spirits around, my friends! Not everyone who was here that day came with a pure heart. Some of us suffered terrible losses that day as a result. This is my close friend and associate Ranga – Ranga, step forward!" Ranga stepped into the central clearing for all to see. "Ranga, my friends, suffered a terrible loss that day. His uncle died in mysterious circumstances! You may ask, how did Ranga's uncle die? That we do not know. All we know is that Ranga lost his uncle that day. As a dutiful nephew, he brought his uncle to the place where he hoped he would get some help. As you know, my friends, the king had made all arrangements for your comfort on that day. For your food, for your shelter, for you to take some rest, and – for the very first time – for you to get the benefit of a healer, in case anybody should fall ill while visiting this great city. This was a great and good thing for the king to have done, I think you will agree!" A loud cheer went up again from the crowd – they all agreed!

"The king ensured that this healer was an extremely competent young woman. You can see her there, my friends, standing in the back, with her loving and supportive family. The young lady's name is Devi. Now, there may be some of you who feel that healing is not an appropriate pastime for a young woman, but rid yourselves of such prejudices, my friends! This young woman – Devi, you can see her standing in the back – she is an extremely competent young woman, and has many followers who visit her regularly at her clinic. She has been well trained for many years through the dedication of her father, the respected Vaman Bhat, who is even now standing at her side." Many curious glances were cast at Devi and her family.

"Ranga ran to the tent of this young woman, Devi, hoping that she could revive him with her skills. But the unfortunate truth, my friends, was that Ranga's uncle had already reached his final abode. There was nothing to be done for him. Whatever the reason, by the time Ranga found his uncle, he had already expired and nothing could have been done to save him. I know there are some of you who are spreading the vicious rumor that this young woman could have saved Ranga's uncle if she had been more skilled. But this is not true! There is no magic known to man, even in the holiest of holy scriptures, that can revive a dead person! So although this young woman Devi pursued an extremely professional course of action, and provided whatever help and succour she could under the circumstances, there was no way that she could have revived Ranga's uncle. He was already dead, my friends, this is something you must all remember, especially when you hear someone trying to cast aspersions on the competence of this young healer."

"So I want to make it clear that this young woman bears no responsibility for the unfortunate death that day of Ranga's uncle. She is a dedicated and skillful healer, even though some of us might feel that healing is best left to men, and home-making is the real domain of the woman. That is only an opinion, and we should not let that color our assessment of her abilities. The king himself has placed his confidence and trust in her. If he can do so, then certainly we can all do so without any hesitation."

"But this is a minor matter, I have something more to say! After the death of Ranga's uncle, there was another death. This time it was the sais of the Ashvamedha horse, the man who had been responsible for that horse's health and well-being. Many of you may have heard of this. And many of you decided to put two and two together and come up with a fantastic story that there was bad luck associated with the Ashvamedha itself. For those of you who were spreading such stories – here is the truth! The culprit has been apprehended! Yes, we have caught the person responsible for those deaths. The Commandant of the guards, who is here to day – there he is, ladies and gentlemen, please show your appreciation of the the wonderful job he and his colleagues do in guarding our beloved king," and here the crowd cheered obligingly, "he launched a thorough investigation and was able to apprehend the real murderer. It was not by any supernatural means that these people met their death. They were murdered by a human being! And that human being has been captured and will face the full majesty of the law for his actions! So you all can stop speculating about the circumstances of those deaths, and you can certainly stop imagining that it is the work of the devil!"

Siddayya looked like he was going to say something else, but then he abruptly left the podium, signaling the end of the meeting. People lingered for a few minutes, and then realizing that the show was over, they started to leave to go about their business. But Devi was not yet done with Siddayya. "Come on," she commanded Udaya, who followed close behind her as she threaded her way through the crowd, making a beeline towards Siddayya's receding back. Vaman Bhat knew what his daughter's mission was. While they had waited for Siddayya to appear, she had told her father and her brother about Kumari's revelation to her last evening. They had been horrified, but completely supportive of whatever move she deemed fit. She was in favor of confronting the man, and they too felt that this was a reasonable course of action. After all, there was no reason to withhold this information as some sort of trump card. With this public assertion of his support for Devi's healing activities, Siddayya had done all that he could for them. Now their only desire was that he leave them severely alone. If their paths never ever crossed again, that would be fine with Devi. So the information that she held could only be used to ensure that he stayed out of their lives.

What better way to ensure that than to alert him to the fact that the diseased daughter whom he had evicted from his house was now a welcome guest at Devi's clinic? His fear of exposure should permanently keep him far away from her, Devi figured!

Siddayya was striding rapidly away, and would probably get away despite Devi's hurrying as fast as she could in his wake. "Sir, sir!" she called out, hoping to catch his attention. She did. He turned around to see who was calling after him, and stopped short when he caught sight of her. He waited for her and Udaya to catch up with him.

"Sir, we wanted to thank you for what you just did," Devi wanted to throw the man off his guard. "It was very good of you to have called this town meeting so that you could make a public announcement to clear my name."

Siddayya turned to show a truly frightening visage, a mixture of fury and dislike in the look he directed at her. "You have no reason to thank me," he retorted in almost a snarl. "I did not do it for you! If I had been given a choice, I would not have done it at all! But a report had to go back to the highest authorities that I had made a public demonstration of this sort, and now I am absolved of any blame with regard to you. Any disasters that befall you in future will be of your own making, and you can dig yourself out through you own efforts. Don't count on any help from me!"

"In fact," and here he stepped closer with a distinct air of menace, "In future, you can count on me to trouble you whenever I get the slightest chance. Do you understand me? I will be watching you. The slightest slip up, the slightest stumble, and I will bring you down without any compunction! In all these years, no one has caused me as much trouble as you have! So you better watch out, because I will be watching you!"

Devi was glad he had started threatening her in this manner, because it gave her the perfect reason to retaliate. "Don't be so sure! I may be the one who will bring you down, sir! Fate brings about all kinds of twists and turns in our lives. We never know when our past may come back to haunt us."

Siddayya did not understand this new direction that the conversation had taken. "What are you blabbering about?" he asked contemptuously. "What is all this rubbish you are talking about fate and the past? You maybe worried about your past, but I have nothing there to frighten me!"

"Are you so sure, sir?" Devi asked him softly. "We all have done things that we later are ashamed of, or regret. Can you really be an exception? I think not."

Now Siddayya was more watchful. He began to sense that she had something up her sleeve, but could not guess at what she was hinting. The things he had to hide, she had no way of finding out. Surely?

Devi continued. "For example, I think it maybe the case that you once had a daughter…."

Siddayya started and blanched a ghastly white. "And perhaps you threw that daughter out, when she was a mere child, into the outer darkness, into the hands of the wolves that lurk there…."

"Now, why did you do that, sir?" Answer came there none. Siddayya looked like he had seen a ghost, and was incapable of rational thought, let alone any speech. "Because you thought she had an incurable disease, a disease moreover that would cast a stigma on your whole family. Kushta roga, that is what you thought, is it not? And we all know what happens to lepers and their families. You would have been drummed out of town, forced to live on the fringes of society, with all the other untouchables. All your plans, your insatiable ambition, would have been cast to the four winds! Far from being an advisor to the king, you would have been an outcast, despised by all."

"So what did you do? You did not even take the poor child to a healer to confirm your fears. The healer might have started to spread rumors! So instead, you gave her to the scavenger, with some money for her upkeep. Do you know what the scavenger did with your daughter and the money? Would you like me to tell you?" Again there was utter silence. Siddayya seemed to be in a daze, as if he had been overtaken by some terrible nightmare. "I'll take that as a yes. He kept the money, and left the girl in the wilderness, to fend for herself. That's what he did! Unfortunately he is now dead, so we cannot go and mete out any justice to him, but hopefully his sins have caught up with him in the afterlife. But the wonder of it is that the little girl, in spite of all the cruelty she had already faced, from her own father, the man whom she should have been able to count on to guard and protect her – that little girl still had a tremendous will to live! Yes, sir – that little girl, whom you had put out of your life and out of your mind for all these years – she is still alive!"

"She has lived for many many years like an animal, abused and mistreated by all those around her, filthy, with only scraps of cloth to cover her nakedness, eating raw meat and food that people had thrown away as not fit to eat. Yet she has survived, and my brother and I have been able to rescue her from her horrific existence and give her a new life."

Siddayya now made a strangled sound, whether pleading or tormented, it was hard to tell. "Yes, she now lives with me. I would have brought her here with me, but I did not want to put her through the trauma of confronting you. The girl that you saw yesterday at my clinic, whom you shunned as being diseased, that is her! After all these years, she was still able to recognize her father when she saw him. And do you know the final irony of all this, sir? She does not have kushta roga at all! She has some abnormality in the pigmentation of her skin, that is all! She is under treatment from my father, and will slowly improve over a period of time. So you lost a daughter, and proved yourself to be lacking in any moral fiber or humanity, all for nothing! If you had had even a vestige of love for anything but your own self aggrandizement, if you had taken the child to a healer, you would have found this out ages ago. The poor child need not have gone through all those horrific experiences. She could have had a happy childhood, with her mother and brothers and sisters by her side. Instead you condemned her to a living hell! Let that be on your conscience, if you still have one, for the rest of your living days!"

Devi saw that Siddayya was at the end of his rope. She decided to end the interview, but not before she drove home her point. "So do not come threatening me with dire consequences, sir. If you try to cause trouble for me ever again, the consequences for you will be far worse. We have Kumari – that is the name we have given your daughter. If you make it your business to undermine me or any members of my family in any way at all, Kumari will be more than happy to come forward and tell her story. We will organize a town meeting just like this one, and announce to one and all the type of man you really are! Your political career will come to an abrupt halt after that, I think I can guarantee. Do not forget this conversation, because I mean every word I say!"

Devi turned on her heel and walked away without a backward glance. She had no interest in what became of Siddayya – let him collapse with shock, let him die! she thought viciously to herself. After what he had done, no fate could be bad enough for him!

Her thoughts were a jumble, and she marched through the markerplace, hardly knowing what direction she was taking. That whole scene had taken its emotional toll on her, and she suddenly felt cold and exhausted. Udaya came breathlessly up to her, and caught her by the arm. "Devi, Devi! Slow down. Calm down! Where are you going? You are just racing off in some direction! Come, let us go home. Mother will give you something to eat, and then you can lie down for a while before you go back to your house. This has been quite a morning for you! Come, let me take you home."

Udaya gradually coaxed her into a more stable frame of mind, and took her to her father's house. There she found her parents waiting eagerly for them to return, and greeted Devi with a barrage of questions. Then, taking one look at her daughter, Sita stopped Vaman Bhat in his tracks. "I think we better let the poor girl rest," she said gently, taking her daughter inside into the cool central hall of the house. "Lie down, child. I will bring you some hot milk to drink and some of the sweet pumpkin halwa I made this morning.

You need to restore your energy! It has all been too much for you, the physical and emotional strain. Lie down and let us take care of you for a while. Even independent young ladies sometimes need to be looked after by their parents!"

Devi smiled wanly at her mother, but submitted to her tender care. It was a relief to have such loving parents, and she was particularly conscious of how blessed she was in this regard – not everyone could count on it!

ii

After a little while, Devi felt well enough to attempt the journey home. Both her parents tried to persuade her to stay the night, but she was adamant. There was plenty of work to be done at home. Besides, she was not an invalid! She had been a bit overcome by the events of the morning, but she was young and fit, and she could take it.

Vaman Bhat saw off his daughter and her helpers and then decided he would go into office. He had been neglecting his duties all day, and there were a few matters that needed his immediate attention.

They set off at a brisk pace, and went only a short distance when they came upon a road block. There were an inordinate number of people milling around as well as a long line of horses and carts, and they all seemed to be heading towards some attraction a little further down the road. Children were shrieking in excitement and even women who looked like respectable housewives were racing along to see whatever it was. Since this was usually a quiet rural road, Devi was taken aback at this unexpected circumstance. After some minutes of futile waiting, Devi instructed the cartman to go and check what the excitement was all about. They sat waiting for a while for him to return, and then Nagi lost her patience and said, "Let me go! This chap of ours seems to have got lost, or so carried away by whatever entertainment is going on that he has decided to abandon us to our fate!"

Devi tried to stop her, since there was no telling when the mood of the crowd would turn, but Nagi would have none of it. She clambered off the cart and set off determinedly to see for herself what the crowd was gawking at. She was quick to return, and when she did she was grinning broadly. "What is it?" Devi asked impatiently.

Nagi let out a guffaw. "What a bunch of fools these people are! They are all willing to drop everything to go watch this complete charlatan in action! Can you believe it – there is some guy dressed up like a complete clown, putting on a show. He has this poor woman lying on the ground, and he is claiming that he will rid her of her demons. She is lying there shaking and moaning and he is chanting some mumbo-jumbo over her. Of course, he has his little basket on the ground for any coins people might want to throw to him! It is completely idiotic – I could not bear to watch!"

Devi smelled something rotten here. "A clown dressed outlandishly? Does he have a name?"

"Yes! And this is the best part! He is calling himself Shambhu Maharaj, can you believe it! What a fake name – but quite a brilliant stroke on his part, I must say. It conjures up all sorts of images, of great wizards and shamans. This whole crowd has fallen for his act alright! More power to him. But meanwhile, we have to cool our heels here, until that woman is finally rid of her so-called demons! Hope he gets it done quick."

"Shambhu Maharaj! That is the same fellow I told you about Nagi, the fellow who had Kumari in his clutches that day when we rescued her!" Kumari had shrunk back into a dark corner of the cart; just the sound of the man's name brought back the most fearful memories for her. "Don't you worry Kumari," Devi assured her. "Nothing will happen to you. Just stay here quietly with Nagi. I want to go and see what my old friend Shambhu Maharaj is up to. This talk about ridding a woman of demons is sounding suspiciously familiar! You all wait here!" Devi hopped off the cart and made her determined way to the front of the crowd.

Sure enough, there was a familiar figure holding forth in the center of the large crowd. "Behold, ladies and gentlemen!" he was shouting for the benefit of those who had recently joined the audience. "Behold this woman! All the people here have been watching her for some time. Look at how she is possessed of the devil! Look how she shivers and shakes – that is the devil in her, the devil that possesses her, body and soul! The devil has made her do terrible things! Only yesterday, she ate a live baby, I tell you! But it was not her fault, ladies and gentlemen – it was the fault of the devil! But today, I will bring about a miracle. With my knowledge of magical incantations, I will rid her of the devil before your very eyes! This is a very dangerous business – I might lose my life in the process! But I am willing to do it – I am willing to even sacrifice my own life so that this woman may be saved from the devil!" A gasp ran through the crowd. Devi rolled her eyes in exasperation and pushed herself further towards the front. Obviously Shambhu Maharaj had seen the rich possibilities of the act she and Udaya had put on the other day – clever showman! She couldn't blame him for trying to make a quick buck, but he should know that she was well aware of the little game he was playing.

With single-minded elbowing, she finally reached the front row. Shambhu Maharaj did not notice her at first, and continued with his nonsense without any pause. Devi realized that he would have to wind up soon, because the woman was slowly losing consciousness and slipping into a deep sleep. He would pretty soon have to declare her devil-free and bundle her off, before she started snoring! Devi decided to make her presence known. "Shambhu!" she called to him. He started at the sound of a familiar voice. Then he looked closely and paled at the sight of this familiar face. He soon recovered himself, and approached her rapidly. "Akka, how are you? So happy to see you! You maybe surprised to see me here and to see what I am doing!"

"Not at all," Devi said to him cordially. "I would expect no less from you. Now I suggest you complete your act quickly before the woman falls asleep! You get my meaning?"

Shambhu Maharaj got her meaning perfectly. Nodding energetically, he hurried back to the center of the clearing, and seizing the woman's arm, he proceeded to chant some long and complicated incantation. Devi did not understand a word of what he said – it sounded like some language she had never heard before. No doubt it was a list of herbs in his own language, or maybe the names of his relatives! Whatever it was, the crowd watched him spellbound, and sure enough, the devil left the woman limp on the ground, and the crowd was suitably impressed by Shambhu Maharaj's amazing feat. He collected many coins in his basket, and then bundled the drugged woman into his cart as the crowd began to disperse. Devi followed him off the path and into a thicket of trees by the side of the road.

"Well done!" she said appreciatively.

"My wife," Shambhu simpered modestly. "My third wife, actually. She is very sporting, and participates in all my activities. I have prospered well after I married her."

"Excellent! You make a good team. But be careful how often you do this trick with her! She could easily become an opium addict, you know. The amount you have fed her to pull off this trick could become a habit!"

Shambhu immediately laughed off this suggestion. "No, no, akka! Don't you worry about that! She has a strong constitution. Earlier I had a different trick for which she had to wrap a deadly snake around her neck and do a snake dance. Many times, the snake is biting her here and there. But you see, still she is alive and kicking! She is not like my first two wives. They would fuss too much! This marriage will be my last, I'm thinking."

Devi laughed out loud at his simple logic. Then she thanked him warmly for the entertainment and left him to cope with his comatose wife. Now that the show was over, the traffic had cleared, and they could finally go home.

## iii

Vaman Bhat returned home late that night. Sita felt a clutch of fear when she saw him – she had never seen him look so abjectly dejected and demoralized ever before. Had something happened to the children.....?

"Husband, what is it?" she cried, rushing up to him and gripping his arm tight in her agitation. "Is it Udaya? Or Devi? Why are you looking like that?"

Vaman Bhat sighed deeply and sat down heavily. "No, Sita, it is not the children," he reassured his wife, albeit absently. "By god's grace, they are well. No, it is something else that makes me sad. I hardly know how to tell you this."

Sita waited impatiently for her husband to gather his thoughts. Then he looked at her bleakly and said, "Krishna Rao hanged himself this afternoon."

Sita gasped and fell back. Whatever she had feared, it was not this! "What has happened, husband? Why did he do such a thing? What have you heard?" The questions came tumbling out.

"There is not much to tell. The story I was told is that he had been involved in a plot against the king. The king discovered this plot and confronted him with it. He could not bear the shame of it – he took his own life."

"A plot against the king? How is that possible, husband? Krishna Rao was the most noble man in the kingdom. He had been elevated to the position of Prime Minister because the king trusted and relied on him above all others in the land! How can it be that he would commit treason?"

"I do not know, Sita, I just do not know. There is something behind the scenes here, something that we may never know. He was disgusted with all the waste of money and empty show the king was indulging in lately. He had even expressed his unhappiness to me. They say that he plotted with the king's enemies to overthrow the king and place his son Krishna on the throne. He thought that Krishna had the people's interests at heart more than

Kakushtavarman. Do you know, Sita, it was Krishna Rao who engineered the death of Thimmappayya and instigated Ranga to cause all the trouble? And when that did not work, he engineered the death of the sais. I believe the idea was to taint the Horse Sacrifice.

"What made Krishna Rao do this? I really don't know what was going on in his mind when he embarked on this enterprise to unseat the king….. They are saying he was not alone, that he had some accomplices who did the actual deeds, but under his direction. But he never gave up the names of his partners, so the king still doesn't know who they were – they are still at large! The only other person implicated is Narayanachar, I believe, the Royal Physician. He will rot in prison for a good long while for the role he has played…....."

"Of course, I realize that what Krishna Rao has done is treason, a heinous crime. But all I know is that I have lost a friend and a respected colleague. I will miss him. Despite all of this, I will still say that he probably had his reasons. I can never believe that he was a villain."

Vaman Bhat retired to his room. He just wanted to be alone, to contemplate this man whom he had always admired, and whose life could have served as an example to all the young men in the kingdom.

# Epilogue

Devi was back in her garden, tending to the holy basil plant. It had to be carefully trimmed so that it didn't go to seed, and she was kneeling on the path, pulling out all the flowers one by one. She stopped to brush the hair out of her eyes, and looked up at the sky. It looked like rain she was happy to see. The spring had been rather dry, and everyone was looking forward to one heavy rain to salvage the crops.

It had taken a while to get over the events of last winter. The excitement of the Horse Sacrifice, the mysterious deaths, the tragic suicide of Krishna Rao; they had shaken up the whole kingdom. It was still a bit of a mystery how that had happened – so many stories and rumors did the rounds initially, but then they all slowly died down, and now hardly anyone even thought about those days any more. The king had chosen another Prime Minister in his place. For a while, there had been strong rumors that the new person would be Siddayya! But luckily, that had not come to pass, and the new person was a highly respected and moderate person, well liked. There were those who said he was not independent minded, the way Krishna Rao had been. But then look where Krishna Rao's independent mindedness had got him!

The clinic was back to serving the sick and the needy in the villages all around. Thanks to Devi's trump card, Siddayya had not bothered them at all. Kumari blossomed into a more and more promising young woman every day. She was quick to pick up everything Devi was teaching her, and very soon would be an accomplished assistant. Her skin had still not healed. She was meticulous in the application of the medicines that Vaman Bhat had prescribed, and examined herself carefully in the shiny copperplate everyday for any signs of the patches abating. Nagi would laugh whenever she caught sight of her doing that. "Mad girl! Be happy with what you have. Remember, beauty is more than skin deep! Anyone who admires you only for your looks is not worth wasting your time on." Kumari would ignore her and persist in her examination.

Devi was content. The king had smiled upon her and had rewarded her handsomely for her services. Now she had the time and the resources to start thinking about expanding the clinic and doing all the things that she had been planning for many years now. There was no hurry, however. There was time enough in which to accomplish her objectives. After all the trials and tribulations of the past many days, she felt she deserved this feeling of contentment. It was well earned.

While she sat there thinking quietly about the year gone by, she saw a man weaving his way through the plant beds, coming towards her. He looked familiar, and as he approached closer, Devi recognized him. It was Mada, the king's trusted servant! What could he want from her, she wondered. Perhaps someone in the palace needed medical help, or some special medicine. She got up and received him with folded hands. After exchanging the usual pleasantries, Mada handed over a letter to Devi, bearing the royal seal.

"The king has instructed me to give you this letter, my lady," Mada said respectfully.

Devi opened the letter with nervous fingers. A letter from the king! She could not imagine what it might contain. She read with growing disbelief.

*To Devi, the Healer*

*I offer the position of Healer to the king, Royal Physician.*

*She will be responsible for my health and well-being; ensuring that my body and mind are maintained at the highest level of readiness to face all manners of challenges, both physical and mental.*

*She will treat me in illness as necessary, taking care to provide all the medicaments and comforts needed until such time as I am restored to good health.*

*She will ensure that my nourishment is safe, sufficient and sustaining, using whatever methods she deems fit.*

*I entrust her with this important office because I trust her knowledge of the medical*

*arts. I have observed her at work and I find
her to be competent and compassionate.
So let it be decreed.*

*Signed and sealed with the royal insignia*

Devi sat down with a thump. Royal Physician! So she would replace Narayanachar! There had been a lot of speculation on who would be selected to do so, but not in her wildest dreams had she expected to be the chosen one. Her mind in a whirl, she thanked Mada and sent him on his way. She would have to inform her mother and father, her brother. They would be supportive, she knew, and would help her face this challenge as they had many others. She would have to make all sorts of arrangements to accommodate this new call on her time. What would become of her clinic? How would she juggle these duties with her commitment to the communities she served?

Calm down, she told herself sternly. This is a good thing, don't let it become stressful. All the things that need to be done will get done, with the blessings of family and friends. All that happens, happens for the best.

There was a lot to think about, a lot to arrange, a lot of work….

But for now, she just wanted to enjoy her garden and finish weeding the bed of holy basil!

FINIS